I Need a Bad Boy in My Life

I Need a Bad Boy in My Life

Ambria Davis

www.urbanbooks.net

Urban Books, LLC
300 Farmingdale Road, N.Y.-Route 109
Farmingdale, NY 11735

I Need a Bad Boy in My Life

ISBN 13: 978-1-64556-399-0
ISBN 10: 1-64556-399-5

First Trade Paperback Printing December 2022
Printed in the United States of America

10 9 8 7 6 5 4 3 2 1

*This is a work of fiction. Any references or similarities
to actual events, real people, living or dead, or to real
locales are intended to give the novel a sense of reality.
Any similarity in other names, characters, places, and
incidents is entirely coincidental.*

Distributed by Kensington Publishing Corp.
Submit Orders to:
Customer Service
400 Hahn Road
Westminster, MD 21157-4627
Phone: 1-800-733-3000
Fax: 1-800-659-2436

This book is dedicated to my two, Nevaeh Davis and Kayson Weber. I couldn't imagine my life without you guys. Y'all make me a better person, a better woman, and a better mother. I do this for y'all, but also for me. My only goal in life is to make sure that y'all never go without, and I promise that I will continue to fulfill that. I love y'all, always and forever.

ACKNOWLEDGMENTS

First and foremost, I want to give all thanks and praises to the Man up above. Without Him, none of this would even be possible.

To my parents: thanks for being so hard on me when I was a child. I now know why y'all were doing it. I love y'all.

To my sisters: this past year hasn't been easy, but thank God that we're still here. I love y'all and I thank God every day for y'all.

To my aunts: thank y'all for everything. I appreciate y'all and even though I don't say it much, I love y'all.

To my cousins: I know we may fuss and fight a lot, but no matter what, we're always there for one another. We're not just Fam(ily), we're best friends also. I love y'all, never let no one tell y'all any different.

To my sissy Racquel: words can't explain how much you mean to me. Thanks again for giving me a chance. I love ya, sis.

To my readers: thanks to each and every one of you, because without y'all, I'd be nothing. I appreciate the support and I'm highly grateful for everything. My readers Rock!

Shout out to My Tigerville Family.

Free Pat-Meat, Big Dog & Casimere 3rd

R.I.P. Lynetta, Earline, Geanetta (Black Gal), Mark, Lil Adam, Teresa, Rowland Morris, Casimere Jr, Ralph, Juan, Gee Gee, Frank & Leontine. Continue to watch over and smile down on us. We love and miss y'all.

CHAPTER ONE

Keys

"Please, don't do this to me," I heard Joey cry out in pain.

"Nigga, fuck you. I told you to leave my girl alone, but ya didn't. You just had to test me. Now I'm going to show yo' bitch ass how I get down," young Cash screamed back at him.

"Oh, my God, Cash, what is you doing? I told you that I was going to handle it," I said, walking into the room.

"Fuck that shit. That nigga played one too many games, and now he's got to pay," Cash said as he continued beating him.

"Cash, don't do this. I don't need you going to jail over this bullshit. Let the law handle him," I begged as my hands clutched my growing belly. I understood why he was doing what he was doing, but I still didn't want him to do it.

"Ma, I'm sorry, but this is something that I have to do," he replied.

I stood back as I watched him do what he did. He was doing this for me, but I didn't need him to, and I didn't want him to. I wanted him to handle things the legal way, but sometimes the law wasn't on your side. In this case, I knew for sure that the law wasn't going to be on our side.

As I stood there watching him take matters into his own hands, something came to me. I didn't know what it was, but I felt that since this had something to do with me, I might as well help him. Walking over to the wooden table that sat in the basement of the abandoned house, I grabbed the gun on it.

"Move, Cash," I hollered from behind him. He looked at me standing there with the gun in my hand before he did what I asked him to do. I walked over to Joey and pumped three hot slugs into his chest. His eyes widened as he looked at me with sadness written all over his face. I stood there watching as his body began to shake. Then his eyes began rolling into the back of his head. I didn't show one sign of regret. If I did, Cash would've known that something was up. Instead, I stood there looking as tough as nails even though I was dying on the inside. When I saw the enormous amount of blood coming from his body, I knew that his time was almost up. That meant that our secret was going to die with him.

"Give me the gun, ma," Cash said, walking over to me. He took the gun from my grasp before kissing my forehead. He then grabbed my hand, leading me to the exit. "Come on, let's get out of here."

I awoke from my dream in a cold sweat. Even though I didn't get to see the end of my dream, I already knew what would happen. I hadn't dreamed about Joey in years. I thought that I had left that part of my life in Louisiana when I left there and moved here, but somehow, this shit was still haunting me.

"Lord, not now," I said to myself. I clicked on the light in the bedroom to find that Cash was nowhere in sight. *If this nigga ain't home, I'm going to fuck his ass up,* I thought as I threw the cover back and got out of bed. It was almost five o'clock in the morning, and I had to be to work at six. I hoped his ass was here, because I needed him to get Moni, and he knew that I couldn't be late. Since I had to get up anyway, I decided to get ready for work. Shit, I already knew I wasn't going to be going back to bed.

Grabbing my robe from the chair that sat in the corner of my room, I headed downstairs. Before I actually went downstairs, I peeped in to check on a sleeping Emoni. I noticed that she had kicked the cover off her, so I went to fix it. I stood there staring at her for a minute. I thanked God every night for blessing me with her. She, among other things, was the reason why I had changed and become the woman I was today. Only the Lord knows how fucked up my life was as a teenager. I was a troubled child. It took almost going to the chair and being raped by my man's best friend for me to slow down, and I was happy that I did.

"I love you, little lady," I said softly to her as if she could hear me. I placed a kiss on her forehead before I left the room. I made sure not to slam the door, because if I did and she woke up, it would be hard for me to go to work. I was happy that today was Friday and I was off for the weekend, because I desperately needed to spend some time with my *chuchi*.

I'd made my way down the hall and was about to walk down the stairs when I began to hear a female shouting. I thought I was tripping or that maybe I had left the television on in the living room. However, when I made it to the living room, I saw that the television was off. I knew for sure that the one in the bedroom wasn't on. *So, where is all this noise coming from?* No sooner had I asked myself that than I walked over to the door and found the answer.

"Cash, don't fucking play with me. I don't care who's asleep!" I heard her say. I took a good look at her before realizing that I'd seen her somewhere before.

"Look, Brandy, I'm not about to play all these games with you. So get the fuck from in front of my house before you wake my girl up!" he said, pushing her toward her car.

Once I heard her name, I realized that I did know her. Well, I really didn't know her. I only saw her a few times. She stayed in the projects out in Shelby County. I'd always see her when Tay and I went to visit our new friend Dominique.

"Yo' girl? Yo' girl, huh?" she asked, scooting up to him. "Was you thinking about that bitch when you was laid up in my bed two days ago for two days straight?"

"Honestly? Yeah, I was," he replied.

"Nigga, fuck you. You ain't nothing but a low-down mutt. I wished like hell that I never met yo' dog ass!" she screamed.

By then, I had heard enough. I opened the door to see her punching on him. I quietly shut the door behind me and began walking over to them. They were so busy scuffling that they hadn't noticed me standing there.

"I don't know how many times I've told you about controlling your hoes. It wasn't bad enough I had to fight hoes in the streets and they're calling my phone and keying my fucking car. Now I gotta deal with this bullshit here. Really, Cash? Really?" I asked, shocking the hell out of both of them. They stopped fighting to look at me. "Fuck, man. You stay cheating on me. The least you could do is get a bitch who looks better than me!"

"Keys, baby, I can explain," he said, walking over to me.

"First of all, don't come near me," I said, throwing my hands up to stop him. "I done tolerated just about everything from you, but for you to let one of your hoes come in front of the house where my child and I lay our heads is where I draw the final line. I can't keep doing this with you. Bad thing is, out of all the bitches you fuck me over with, none of them hoes look good. They don't have nothing, and they ain't nothing, and yet you cheating on me with bitches like that. Them hoes be looking like they belong in the gutta. Fucking gutta rats are what they are, and here yo' dumb ass steady fucking with them. Fuck me if I think being with you is a downfall, but I've been through nothing but rough times since we've been fucking around, and I'm through with this shit. I now realize that nothing good will come out of me fucking with you."

"First of all, ho, who are you calling a bitch?" his ho had the nerve to ask.

"I'm talking to your no-class-having ass. You know, y'all bitches really do kill me. It's bad enough that y'all muthafuckas be cheating with the next bitch's man, but then y'all hoes be wanting to cause scenes and shit, like creeping with the next bitch's man is what's up!" I said, walking closer to her ass. Cash walked between us, but he made sure not to touch me. I rolled my eyes at his bitch ass before I spoke over his shoulder to his ho. "Ain't nothing cute or good about sleeping around with the next bitch's man. Sad thing is, I'm black and you black. Bitch, respect me or something. You shouldn't have come in front of my house."

"Bitch, you can save that speech, because just like him, I don't give a fuck. I don't know you. Therefore, I have no loyalty to you. Yo' nigga didn't care, because if he did, he wouldn't have fucked with me in the first place. That's who you should be giving a speech to, not me," she replied.

I clapped my hands to applaud her no-class-having ass. That was probably the only sense she knew how to make, and even though I hated to admit it, her ass was right.

"Yeah, you're right, and I know you don't know, because if ya did, you wouldn't have fucked with my nigga. Now while you fucking that nigga, I hope you made him strap up, because he's around here burning bitches. Ain't nobody safe out here," I said before I shook my head at both of them and headed inside. She was right. She didn't know me, nor did she have any loyalty to me. It was Cash, and since he was fucking her and all the rest of them bitches, obviously he didn't care about my ass either.

Once I made it inside, I went upstairs to take a shower. I had to work, and since Cash always did some shit like that, I wasn't about to let it spoil my day. I was already used to the shit. I just hoped that he didn't expect me to stay with his ass after all this shit. Really, the nigga was real sad for that shit. People always said never to shit where ya stay, and that was exactly what he was doing.

Fuck his ass though, I thought as I went to turn the shower on. I waited until the water was warm enough before I stripped out of my clothes and got in. Knowing that I didn't have enough time on my hands, I went right to work, grabbing the washcloth and Dove soap. I lathered the cloth up before I washed every inch of my body. When I had gotten everything, I rinsed off and repeated the process. I was about to turn the water off and get out when I felt Cash get in. I tried to bypass him, but he stopped me.

"Move, Cash," I said to him, but he ignored me. He began sucking on my neck. That nigga wasn't slick. He knew how to get me in the mood even when I was mad. Spreading my legs with his, he grabbed my arms and went down below. *Good boy,* I thought the minute his tongue connected with my pussy lips. He dove in hungrily, eating my pussy and licking as if it were his last meal. Even though the water was still on, I could hear the smacking sounds he made as he lapped up my juices. The nigga was trying to make up desperately.

I couldn't lie. That nigga was trying to suck my soul through my pussy. I clawed at the shower walls as he devoured my pussy from the back. My head started spinning when he began nibbling gently on my pearl tongue. Cash had never eaten my pussy like this before, and it was beginning to scare me.

"Ohhhh, fuuuuuuuck," I yelled, arching my back more so that he could get everything. Moving along, he used his tongue to part my lips before he began tongue fucking me, nearly driving me insane. I began moving my hips in a circular motion, riding the shit out of his face.

"Ummm," he moaned. I had to humble myself, because if I didn't, I was going to bust early, and I didn't want that to happen.

Raising my right leg, I placed it on the wall as I brought both my hands down and touched the floor. I didn't care that my hair was getting wet. Right now, Cash's tongue was working miracles. My pussy was so wet that when I opened my eyes I spotted my juices running down the side of his mouth. Again, I began rotating my hips as I felt my nut building. Before long, I busted all in his mouth, and just like the dog he was, he made sure to get every drop. I moved to get up when he plunged his nine-inch tool deep inside of me, making me gasp.

"Shit!" I yelled, as he began giving me slow, deep thrusts. I bit down on my lip hard as my pussy cried out for more. She received all nine inches of daddy's dick. "Oh, Goooood, fuck me please," I said as I started winding my hips on his dick. Round and around my hips moved as I felt my nut building up.

"Fuck me!" I begged him, and that he did. He grabbed ahold of my hips and began fucking me as if I had owed him something and never paid him. Not wanting to be outdone, I began throwing that ass back in a circle. I wanted to fuck him instead of him fucking me. The faster he pumped, the harder I thrust. I was trying my hardest to leave that nigga wishing that he never fucked me over. "I'm cumming!"

"Me too," he said, pushing his dick so deep that I could've sworn I felt it in my stomach. A few seconds later, we were cumming together. I stood there bent over, trying to catch my breath. I almost fell over trying to stand up. It was a good thing that Cash was there to catch me, or else I would've been tasting that floor.

"I love you, ma," he said, trying to kiss me, but I moved my head out of the way. Those words weren't going to get me this time. Cash didn't know love. I didn't think he ever did. As I looked into his eyes, I couldn't help but imagine him and Brandy together. I wanted to ask him what it was about other females he found appealing that he didn't find in me, but I didn't. I kept my mouth closed. I wasn't ready to ask a question I didn't want to hear the answer to.

Coming back to my senses, I realized that I was going to be late if I spent any more time playing with his ass. Even though I barely had any energy, I grabbed the wash towel, grabbed my Summer's Eve body wash, and cleaned my body. Grabbing a douche from the counter, I douched before I passed the soapy cloth on my body again. I was pissed that my hair had gotten soaking wet, but I'd have to think about that later. Turning the water off, I grabbed the towel that was hanging on the shower door and got out. Grabbing my things, I headed into the bedroom. No sooner did I make it in there than Cash came in, following me. I knew his ass hadn't taken a shower that fast because I hadn't heard him cut the water on.

"Keyon, let me talk to you for a minute?" he asked.

I looked at him before I walked around him and headed into the clothes closet. I grabbed my scrubs and went back into the bedroom, and he was standing there in the same spot. Again I walked around him to the bed, where I laid my clothes out and started getting dressed.

"Come on, ma! Are you really going to do this?"

"Look, Cash, I'm not in the mood for your bullshit. I have to go to work. Ain't nothing you can say to me that can fix any of this. Just because I let you give me some dick doesn't mean that changed anything. I caught you red-handed this time. So don't try to lie your way out of it," I said as I began putting on my bra and panties. I grabbed the lotion off the dresser and began to put it on my body. I was ass backward right now. I tried hard to show Cash that he and his bitch hadn't affected me, but they did. "Just know that when I get off work today, I'll be packing my and my daughter's things and we're moving. I don't have time to deal with this shit anymore."

"Ma, chill. You don't have to leave," he said, grabbing my arm.

"Really? What do you take me for? Who do you take me for? You really think I'm going to continue to allow you to disrespect me like this?" I asked in a rage. "I'm not a stupid bitch. Cash, I only put up with your shit because of everything that we've been through and the love that I have for you. Make no mistake though. I'm far from being a dumb bitch."

"Ma, I didn't say you were a dumb bitch, and why did you let me fuck if you knew you were going to leave?" he asked, trying to explain himself.

"You didn't have to say those exact words. You said it when you said I didn't have to leave you after all the things you put me through, and I only let you fuck because I needed a nut," I told him as I began putting on my clothes for work. I was tired of Cash and his shit. I knew life wasn't supposed to always be peaches and cream, but damn, it was as if I barely got any good times. I was always in the storm and rain. I didn't see an inch of sunshine.

"Keyon, look—" he began, but I really didn't want to hear anything he had to say.

"I'm through being your doormat that you think you can just walk all over whenever you feel like it. I'm a human being. I have feelings, feelings that you don't consider. So since you're always saying fuck me, it's time for me to say fuck you." With that being said, I took one last look at him before I grabbed my bag and headed to work. I wasn't even in the mood to eat breakfast. My appetite was completely gone.

Before I left the house, I went back into Emoni's room. I never left in the morning without kissing my daughter and telling her that I loved her, even if she was asleep. It was something I did on a regular, and just because I was mad with Cash didn't mean that I wasn't going to do it. After doing that, I left the room and headed downstairs. I immediately rolled my eyes at the sight of Cash standing by the front door.

"What?" I asked with an attitude. "What do you want, Casimere?"

"Ma, just talk to me."

"Look, I don't have time to do this shit right now," I said, trying to move past him, but he jumped in my way. "Get the fuck out of my way, Cash!"

"Okay, you got that," he said before he moved out of my way. On my way out the door, I made sure that I bumped his shoulder. I damn near broke my collarbone, but I didn't care. He was lucky that I wasn't a big bitch, or else we would've been up in this house rolling.

A man only does what you allow him to do, a little voice in the back of my head said. I knew what that voice was saying was true. I needed to grow a backbone when it came to Cash and put my foot down. *Soon,* I thought as I hopped in the car and headed to work.

Once I made it to work, I was not in the best mood at all. Normally I'd be all jolly and happy to be at work, but Cash had completely ruined my morning for me. The only thing that kept me good was the sight of my patient, Mrs. Earline Davis. She was one of the few people who kept me sane. This old lady was really like a grandmother to me. She knew when I was in a bad mood. She also knew the right words to say to get me out of my funk. That was why I looked forward to seeing her every day I came to work.

"Hey, mama," I said, greeting her with a smile. I walked over to her, placed a kiss on her cheek, and sat down in a chair beside the bed.

"Good morning, my baby," she replied. "How are you?"

"I'm good," I lied. She was already old and sick. I didn't want her to worry about my problems and what I was going through. All she needed to worry about was getting healthy so that she could get out of here.

"Child, you know me better than that. Tell me what's going on," she said, motioning for me to raise her bed. I did as she asked me to and then sat on the bed next to her. I began telling her all about Cash and me. I told her everything. I started with the day I met him and went up until this morning. I made sure that I didn't leave out anything. I wanted her to hear everything that I'd been going through so that she could give me her take on things. When I was done, I just sat there in the bed looking at her, waiting for her to tell me whatever it was she had to tell me.

"Chile," she said before she became completely silent. Her eyes traveled from me to the window, then back at me. I was somewhat scared to hear what she had to say with the way she was stalling. "I'm going to tell you a thing or two, and I want you to hear me. Okay?" she said, grabbing my hand. I nodded my head, then placed my clipboard down on the bed and scooted a bit closer to her. I knew that whatever she was about to tell me was something wise and that for sure I needed to hear this.

For about an hour, she sat there telling me all about her and her late husband, John. She didn't hold anything back either. She told me about the many things they'd been through and how they had overcome them. She said that if a man and woman really loved each other, they were going to find a way to work out whatever problems they had. She said to never give up on the person you loved, because living miserably with someone else was not a good feeling.

I was somewhat confused, because she heard everything that Cash and I had been through, and yet she was basically telling me to fight for him. She must have noticed the look on my face. She made me face her, looked deep into my eyes, and said, "Oh, but make no mistake, Keyon. I didn't say that you had to be dumb in love. If you are the only one trying to protect what you and this young man have, and he's not trying to put in any effort, then the best thing you can do for yourself is leave him. No woman should ever be unhappy and in love by herself."

"I love you," I said sincerely. This woman was like the grandmother I never had. I really hoped and prayed that the good Lord would heal her and keep her on this earth a little while longer.

"And I love you, dear," she replied. I placed a kiss on her cheek before I grabbed my clipboard and told her that I would see her later. The wisdom she'd just spoken to me had my ears ringing. I knew what I had to do.

For the rest of the morning, I thought about everything that she had told me. I wanted to live my life. Hell, I needed to live my life for Emoni and me and no one else. I just didn't know how to. I'd been wrapped up in Cash for ten long years. He was all I knew.

It wasn't until I was on my lunch break that I finally decided to live my life to please me and me only. I took the rest of the day off, and I decided to treat myself. I went shopping for the perfect outfit first. I then went to get my nails and toes done. When I was done, I went to the beauty shop and got my hair slayed by one of Tennessee's best stylists. While I was at the shop, I called Tay to let her know of my plans. She agreed, and just like that, my day was about to get started, or should I say my night. We were about to go club hopping, and I was in dire need of a few drinks. I just hoped that my day wouldn't be as eventful as it was this morning.

Later That Night

I really thought my night was going to be great, but just like the rest of my life, Cash had to come and ruin it. I sat in the back of the VIP section of Club Rae's, nursing a drink as I watched the people around me. I was chilling as the DJ spun Boosie's "No Juice" throughout the club speakers. Any other time, I'd be rapping along with the lyrics, seeing as he was my favorite rapper and this happened to be my favorite song, but that night I wasn't. I really wasn't in the mood to do anything but chill and sip some much-needed drinks. I really thought that going out was going to cheer me up, but I was still in a sour-ass mood about the shit with Cash. To make matters worse, he had the nerve to be all up in some bitch's face as if I weren't anywhere around. This was the first time that Cash had ever disrespected me in my face, and I was heated. I had a mind to go over there, snatch him, and fuck the both of them up, but I wasn't even about to let this nigga see me sweat. Besides, I wasn't one to make a scene, especially not behind a nigga. I wasn't the type of bitch to run behind one nigga knowing there was a whole sea of niggas out there and I probably had access to a bunch of them. Cash had me fucked up if he thought I was the type of bitch to run behind him, because I wasn't. I may have been stupid a time or two and took him back after he mistreated me, and I may have fought a few of his hoes, but chasing him wasn't anywhere in my blood. I'd leave that to his other females to do.

Oh, excuse me. I'm so busy running my mouth, but please allow me to introduce myself. My name is Keyon Miller, but people call me Keys for short. I'm 26 years old, stand at about five feet seven, and weigh about 160 pounds. I have a caramel complexion, shoulder-length brown hair, and an hourglass frame. I'm an only child. I was born and raised in Baton Rouge, Louisiana, but later moved to Memphis, Tennessee, where I went to school and became a registered nurse. I was able to purchase my own home just two years after graduating college, and I was quite proud of myself.

I was currently in a relationship with my long-time boyfriend and baby's father, Casimere Edwards. Well, at least I had been. When I first met Casimere, or Cash as many called him, I thought I'd found my one true love. He was everything I wanted in a man. He was loving, caring, supportive, manly, and thuggish, just like I liked them. He also had a soft side to him, and he was attentive to my every need. On days when I wanted to give up or thought school was too hard, he was there to push me, motivate me, and be my crutch, especially after I had my daughter. I had to balance being a first-time mother and a full-time student. Many nights when my daughter would be up late and I'd have to study, he would take care of her and let me study. He would even help me study sometimes, while balancing a bottle between his shoulders and head. My man even made sure that I had a hot breakfast the next morning, and he kept our daughter all through the day while I was at school. I didn't have to put her in daycare until she was about 2 years old, which was why, when I was able to, I got two jobs and helped my man get on his feet. He now owned two apartment buildings and was the co-owner of two clubs. He'd been through a lot, and he'd come far. I was extremely proud of him.

My man made sure that my daughter and I never went without anything. We always had everything we wanted and needed, and even though I had my own money, he never let me spend it. He even bought us another home. I never understood why, because I had already gotten us one. At first, I was going to sell my house, but my first mind told me to keep it, and I was glad I did. Cash was my black knight. He was everything to me. I never thought he would change on me, but boy, was I wrong.

For about two years now, he'd been changing. He didn't do what he normally did. I had no doubt in my mind that he absolutely loved me, but as I said, he'd changed. It all started when he and his boy Jamel went to Chicago. They were trying to open their third club. Both of them wanted it somewhere different, and they decided on Chi-town. They went to look at a few properties. They didn't find anything until about their third visit, when they were able to find a spot. It took them all of a few months and a lot of money, but that following year they were able to open. When they had their grand opening, he wanted me to fly out there with him, but I couldn't. I had to work a double, plus I had Emoni, and I wasn't trying to leave my baby behind while she was so little. I didn't go, and things between us hadn't been the same. When he returned home from Chicago, the following two weeks he started cheating and staying out until all hours of the night. Hell, sometimes he didn't come home at all, but I wasn't tripping. I gave him all the rope he needed, and when he would hang himself, I'd pack up my and Emoni's things and go back to my own house. When he would come begging, I'd go back home. Cash and I had broken up three times over the past two years. This time I didn't leave the house because I knew he would try to beg me to come back, and like a fool, I'd go back. Instead, I left my shit there.

I didn't know where Cash and I went wrong. After I reached my goals in life and became a mother, he started acting differently. I didn't know what I did to make him feel that way or do the things he did, but every night I prayed to God, hoping that he would change. Deep down I knew that he wouldn't, but that didn't stop me from praying for him. After all the praying I'd done, today I couldn't deny it anymore. Cash was always going to be Cash, and as I sat there looking at him totally disrespecting me as if I weren't here, I knew that the man I fell in love with was gone.

I lowkey watched as he whispered all in the chick's ear while feeling all on her ass. Again, I wanted to make my way over there, but instead I grabbed my drink and threw it back. It took everything in me not to go to him. I knew he was just trying to make me jealous, so I wasn't about to give him the satisfaction in knowing that he had succeeded. I could've easily flipped the script and had a nigga feeling all on me, but I knew he would trip a little too hard, and I wasn't in the mood to fight with him. If a scene was what he was trying to get out of me, he'd be heartbroken when he saw that I wasn't giving in to his bullshit. I was cool. He could do whatever he wanted to do, because from this moment on out, I was officially about to do me. Just like he wanted to play, I was going to play too. I was going to show him that two could play his game.

"Bitch, what's the matter with you? Why you sitting over there looking like you done lost your best fucking friend?" my best friend Tay asked me. "'Cause hello, bitch, I'm right here. You ain't lost me!"

"Ain't shit up. I'm just chilling, that's all," I said to her with my eyes still focused on Cash and his female companion. She must have noticed that my attention was elsewhere, because her eyes traveled to where I was looking. The moment she spotted what I was looking at, she got mad.

"Oh, hell no. I know this nigga ain't all up in some other bitch's face while you're up in here. You want to go over there and check his ass?" she asked, jumping up from her seat. I knew she was going to feel like that because I didn't tell her about what happened today. "I told you that this nigga wasn't shit!"

"Nah, I'm good. I ain't even about to trip behind Cash's old, tired ass," I replied, getting up from my seat. I ignored her last comment, because what she'd been saying for the past few years was true. Cash wasn't shit. I just didn't know why it was hard for me to leave him. "I'm about to run to the bathroom right quick. Order me another drink and get ready, because I'm about to show this nigga I ain't sweating one bit."

"All right, I got you, but if you want to, we can still go fuck them up," she replied. I had mad respect for my bitch. She was the definition of a true friend. She wouldn't let anyone play with me. She'd quickly try to set shit off and wouldn't think twice about it.

"Nah, I told you that I'm good. Fuck Cash's ol' tired ass. You just be ready to tear the floor up when I get back," I said and walked off, making my way toward the bathroom. I couldn't lie. These drinks had me feeling real good right now. *I might end up taking one of these fine-ass niggas home with me tonight.*

"Hold up, where are you going?" I heard a voice say behind me. I didn't have to turn around to know that it was Cash's ass. Turning around, I rolled my eyes and grilled his ass.

"What do you want, Cash? Why are you worrying about me when you already got ya hands full?" I asked, pointing toward the woman he had sitting next to him. She looked at me and turned her nose up, but I wasn't worrying about her. If anything, she should've felt some type of way about this nigga whose face she was all in while he was checking me about my whereabouts.

"As long as you're the mother of my child, I'm always going to worry about you. So you might as well drop the attitude, ma," he replied, taking a sip from his drink.

"You're right. I'm the mother of your child, not your woman. Therefore, your concern should be about your child and not me," I said with an attitude. The fuck he tried to be concerned or worried about me when this nigga was being a dog right in my face.

"Whatever, ma. Like I said, as long as you're the mother of my child, I will always worry about you," he said, looking at me while licking his lips.

"Cash, who the fuck is this?" the chick asked him.

"Why the fuck are you worrying about who I am?" I answered before he could. "The question is, who the fuck are you?"

"Because, bitch, I know you just seen us talking, and I'm his girl. That's who the fuck I am!" she answered boldly.

I couldn't do anything but laugh. I swore Cash had all these bitches coming out of the woodwork. Every time you looked, there was a different bitch or problem.

"What the fuck is so funny to you?"

"You! That's what's funny. You think I really give a lovely fuck? I don't care what the fuck you are to him!"

I told her matter-of-factly. This bitch had me confused, because if she thought I gave a fuck about whomever Cash fucked with, then she was most definitely wrong. "Cash, you really need to keep ya bitches in line, because this here is becoming a routine thing. Every time you look, there's a bitch coming at me over some bullshit behind your trifling ass. The bad thing about it is them bitches really think I give a lovely fuck about them telling me they fucking or done fucked with you. What they need to know is that I'm fed up and I don't give a fuck about what you do anymore, because like I said, I'm not your woman anymore. So you can fuck however many bitches you want to fuck. It don't matter to me one bit!"

"Bit—" She began to roll her neck, but I cut that ass off before she could even begin to run her trap.

"Don't make the mistake of calling me a bitch again, because I promise you that that'll be the last word you will get out of your mouth. I will beat the brakes off your ass and have your ass lying in a hospital bed, where I'd probably end up being ya nurse!" I said, stepping a bit closer to her. By that time, Cash was already up on his feet. He wasn't crazy. He knew how I could get when a bitch tried to play with me.

"Shorty, I'm going to need for you to hush ya mouth before you let it write a check your ass can't cash," he said to her. "Furthermore, who gave you the idea of you being my girl? I know I didn't. My girl is standing right in front of you. You're nothing but a freak of the week. Respect her or keep it pushing."

"Well, it's about damn time," I said, applauding him. "I can't believe you finally stood up to one of your side pieces for me. It only took you a few years to get it right, and the crazy thing is I'm not even your woman anymore."

"Whatever, Keys," he said, taking a sip of his drink. "You coming home with me tonight?"

"Nigga, please, you better get ya little groupie to go home with you, because I plan on taking one of these fine-ass niggas with me," I said, trying to mess with his head. He placed his drink down on the bar and stood up. *Oh, shit!*

"Baby, please don't get you and whatever nigga you try to leave up out this bitch with fucked up," he said a little too calmly for me. I didn't know why he was in his feelings when he was the one clearly being disrespectful. He shouldn't have a problem with me leaving with anyone since he was doing what he was doing.

"Whatever. Like I said, you don't need to be worrying about Keyon. Worry about whatever this broad's name is, and leave me the fuck alone," I said and walked off.

It took me a good minute to get to the bathroom. There were so many niggas in the club trying to get me to dance that I had completely forgotten about Cash and his bullshit. When I made it to the bathroom, I hurriedly entered the stall to relieve my bladder. It felt like I was peeing forever. That was how long it took me to finish. When I was through, I grabbed a Summer's Eve wipe out of my clutch, wiped between my legs, trashed the wipe, and fixed my dress.

Walking out of the stall, I went straight to the sink and washed my hands. Seeing that my lips needed a little more gloss, I pulled out my MAC lip gloss and applied some. I then fixed my hair and looked at myself in the full-length mirror.

"Girl, you know you bad," I said, blowing a kiss to myself. I was too cute in this dress, but don't let looks fool you. Just like a man, I could make a nigga taste that dirt if he played with me, and that was on everything.

"Yes, you are," I heard behind me, and just like that, Cash was in my face again. *Don't even worry about him.* Cash knew what he was doing, and I wasn't trying to entertain that fool.

"Cash, why are you in here bothering me? This is the women's bathroom, and I could've sworn that you had a woman waiting for you at the bar," I spoke, frustrated.

"Nah. My woman is right here. That bitch ain't shit to me," he said, walking up to me.

"Did you remember that we're not together? We broke up earlier today," I retorted, taking a step back from him.

"As long as I'm alive and breathing, you will always be my woman," he replied, grabbing my arm.

"Let go of me, Cash. I will never be your woman, not as long as you keep doing the shit that you do. I can't for the life of me understand why you can't be comfortable with one woman. Instead, you need a herd of bitches, as if that's supposed to be manly. That shit ain't cute. Keeping up with all these females must be hard to do," I said, trying to break free from him.

"Why are you doing this, Keyon?" he said, calling me by my real name. The nigga knew I didn't want him to call me that shit.

"Because I'm tired of playing these games with you, Cash. I've been with you for years now. I thought you were my everything and I was yours, but just like the rest of them niggas, you had to fuck that shit up. I don't know why I keep taking you back, but I promise you that you'll regret the day you started fucking me over. I don't need a man who wants to have his cake and eat it, too. I can do bad all by my damn self," I said, pushing him off of me.

"Baby, you can't do this shit to me. You know how many times we've broken up just to get back together again the next day," he said.

I turned around and walked over to him. As I looked straight into his eyes, one lone tear fell from my eyes before I placed a kiss on his lips.

"That's the problem. After everything that you've put me through, I'm always taking you back, and you end up doing the same thing a few months later. That's why you constantly do the shit. I'm tired of fighting all ya bitches, ya late-night creeps, the late-night phone calls, et cetera. I'm just tired. it's time for you to accept that and move on, Cash. This journey that we've been living together has come to an end. Unfortunately, it's time for us to go our separate ways."

"I love you, ma," he said, fighting back the tears threatening to fall down his face. This had to have been hurting him, because it was very rare that I'd seen him cry, but even his tears weren't going to stop me. With one final kiss, I said goodbye and left the bathroom. I meant what I said. I couldn't be with Cash without him hurting me, so in order for me not to hurt, I guessed I had to leave him.

Walking out of the restroom, I bumped into the chick Cash was entertaining. I guessed she was looking for his ass. She looked me up and down and rolled her eyes before she walked off. I played as if I didn't notice the look that she gave me, as I walked back toward the VIP section. I was not about to entertain her petty ass behind a nigga I didn't even want anymore. Besides, if I did, I could have him with the quickness.

"I was just about to come look for you. I thought that you had gotten lost or some shit," Tay said once I had sat down. I chuckled and turned so she wouldn't see that my eyes were still glossy. "Keys, what's wrong?" she asked once she noticed that I wasn't looking at her.

"Nothing. I'm good," I said, my voice cracking.

Knowing that something wasn't right with me, she turned my face so that I was now facing her. "Why do you look like you've been crying? Did Cash do anything to you?" she asked me, spazzing out. That was why I didn't want to look at her in the first place. I knew she was going to blow her top. Besides, she never did like Cash.

"I have, and no, he didn't do anything," I said to her.

"Well, why were you crying?"

"I just told him that we are over. For good this time, and I'm not sure if I really meant the shit or not," I said with tears falling down my face. I didn't know if I could really let him go. I knew what I said in the bathroom, but my heart was singing another tune.

"Aw. Do you want to get out of here?" she asked me, giving me a look that said, "It's about goddamn time."

"Nah, I just want to get my drink on and get fucked up," I said, grabbing my drink from the table. I was already close to it. Lord knows I couldn't drink to save my life. Removing the straw from my cup, I took the whole thing to the head.

"Will you be all right?" she asked, passing me another drink.

"Yeah," I said, placing the empty cup back on the table. "Order me another one."

"Okay," she said, looking toward the entrance of the VIP. "The fuck do this nigga want?"

"Who?" I asked her.

"Your baby daddy," she replied. My eyes followed in the direction she was looking. I spotted Cash by the entrance of the VIP section. I rolled my eyes before I got up to meet him.

"What are you doing, Cash?" I asked the minute I reached him. He was really beginning to blow me. I hated when he did that shit.

"Keys, baby, I can't let you go. I know that I've messed up in the past years, but I promise you that I will change. Just give me one more chance, and I promise you that I will change. Please!" he begged.

"I can't, Cash. I meant what I said. We're over!" I said to him and walked off. He grabbed my hand and was about to respond when the DJ called me over by the stage. I was puzzled as to why he was calling me. I knew for sure that he wasn't trying to call me to sing. At least, I hoped not. I wasn't in the mood. I moved and almost fell on my face. I was half drunk, but I went anyway.

As I made my way over to the DJ booth, all eyes were on me. To say that I was nervous would be an understatement. My heart was beating so fast I thought I'd catch a heart attack. When I made it to the booth, he handed me a mic and instructed me to walk to the middle of the stage. Even though I didn't know what was going on, I did as I was told. I paused as Tamia's "Still" came playing through the speakers. That was our song, and at a time like this, it didn't need to be playing. Any other time, I'd have happily sung it to him, but seeing as I had just broken up with him, my heart ached more. Since my heart was playing one tune and my mind was playing another, I decided to sing anyway.

I stood still as Tamia began singing.

Usually when two people are together for a long time
Things seem to change

Tears started to sting my eyes. That was Cash's favorite part. He loved to hear me sing it. Singing was always a way for me to escape my problems. It took me to a whole other world where nothing mattered to me but the sweet sound of my own voice. I brought the mic up to my lips as I began to sing along with Tamia.

Still feels like the first time we met
That I kissed and I told you I love you
We still run around like teenagers even though we're grown and married with kids

The minute I saw Cash walk up onto the stage, the tears that I was holding back came flowing down my face. I was an emotional wreck. I just wanted to grab him and never let him go. Who was I kidding? I was never going to leave my man. This was my soul mate. He completed me. Whatever he felt, I felt. If he was hurt, then I was hurting also. Even though we'd been through a lot, he was mine. There was no way in this fucked-up world that I was going to be able to find another love or man like that. That was my man. He wasn't perfect, but yes, he was mine. As he stood in front of me, I continued to sing.

One would think that I was the artist who recorded that song, the way I sang it. With every word that I sang, I put my heart into each note. After that part, the DJ decided to cut it off, but I didn't stop singing. I closed my eyes and sang it a cappella. I put all my feelings into every word that came out of my mouth. I wanted them to feel the words instead of hearing them.

I stopped singing and opened my eyes to find Cash down on one knee with a small box in his hands. I wanted to believe that I was dreaming, but by the cheering of the crowd in the background, I knew that I wasn't. I spotted Tay off in the far corner by the DJ booth with this look on her face that I couldn't read. I knew she wouldn't approve of this, because Cash had hurt me too many times. However, it was my life, not hers. She would just have to accept the decision I'd make.

"Keyon, I know that we've been through a whole lot of shit in our lives together. I know that you're just about tired of all my shit, but, baby, I can't see myself being with nobody but you. I know that I have a lot of shit to get straight, and I'll admit that I do, but if you could just work with me, I promise that I will clean up my act and be the man you need me to be. I promise to leave all these chicks alone and to start coming home at a decent hour. I'm not saying that the shit will happen overnight, because I know that it can't, but I'm willing to change if you'd give me another chance. So what I'm asking is, will you do me the honor of becoming my wife?" he asked.

I just stood there. I'd been with Cash for ten years and some change. He was the only man I'd ever been with in my whole 26 years of life, and I couldn't help but remember all the shit he'd put me through. I loved him more than life itself and more than anyone else, well, besides my daughter, but could I really trust that he would change? Could I really believe him when he said that he would change? Those were all the things that ran through my mind as I tried to figure out what I wanted to do. With tears now fully running down my face, I moved my head to say yes when a female voice stopped me.

"I don't know how you do it, Cash. Keeping up this lie and living a double life must be hard," she said, making me turn toward the steps leading onto the stage. The chick who stood in front of me was drop-dead gorgeous. Looking at her really made me feel intimidated, but I wasn't about to let her see that. She had to stand at least five foot six. She had a high-yellow complexion with an all-right body, and she sported dark brown shoulder-length hair. She resembled Christina Milian, and I thought I'd seen her somewhere before.

"Mia? What are you doing here?" I heard Cash ask behind me.

I turned to him with a look on my face that asked, "What, you know this bitch?" When his face went down to the floor, it let me know that he indeed knew her. The question was, how?

"I came here because it was time for you to stop living a lie and to start owning up to ya shit. I need you to tell Keyon the truth and nothing but the truth," she replied. When I heard her say my name, I turned around so fast that I almost caught whiplash.

"Umm, excuse me. I don't believe we've met. Who are you, and how do you know me?" I asked, puzzled.

"I've known about you for a while, Keyon, or would you like for me to call you Keys instead?" she replied, walking onto the stage. In the corner of my eye, I spotted

Tay walking over to me. I knew she wasn't too far behind. When I saw Mia move, Tay moved right behind her. That was how she worked. She wasn't about to let anything shady happen, not without her being in the mix.

"That doesn't answer my question," I said to our uninvited guest. "Who are you?"

"Why don't we ask Cash who I am?" she asked, looking at him. I looked over to see that he had this stupid, confused look on his face.

"Well, are you going to tell me who she is?" I asked him. He looked like a deer caught in headlights. He said nothing as he put his head down in shame.

"Cash!" I yelled to get his attention.

"Keyon, can we please just talk about this at home?" he asked. "If you haven't noticed, we're in a club full of people."

"Nigga, I don't give a fuck if we were in a church full of pastors. I want some answers and I want them now, Cash. Who is she?" I asked again, but still he didn't say anything.

"Since it looks like he won't tell you who I am, I guess I'll have to tell you," she replied.

"Well, speak ya piece then. I don't have all night. I have a daughter I have to get home to," I said, trying to hurry her ass up. I wanted to know why she was here, and since Cash didn't want to tell me, I knew she would. If she was one of his pieces, she was definitely going to tell me. That was how side bitches were. They always wanted to make themselves known and shit.

She stood there silently for a few seconds before I looked at my wrist, showing her how impatient I was becoming. I looked over at Cash, who was now up on his feet. I was starting to become impatient with both of them. "Look, if you don't hurry up and say why you're here, I'm going to leave."

"Well, as you already know, my name is Mia. I'm from Charlotte, North Carolina, and I'm Cash's baby mama. We have a one-year-old son named Casimere Edwards Jr., but we call him CJ," she said, pointing between herself and Cash.

"Umm. Come again?" I questioned, not believing that I heard her right. "You said what now?"

"You heard me right the first time, honey. You and I have the same baby daddy," she stated proudly like that shit was something her ass was supposed to be proud of.

"So you're telling me that Cash, my Cash, the man I've been with for years, fathered a child by you?" I asked, wanting to know if I was getting the shit right.

"Yes, that's just exactly what I said," she replied.

I simply nodded my head and turned to Cash. "So what do you have to say for yourself?" I asked him.

"Ma, what can I really say?" he asked, looking at me with pleading eyes.

"Is the fucking shit true or not?" I asked calmly. "Tell me that this shit isn't true!"

"Yes, it's true," he simply answered. "But I don't want to be with Mia, Keyon. You're the woman I really want."

"Oh, yeah? You wasn't saying that shit when you came to see me and CJ last week," Mia blurted out.

I couldn't do anything but shake my head as I walked off. I couldn't believe that I had actually considered saying yes to this two-timing-ass nigga.

"Keyon, baby, where are you going?" he asked, grabbing my arm and trying to stop me.

"All I'ma ask is that you get your hands off of me before both of your kids be minus a parent," I said, jerking my arm away from him.

"Baby, don't do this. Don't make a mistake that you'll regret," he said, which made me pause.

I turned around, looked him straight in the eyes, and said, "A mistake? All I've been making is mistakes when it comes to you, and I promise you that this here won't be one. See, the first mistake I made was a long time ago, when I didn't leave after you cheated with Gabrielle. The second mistake I made was when I took ya back after you supposedly fathered a child with Chilly. Lord knows I love Emoni to the highest power, but the third mistake I made was when I let you knock me up. My final mistake was just now when I actually considered saying yes and thinking that a nigga like you would ever change. I can't believe it took me ten years—a whole fucking decade—to figure out that I'm better off without you in my life, but it's better that I found out now. I know that it will hurt, because you're the only man I've ever loved and given my all to, but fuck it. I just can't go through this shit no more."

I turned to his baby mama and said, "I don't know what you thought was going to happen by coming here and exposing him in front of a crowd of people, but I can definitely tell you that you've accomplished nothing. If you want him, you can have him. Just remember, though, that how you get 'im is how you lose 'im. Don't think that just because he's with you, he's going to change or be a better man. I was with him for years, and I loved him unconditionally. If he cheats on a woman who was with him when he ain't have nothing, he'll cheat on anybody. What he's done to me he will do to you."

She said nothing as she stood there with a smirk on her face. I wanted to walk over there and knock it off her face, but I took the high road. Besides, that's where females got shit fucked up. They always go after the female when their problem should be with their man instead.

"If I were one of those thirsty broads who didn't know any better, I'd come over there and smack that smirk off your face, but since I know better and I'm a bitch with class, I'll just leave like a lady instead of beating that face, because I'd send you straight to the hospital, and I wouldn't think twice about it."

"Bitch, please, I hope you don't take me for one of them bird broads. If you put your hands on me, you can bet your last dollar that I'd be the last bitch you'd ever hit. Play with me if you want to," she said, balling up her fist.

I took a few steps closer to her, but before I could make it over to her, Tay stopped me.

"You don't need to be getting all out of character over some bird bitch and fuck nigga, especially not in front of a group of people," she whispered in my ear. "There is a time and place for that, and believe me when I say that I want to fuck them up as bad as you do, but now is not the time for it. God makes no mistakes. You better believe you will see him again."

I had to think about what she was saying, because my emotions were all over the place. I wanted to fuck this bitch up, but like Tay said, now was not the time. These people had already seen all my business. *Should I continue to let them? Or should I walk away and handle the shit another day?* I turned to see the many people out in the crowd and decided against it.

"You're right. I have way more sense and class than to let them take me down this road," I said to her. *This shit ain't over though,* I thought as I walked off the stage. Then a thought came to me, and I walked over to the DJ booth. I whispered into his ear and asked him to do me a favor. He shook his head and played with a few keys on his computer before he handed me the mic, and I walked over to Cash. Since this nigga wanted me to sing a song, I had the perfect song for him. I couldn't lie. My heart was hurting me so bad. To know that I was leaving the only man who I had ever loved was killing me, but this was it. No more being a fool, no more taking him back, no more anything. I was tired, I was through, and this was the end of us.

"I used to wonder day in and day out why you would constantly cheat on me. Like, was I woman enough? Was I pretty enough for you? Was it my hair, how I kept my nails, or the color polish on my toes? Was it the way that I cooked daily for you, kept the house clean and your daughter right? Was it because I decided to be something, bought myself a house or a car without your help? Was it my independence and the fact that I didn't need a man to survive that got you all fucked up? You know, petty shit like that had me questioning if it was me that made you stray. It took me a while to figure it out. I was so busy thinking that I was the problem that I didn't get it. Until, one day, I answered my own question and decided that I wasn't the problem at all. The problem was obviously you. You were a typical man. You wanted to do what most niggas did, and believe me, I ain't mad. Hurt, yes, but I'm not mad. You can do whatever you want to do. Just know and remember that I won't be there when you need me. When nothing in your life is going right for you, you won't be able to call on Keys, because from this day forward, I'm dead to you and you're dead to me. If you wanna see Emoni, you can have your mother call me, and I'll drop her off at her house because I won't keep your daughter away from you. But under no circumstances should you be calling my phone or popping up at my house for me, because like I said, we're dead to each other."

I raised my hand up to let dude know I was ready. Two seconds later, Chrisette Michele's song "Blame It on Me" from her album *Epiphany* came flowing through the speakers.

Sometimes you can work it out
Sometimes you can't
Sometimes you're forced to watch everything fall apart

When the song was done, I dropped the mic at my feet and walked off the stage. I couldn't even finish singing. That was how emotional I had become. My nose was running, and tears were falling freely down my face. Cash had really put me through it these past few years, and I'd always taken him back. I couldn't believe I was finally saying goodbye. It was the best thing, and this time, I was going all the way through with it. No matter how hard it hurt, or how much he begged, this time there was no turning back. I was too good of a woman, and Cash wasn't the man for me.

"Keys, baby, where are you going?" I heard Cash yell out behind me. I didn't even pay his ass any mind. I kept on about my business, because I knew that if I turned around and went back, all that shit Tay was just saying to me would be dead. I would light into both of their asses, not giving a fuck about where we were or who was watching.

I made my way through the crowd of people like a madwoman. I was trying to get the hell out of this club before I messed around and did the unthinkable. Either it was the way my face was screwed up, or the crowd just knew I was pissed after they witnessed what had happened, because they were parting the way like the Red Sea. I didn't even have to fight my way through the crowd. They just moved out of my way with ease. I was glad, because from the way I was feeling, anybody could get it right now.

"Can you please get me my car before I fuck around and catch a body or two out here," I said to the young boy who had parked my car for me when I first made it here.

"Yes, ma'am," he stuttered before he ran off to get my car.

"Keys, baby, can you please talk to me?" Cash asked from behind me.

I could've sworn that I told him to leave me the fuck alone, and yet his ass is still here bothering me. Fuck, if somebody told me they didn't wanna be bothered with me, I would've left them alone the first time.

"Cash, I already told yo' ass to leave me alone. That's ya best bet before you make me do something that I'll later regret. Again!" I yelled, not even turning around. I didn't want to face him. I couldn't. How could I not look at him and feel hurt, anger, and pain? The man I wanted to spend the rest of my life with had hurt me to the core, and all I could think about was getting even somehow. Tonight this man took my heart and tore it up into a million pieces, and I didn't know which piece to pick up to begin gluing it back together.

"Baby, I know I fucked up, and I'm sorry. Please don't leave me like this," he begged.

I continued to ignore him because I didn't have anything to say to him. I wasn't about to put my time nor energy into this man anymore just so he could go back and do the same thing a few months later. Oh, no! That was not about to happen. I didn't need that in my life.

"Tell me what I gotta do, baby! Tell me what I got to do to make it right, and I will do it. Just don't walk out on me. I'll do whatever. I need my girl in my life."

By then, the man had pulled up with my car and was now holding the door open, waiting for me to get in. I turned around and looked at Cash. I noticed his baby mama standing behind him. I could've been like any other bitch and fucked her up, but my problem wasn't with her. It was with my man.

I began shaking my head. I used to love this man unconditionally. There was a time when he could do no wrong in my eyes, because I knew he loved me too and would never do anything to hurt me, but that man was gone and so were the thoughts of him never hurting me. I didn't know what to think about him right now, but I did know that I didn't want him anymore.

"There's nothing in this world you can do to make me stay. I've played the fool for you too long, and it's time for me to move on with my life. You did what you did because obviously I wasn't making you happy. So this is me letting you go to be free and happy. Do whatever you want. I don't care. I won't hound you or worry, because you're no longer my business, and I expect the same in return. Have a nice life, Cash."

With that being said, I hopped in my car and pulled off. Lord knows I was hurting inside from those words, but this had to be done. In my heart, I knew it was going to take me a while, but with time, I was going to get through this. I couldn't go on playing the fool for Cash any longer. I was too good for that. I was going to find a man who was going to love and appreciate me. One who deserved me.

Tay

I wanted to believe that what this chick was saying to Keys wasn't true, but I knew better. Hell, we all knew better. Everybody in the state of Tennessee knew that Cash was a dog and he couldn't keep his dick in his pants. Hell, this wasn't the first time a chick came at Keyon, saying that Cash was the father of her child, but this time, unlike the last time, I knew it was true. The nigga didn't even try to deny it. He just stood there looking like a helpless puppy, while his side bitch made my friend look like the biggest fool in the world in a club full of people. I wanted so badly to smack the fuck out of her and shoot his punk ass, but I couldn't get into trouble because I worked at the hospital. Don't get me wrong. I still fucked bitches up. I just made sure there weren't too many witnesses around in case the police were to get involved.

As I watched my best friend of nine years walk out the door with tears running down her face, I knew that this time Cash had pushed her past her breaking point. I just hoped and prayed that she didn't take him back, because I was tired of seeing her get hurt by the same man for the same reasons.

I wanted to follow her out of the club, but she needed to be a big girl and do this on her own. Yes, I was always going to be there if or when she needed a shoulder to cry on or an ear to listen to her. However, when it came to Cash, she never listened to anything I had to say, so I stopped putting my two cents into her business. I didn't know how many times I begged her to leave him because of this same bullshit. She would just shoo me off and say that she loved him too much to walk away from him. That was why I only voiced my opinion if or when it was really and desperately needed. Right now, she needed to get her head together. She needed to see what everyone else saw. Cash was a nobody. He was going to keep hurting her unless she put an end to that shit herself.

I took one last look at the bitch Cash fucked my friend over with before I left the stage. Most likely, since she and Cash had a son together, we'd be seeing her ass around. She wasn't going to be lucky all the time. You'd better believe that she was going to get caught slipping. As for Keyon, I was going to pray that my friend got it together before Cash took her all the way under. I'd call her tomorrow and see what was up then. I just hoped like hell she learned her lesson and left that straying mutt alone. She was too good of a woman to be going through all the things that she was going through behind a good-for-nothing man.

CHAPTER TWO

Keys

When I pulled up to the house, I drove my car all the way to the front door. I ain't care about no fucking grass or nothing. I had three things on my mind: get Emoni, get some of our shit, and get out of there before Cash showed up like I knew he would. I knew he wasn't going to heed what I said back at the club. He was like most men. He wanted to play until it was time to pay, and like always, they don't miss shit until it's gone. Now that I'd walked out on him and said that I was through with him, he was going to try to do whatever he could to make me stay. That was how he operated.

I walked up to the door and busted it open like I was the damn police or something. The door hit the wall so hard that it knocked down a portrait that was hanging up. I didn't care about any of that shit. It wasn't my house to begin with.

"Where's Emoni?" I asked the chick Monique who would babysit for us from time to time. I must have scared the poor girl, because she came running to the door shaking and stuttering.

"She's upstairs in her room. What's wrong? What's going on?" she asked, barely getting her words out.

I didn't say anything to her, I ran up the stairs, straight to my daughter's room. Trying not to wake her, I walked over to the closet, grabbed her custom-made Doc McStuffins suitcase, and began pulling clothes off the hangers and placing them inside. When it was filled, I grabbed another one, walked over to her dresser, and began pulling clothes out and dropping them inside.

"What's going on, Ms. Miller?" Monique asked from the doorway.

I looked back at her, gave her a look that said, "Bitch, shut the fuck up," and continued on about my business. When I was through packing what I could, I placed the suitcases by the door, instructing her to take them downstairs and place them by the front door. I then walked back over to the bed to get Emoni.

"Moni, wake up, baby," I said, gently shaking her. She tossed and turned in her sleep a bit before she fell back asleep. "Moni, it's Mommy. Baby, wake up."

"Mommy?" she asked, sitting up and wiping the sleep from her eyes.

"Come on, let's go," I said, grabbing her arms.

"But I'm tired. I want to go back to sleep," she said groggily.

I felt bad that I had to wake my 4-year-old daughter up at this time of the morning, all because of her stupid-ass father. "Come on, you'll get to sleep when we get home," I said, picking her up.

"But we are home, Mommy. Where's Daddy?" she asked, more alert this time. For only 4, my daughter was very bright and smart as hell.

I ignored her question and decided that I was going to have to carry her out to the car. After wrapping her into her blanket, I picked her up and carried her out of the room and down the stairs. We bumped into Monique, who was still standing by the door, but this time she was talking to someone on the phone.

"Umm, excuse me, Ms. Miller," she said, stopping me in my tracks. Then she handed me the phone and said, "Mr. Edwards would like to talk to you. He says it's important."

I looked at the phone in her hand, and then I looked at her as if she were crazy. "Tell Cash I have nothing to say to him."

"He said please."

"Look, I don't have time for this shit. Tell Cash to leave me the fuck alone," I said, pushing past her. "While you're at it, you can tell him I said to jump on a first-class flight straight to hell please. Better yet, jump off a bridge. It might make me feel better." With that I left.

When I made it to the car, I opened the door and placed Emoni on the back seat. When I made sure that she was in there safely, I ran and got her bags from by the door and placed them in the trunk. Leaving it open, I ran back inside and up to what used to be my bedroom. I grabbed one of Cash's overnight bags and filled it with as many of my clothes as possible that could fit in there. I then moved to the closet and proceeded to open the safe. I removed a couple of bands, my bank statements, the keys to my safety deposit boxes, and the keys to my house and threw them in my purse, which was sitting on the dresser. I wasn't worrying about jewelry or anything else. I could get those material things again. All I wanted to do was get what was mine and be on my way. I wasn't even going to worry about the rest of my clothes. I was just going to have to buy some for myself, as well as Emoni.

After making sure I had everything that I needed, I grabbed the overnight bag, along with my purse, and ran back downstairs. I was guessing that Monique had left, because I didn't see her anymore. It was either that or she was in another part of the house. Whatever the case, I didn't care. All I cared about was getting the hell out of dodge.

Once I made it back outside, I threw my bags in the trunk, closed it, hopped in my car, and backed up onto the street. Cash had better hope that Monique was still there, because I didn't even bother to close the door. I left that bitch wide open. As far as I was concerned, I no longer cared what happened. I didn't care if somebody went up in there and stole everything or the bitch burned down. After taking one last look at the house that was my home for a few years, I threw my car in gear and sped off. *It's going to be a long time before I ever step foot near this bitch again,* I thought as I drove off.

I peeped in the mirror and saw that Moni was sound asleep on the back seat. I couldn't believe that I was dragging my child out of the house at three in the morning. Lord knows if my mama knew that, she would kick my ass, but she lived back in Louisiana, and I was happy about that. In that moment, as I looked at my 4-year-old daughter sleeping, I made a promise to myself that I was going to set an example for her. I wanted her to know what a queen was and how one should be treated. She didn't need to see what I was going through with her father, because Lord knows that wasn't how a queen was supposed to be treated.

"It's okay, pooh. If I have to be alone, I promise I will do that before I ever let a nigga come in my life and mistreat me again," I said as if she could hear me. I meant what I said though. I wouldn't let another man come into my life and fuck it up as Cash had done these past years. In fact, I wasn't even going to look for a man. I was going to let him find me.

Cash

As I stood there watching the only woman I'd ever loved besides my mother and daughter walk out on me, I wanted to break down and cry or at least hurt something. I didn't mean for Keys to find out about Mia or li'l Cash. Well, at least not yet. I wanted to settle down, make her my wife, have another baby, and then I was going to tell her about li'l Cash. This was too early. She wasn't supposed to find out this way. I had just bought her a ring and was planning to marry her in the next few months. Even though we had gotten into it and she had broken up with me earlier, I wasn't tripping. We'd been through a lot of shit, but I knew I was going to marry her. However, that stupid bitch Mia had to come in and fuck everything up. Only God knows what I was going to do to that bitch when I got close to her and there was no one around. I was going to make sure that she respected me the next time, and that was on everything.

I didn't even know how the bitch found out where I stayed. She knew about Keyon because I was the one who told her about her. I made that the first thing I mentioned when shorty first came at me. I let it be known that I already had a woman who I was not leaving, but shorty still wanted to fuck with ya boy, so that was what we did. We fucked around for maybe about a year, but then she started to catch feelings. I told her I wasn't having that, so she started threatening me, saying that she was going to tell my girl all about our relationship. I ended up whooping her ass and leaving her alone for a few months. However, one time when I was in town, we ended up fucking, and a few weeks later, she ended up pregnant. That bitch had trapped me, but I didn't have any proof. How the fuck did I stop fucking with her for months, and just when I decided to fuck with her and give her some dick, she ended up pregnant? That shit still didn't sit right with me, but there was nothing I could do about it. Li'l Cash was here, and nobody could do anything about it, not even Keyon.

"Cash, where are you going?" Mia asked, walking behind me.

"Look, Mia, just leave me alone, all right?" I shouted at her.

"Nah, fuck that. I'm tired of you pushing me away. You're going to talk to me, and I mean right fucking now!" she replied.

I turned to her and stared at her for a minute. Had I known that this bitch would pull some shit like that, I wouldn't have fucked with her from the beginning. She grabbed my arm, but I quickly pulled it back.

"Come here, Cash!"

"Dawg, for real. I'm not even trying to be near you right now, because I'm afraid of what I might do to you!" I said, waving her off as I walked off toward my car.

"Too bad, because I'm not going no damn where!" she screamed and followed me. "What is it about her that has you like this, huh? I thought you said you loved me, that you wanted to marry me. That we were going to be a family. Cash, I'm the mother of your child. I deserve some type of respect, and I damn well deserve some answers. Hell, you even bought me a ring!"

"Look, bitch, you just basically cost me my girl and my life. The best thing you can do for me right now is to get ghost before I fuck around and have our son motherless," I told her in the nicest way that I could've. "You want some type of respect, hollering about you're the mother of my child. What the fuck about Keyon? She's also the mother of my child. You didn't give her any respect when you rolled your sad ass up in here and pulled that shit in front of basically everybody who lives in Memphis, but you over here demanding that I respect you. You don't give me anything to respect, and for your information, I only bought that ring to make you shut your funky-ass mouth. I never had any intention of marrying you. Fuck. That ring ain't even real, homegirl."

"Boy, you know better. You ain't going to put your hands on me. I don't give a fuck who she is. You owed her respect. I didn't. You weren't worrying about my feelings, so why should I worry about sparing her feelings, Casimere?" she said, placing her hands on her hips.

I was about to show her better than I could tell her, but dude pulled up with my car, so instead of giving in to her bullshit, I walked over to my car and hopped in. As I was about to close the door, she stopped me.

"Cash, you better not walk away from me. I need you. Your son needs you. You can't and won't do this shit to us!"

"Dawg, you taking me for a joke right now. You really lucky I'm not breaking your fucking neck and shit from the shit you just pulled. So, I'm telling you now to get the fuck away from me!"

"I already told you that I'm not going nowhere. So you might as well talk to me now."

I looked at her for a minute. I had love for my baby mama. I mean, she did birth my one and only son. She kept him right, and whenever I was in town, she devoted herself to me, but right now, I felt totally different about her. I never in my right mind thought she was one of them sheisty females or that she would try to fuck over a nigga, but, boy, was I wrong. The shit she pulled tonight had me on one. It wasn't as if I didn't tell her ass before that I had a woman in my life—a real woman. Shit, she couldn't compare to Keyon. She couldn't do half of the shit that Keyon did for me when I was broke and didn't have anything. Keys was my ride or die. I wanted to leave that ho stanking, but because of li'l Cash, I wouldn't. If she kept pushing on my nerves though, I would have to go back on my word.

"The best thing you can do to keep your life right nice is to go back to Chicago and be with our son. When I'm through putting back the pieces of my life you just fucked up, I'll come and see y'all, but until then, stay the fuck away from me and Keyon and go back home." I didn't even give her time to respond before I closed my car door and pulled off, never looking back. I didn't have time to be wasting on her right now. I needed to get home and stop Keys from leaving me and taking my daughter with her.

I made it home in literally fifteen minutes. Lord knows it was supposed to take me much longer, but I damn near broke every traffic law trying to get home. I even sideswiped a car on my way, but I didn't stop. I just kept it pushing and prayed that no one saw me and called the police on me before I got home. The only thing on my mind was getting home to Keys and my daughter.

When I pulled up to the house, Keyon's car was nowhere in sight, and the front door was wide open. I hurriedly threw my car into park, jumped out, and ran inside. "Keyon!" I yelled once I entered the house. I spotted a few portraits on the floor that were once on the wall, but I wasn't worrying about that. "Keys. Emoni!"

"Umm, they're not here. They left about ten to fifteen minutes ago," the babysitter said.

"Left? Where did they go?" I questioned her.

"I have no idea."

"Fuck!" I yelled. I walked over to the wall and punched a hole in it. I instantly regretted it when an excruciating pain shot through my hand. "Ahhh fuck!" I screamed out in pain.

"Hold on, let me help you," Monique said, running to the kitchen. A few minutes later, she came back with a Ziploc bag with ice in it. "Here, place this on it."

I grabbed the bag from her and placed it on my hand. Even that shit was hurting, but nothing compared to the hurt I was feeling without my girl and my daughter being here. I couldn't believe that Keyon actually left me and took Moni with her. I knew she said it, but I thought she was just playing on her emotions as she always did. I never really thought she would actually go through with it.

Ignoring the pain in my hand, I stood up. I then reached into my pockets and pulled out the money that I had collected from my boy earlier. I peeled off a few hundreds and then handed them to Monique. "Thank you for watching Emoni, and thanks for the ice. You can go home now."

"Are you sure? I mean, do you need me to take you to the hospital for your hand or something?" she asked, concerned.

"Nah, I'm straight, but thanks for caring."

"Okay. Well, be careful and take care of yourself, Mr. Edwards," she said, standing up. She then grabbed her purse from the floor and left.

I sat down on the floor, feeling defeated. Keys was my everything. Without shorty I didn't know how I would've survived. Baby girl always kept me on my A game. When I didn't have a dime, she bought me everything that I needed, and if she didn't have it, she would steal it for me. Shorty was my gangsta bitch. She was my thug. She wasn't my wife, but when shit was tight, she was always there to make it all seem right. To know that she had finally reached her breaking point with me was devastating. I always imagined that we would be together forever, until we were old and gray, sitting in rocking chairs on our front porch, raising our grandkids together. My actions barely showed up, but shorty was like my ribs. Without her, there was no me, and I couldn't just sit back and let her go like that. I was not about to lose my woman like that. Fuck all that shit. I wasn't one of those types of niggas who would just sit there and do nothing. I was going to fight for what was mine.

As I sat there on the floor, I couldn't help but think about Keyon and Louisiana. The Keyon who was here today wasn't shit compared to the Keyon back then. My baby was a bad girl, but she had calmed down a lot. Baby girl was a live wire, and everyone in Louisiana knew the shit. That was how I met her. She and one of her friends were at a party down at Southern University Campus in Baton Rouge. Me and my friend Joey were there also. Well, at least then we were friends. Anyway, the campus was popping, and there were food and drinks all over. When I tell you damn near every teenager from Louisiana was there, they were.

"Damn, nigga, I'm so glad we decided to come to this party," Joey said, eyeing the females in attendance.

"Shit, I'm glad my damn self. It ain't like we had nothing better to do," I answered, enjoying the view myself. *"I can't wait until we're able to get with Big Dog and get this money."*

"Nigga, me neither," he replied just as we heard a commotion coming from behind us. We turned to find two females fussing.

"Bitch, next time, you'd better watch where you're walking," a bright chick said to a chick with a caramel complexion.

"Look, Brittney, you better go ahead about ya business. I'm not in the mood, and you know damn well you bumped into me," the chick spoke calmly.

I tapped Joey and told him to follow me over there. I wanted to see the shit up close.

"Keyon, I didn't do shit. You bumped me," ol' girl said, inching closer to the dark chick.

"Fuck it," the chick named Keyon responded, taking off her earrings. She handed them to her friend, then walked over to the other girl. *"You know this ain't about you bumping me, Brittney. So tell us why you're doing it, because I'm sure everyone would love to know."*

Brittney looked from her friend to Keyon, then back to her friend. She didn't say anything. She just folded her arms across her chest and rolled her eyes. Keyon looked around, and that was when our eyes connected. For a minute she stood there staring at me. It was like she was talking to me with her eyes.

"That's this ho's problem. She's always in somebody's man's f—" *Brittney began to say but was stopped when Keyon's fist connected with her mouth. Next thing we knew, they were having a brawl right there in front of everybody.*

"Bitch, we both know your dumb ass is only fucking with me behind that nigga Blandy," *Keyon said as she continued to beat the brakes off her. I couldn't lie. She ain't got a lick off her. She wasn't even swinging back. It was like she knew she was about to get her ass whipped.* "Next time, you're going to think twice before you fuck around and play with me behind a nigga I don't want."

I looked around at all the people watching the fight. Nobody was trying to stop them. Everyone was standing around just looking like they wanted the shit to happen, but I couldn't continue to watch that shit any longer. Why would I let them continue to fight and risk them going to jail or something?

"Come on," *I said, grabbing her off the girl.*

"Nah, let me go so I can give her what she wants," *she yelled, trying to break away from me.*

I pulled her close before whispering in her ear. Instantly she stopped putting up a fight and walked off with me. For a minute we didn't say anything. We only walked. We walked until we were away from everyone.

"You good, li'l mama?" *I finally asked her.*

"Yeah, I'm good. Thank you," *she replied, twirling a finger in her hair.*

"You don't have to thank me. I just couldn't stand there and continue to let a beautiful girl like yourself be out here fighting like that," I said, which caused her to blush. "So, if you don't mind me asking, what was all that about?"

"You know, the usual. She was just mad because her boyfriend likes me and told me so in my Facebook inbox," she told me. I would have figured that it had something to do with a man even if I hadn't heard them fighting. That was how females were. They were quick to fight behind a nigga.

"So are you single?"

"Yes."

"Why?" I asked.

"Why what?"

"Why are you single?"

"Because I don't have time to be playing games with these niggas. All of them were confused and wanted more than one female. I wasn't trying to be nobody's option," she explained.

"Well, what if I said I wanted you to be my one and only girl?" I asked. I couldn't lie. When I first laid eyes on her, I wanted her. I was glad to hear that she didn't have a man or anything, because I was trying to get to know her on another level.

"I don't even know you. For all I know you could be a killer or something," she said, smiling.

"That's okay. We can get to know each other."

"Okay, give me your number, and we can start from there," she said to me.

"Okay," I said, pulling out a pen and paper. I wrote my number down before handing her the paper. She then took the paper and pen and did the same. "Make sure you call me, beautiful."

"I will," she replied. She leaned in and kissed my cheek before she walked off. She ended up calling me the next day, and ever since then we'd been together.

After a few minutes of sitting on the floor and debating what I wanted to do, I got up and walked up the stairs to my room and into the closet. Walking over to the safe, I unlocked it to get the set of keys that Keyon had in there. She thought I didn't know, but I knew she'd always had a spare set in there. To my surprise, when I opened the safe, the keys were gone. So were a few other things that were in there a few days ago.

Closing the safe, I looked around the closet and noticed a few empty hangers. I walked out of the closet, down the hall, and into Emoni's room, where I found the closet door open and a few open empty drawers. Passing my hand over my face, I walked over to Emoni's bed and took a seat on it. I then pulled out my phone and dialed Keys' number. The phone rang a few times before it went to voicemail. Deciding not to leave a message, I hung the phone up and tried her number again. This time, it rang two times and she sent it to voicemail, which let me know that she saw me calling. I wanted to feel some type of way, but I couldn't. I knew that what I did and had done to her these past few years was going to catch up with me. I just didn't think that it would happen this soon. I thought our love was going to conquer everything, but obviously, I was wrong.

After sitting in Emoni's room for a few more minutes, I got up. I wasn't about to just sit there and let my girl go like that. I had to do something. Even though I didn't know what it was, I was going to think of something.

Going into my room, I grabbed an overnight bag, threw a few items in there, and left, making my way down the stairs. I made sure that all the doors and windows downstairs were locked before I set the alarm and headed out the door. I hopped in my car, threw the bag in the back seat, and drove off. It was late, but I was going to Keys' house. Hopefully, she would think about all the good times we'd been through and take me back. That was a far stretch, but I was hoping and praying that God would work some type of miracle for me.

CHAPTER THREE

Keys

It was almost three o'clock in the morning when I pulled up to my apartment. I was tired and worn out both mentally and physically. All I wanted to do was crawl in my bed and forget this day had ever happened. I knew I couldn't, but that wasn't going to stop me from trying.

I was happy that my apartment was on the first floor, because when I looked in the back seat, Moni was still knocked out. My poor baby was tired, so I didn't even try to wake her. I wasn't going to be able to get more of our things from Cash's, so I would just have to wait until later that evening. I grabbed my purse and keys before I got out, opened the back door, and grabbed Emoni. *Damn, I didn't know my baby was this heavy,* I thought as I struggled to place her on my shoulder. When I had her somewhat situated, I closed the door using my legs and made my way toward the building.

I was almost to the entrance when I almost fell. Thank God I didn't, because both Emoni and I would've been on the ground together. Instead, my purse and keys ended up on the ground. "Fuck!" I cursed as my eyes began to get misty. I absolutely hated feeling helpless, and right now I was as helpless as a baby who was left in the house all alone. I stood there, bouncing my daughter from shoulder to shoulder, as I wondered how I was going to get my things off the ground without waking her, when a voice behind me scared the shit out of me.

"Let me help you out there, little lady," he said, bending down and picking up my things and then handing them to me. It was in that time when our fingers touched for a moment that I felt an electric shock jolt through my body. "Here you go."

"Oh, my God," I said, jerking my hand from his. "Umm. Thank you."

"You're welcome." He smiled, revealing a pair of pearly white teeth. "My name is Kane."

"Keys," I said, reaching my hand out for him to shake. I wasn't trying to give his ass my government name. Hell, I didn't know who the fuck this nigga was.

"Kane and Keys—that sounds good together," he said, shaking my hand.

"I bet," I said sarcastically. *I know this nigga is not trying to flirt with me,* I thought as I stood there.

"So what's a pretty lady like yourself doing out here this time of the night and with your daughter?" he asked.

"I was trying to go inside, but that was proving to be a task in itself," I answered with a slight attitude. Right now was really not the time for this nigga to even be trying to flirt with me. If he were a real man, he'd be trying to get me inside instead of flirting with me out here in the streets.

"Right, I'm sorry, ma," he said. "Let me walk you inside."

"Nah, I'm good," I said, declining his offer. I didn't know this nigga well enough to be letting him walk me inside. For all I knew, he could be trying to kill us or something.

"Look, ma, I know you don't know me, but all I want to do is make sure that you and li'l mama get inside safely," he said as if he could read my thoughts.

I stood there for a minute contemplating whether I should let him walk me inside. As I said, I didn't trust him like that, but if he wanted to harm us, he could've done that already.

"Okay," I said, shifting Emoni yet again before I began walking toward the front entrance. For my baby only being 4, she was beaucoup heavy. Crazy thing was she barely wanted to eat. Sometimes I had to force her to eat, so I didn't know where all her weight was coming from.

"So! How come this is my first time ever seeing you? Like, I've been living here for years, and I haven't seen you around here once before this," he said, trying to spark up a conversation.

"Because I just moved here, and that's none of your business," I told him matter-of-factly.

"Oh, shorty, my bad. You don't have to bite my head off. I was just asking," he said, throwing his hands up in surrender.

I immediately regretted that shit. "I'm sorry," I said, apologizing to him. I was still mad with Cash, and I was taking it out on him.

"It's cool, ma," he said before he became quiet. He was probably cursing my ass out in his mind, and I didn't blame him one bit. I couldn't believe I really caught an attitude with him when he'd been nothing but nice and helpful to me. Hell, if the situations were reversed, I would've left my ass right fucking there with my child and everything.

It wasn't long before we made it to the door. Like the gentleman he was, he opened the door and allowed me to walk in. "Well, I'm going to get going. Have a great night," he said, trying to leave, but I stopped him.

"Hold up. Wait a minute," I said, grabbing his arm. "I'm really sorry for the way I've been acting. I promise you that I don't normally act like that. It's just that I just found out that my boyfriend was cheating on me yet again. We've broken up for good, and I'm still feeling kind of blue." I didn't know why I felt the need to explain myself, but I did. Besides, I didn't want this man to think I was stuck-up after he'd helped me out.

"I was wondering why a pretty lady like yourself had an attitude like that, but it's cool, ma," he said, causing me to blush.

For the first time, I took a good look at him, and I had to admit that homie was fine with a capital F. Baby boy stood at about six foot two, had a caramel complexion, sported a curly Mohawk, and he was muscular with a set of bedroom eyes that could make a bitch nut by just looking in them. Oh, and his smile. When he smiled, he showed off a great set of deep dimples. I couldn't help but check him out. *My God!* I thought, squeezing my thighs together.

"I'm sorry. I swear I'm a good person. I've just been in a bad mood lately," I said, apologizing yet again.

"You can stop apologizing, ma. I already told you that you were good. I ain't tripping off that," he said, showing off those dimples again.

For a minute, I stood there lost. I watched as his mouth continued to move, but I didn't hear a thing that was coming out of his mouth. His lips were so juicy and looked so soft. I could only imagine how good they'd feel kissing up my thighs or pressed against my lower set of lips. I was so busy thinking about all the things I'd do to him if given the chance that I didn't hear him.

"Yo, ma, you still there?" he asked, waving his hand in front of my face.

"Oh, yeah. My bad," I said, embarrassed. I couldn't believe I was caught slipping like that. *You gotta get it together, Keyon.*

"Oh, it's cool. I have that type of effect on women these days," he replied, laughing.

Cocky nigga, I thought, rolling my eyes.

"Uh-huh. Well, I think it's time for me to head inside," I said, changing the subject. I definitely was feeling him, but I didn't want him to know that. Like I said before, I was not going to look for no nigga. I was going to wait for him to find me.

"Oh, yeah. I'm sorry for holding you up," he apologized. "Let me walk you to your door," he offered.

"Nah, I'm good. Besides, my apartment is right down the hall," I said, pointing toward my apartment door. "I've already taken up enough of your time."

"I've enjoyed every minute of your company, ma," he said, just as Moni began to move. "But, ummm, go ahead and get li'l mama to bed. I'll see y'all around."

"Okay, Kane. It was nice meeting you, and thank you for the help."

"Likewise, Keys, and you're welcome," he said before he winked and left.

I stood there for a few seconds thinking about him. Then my shoulder began hurting, bringing me back to reality. Shaking Kane from my thoughts, I hurried down the hall to my apartment, opened the door, and laid Emoni down on the sofa before shutting and locking the door. Once I was done, I picked Moni up and brought her to my bedroom. Thank God I followed my first mind and furnished this place when I first got it. Otherwise, we would've been sleeping on the floor tonight.

Placing Moni on the bed, I removed her sweater along with her shoes and placed her underneath the covers. I clicked on the TV in case she woke up and I wasn't there, and then I headed back into the living room to get my purse. Just as I made it there, my phone began to ring. Grabbing my purse from the sofa, I fished my phone out and answered it.

"Hello?"

"You good, boo?" Tay asked me.

"Honestly, I have no choice but to be," I said. "I'm hurt, yeah, but I shouldn't have expected anything more from Cash than what I got. After all the things he's put my ass through these last couple of years, I shouldn't have been surprised. Hell, he might have more kids waiting out in the cut somewhere. Don't be surprised!"

"You ain't never lied," she said, cracking a joke. "I don't know how you can be so strong. If that had been me, my nigga would've been in the city morgue, and I would've been in someone's holding cell waiting to be processed. You way better than me, honey!"

"Now that I do know, I can't keep making an ass out of myself behind Cash anymore. I've been doing that for too damn long, and quite frankly, I'm so damn tired," I said, feeling the tears well up in my eyes, but I just refused to let them fall. I was done wasting my good tears on a good-for-nothing man.

"So what are you going to do?" she asked. That was a good question, one I didn't even have a good answer to.

"Honestly, I don't know, but what I do know is that I don't want Cash. I'm through with that heartache and pain. It's time for me to start being happy with my life," I said, meaning it.

"Girl, I feel ya. There comes a time in life when playing the fool gets old and played out," she said just as my phone beeped.

I pulled the phone from my ear and noticed that it was Cash calling. I knew he wouldn't be too far behind, but I was not about to fall for that shit, nor was I going to answer the phone.

"You over at the apartment?"

"Girl, yes, and I'm glad, too, because Cash is blowing my phone up as we speak. I know he's probably on his way to my old house, but his ass is going to be shocked when he realizes that I don't live there anymore." I laughed just as my phone began beeping again. Knowing that it wasn't anybody but Cash, I hit the button to ignore the call. I wasn't trying to hear him beg and plead just to go back and do the same thing a few months later.

"Yeah, I already know his game. It was a good thing you played him before he could play you," she concurred.

"I know, right? His ass is going to be mad when he gets over to the house and notices that I don't live there anymore," I laughed.

"Yes, indeed, and it was a good thing we decided to furnish the apartment when ya first got it, or else ya would've been shit out of luck." She laughed with me.

"I thought the same thing when I walked up in here earlier."

"Where's Emoni?"

"She's in bed."

"Is she all packed to go to her Momo Charmaine's day after tomorrow?" she asked.

"Oh, shit!" I screamed. With everything that had gone down, I totally forgot that Moni was supposed to be going to Louisiana to stay with my mother. "Girl, I done forgot that Moni was leaving this weekend with everything that's been going on. I ain't packed a damn thing!"

"Shit, just go get her things from home then," she suggested.

"No. I don't wanna be nowhere near Cash. I'll just go to the mall and get her a few things when she wakes up in the morning."

"Well, call me when you girls get through, and I'll come over to the apartment and help you pack her things."

"Okay, girl. Good night," I said, yawning.

"Good night, Keys. I love you, girl."

"Love you too," I said before we hung up.

After getting off the phone with Tay, I went and took a ten-minute shower. When I was finished, I brushed my teeth, threw my hair into a ponytail, and got into bed next to Moni. Before I could get comfortable, my phone began ringing. I already had a feeling that it was Cash calling again. Sure enough, when I turned over to check my phone, his name was there. I guessed his ass wasn't getting the message that I didn't want to be bothered with him, and I knew he wasn't going to stop calling me. I decided that I was going to turn my phone off. Right now, all I wanted to do was get some sleep and not think about Cash and his drama at all. Sleep was the only thing on my mind, and that was where I was going.

Cash

Only the Lord and I knew how mad I was when I pulled up to the house that Keys and I had first lived in and spotted that big-ass FOR SALE sign in the front yard. At first glance, I thought I was tripping, but once I looked at the address a few times, I knew that I wasn't. I had no idea that Keys was even selling the house. I pulled out my phone and attempted to call her, but she didn't answer. That pissed me off, because now I didn't know where either she or my daughter was. *This bitch is really going to make me put my hands on her,* I thought as I sat in the truck. I was both confused and outdone. I always thought that she was going to keep it as a backup for when things like this happened, but again, I'd underestimated her. I guessed shorty was really trying to prove to me that she was done, but like I said, I wasn't giving up, nor was I going to let the next man come slide his way in and get what I'd invested years in. Keyon was mine whether she believed it or not, and we were going to get married soon.

Trying my luck, I called her again, but she continued to ignore me. I wanted so badly to leave a message, but I didn't. I was going to give her the space that she needed. *A week or two,* I thought as I thought about where she could possibly be. That was all I was hoping to give her to get over this little situation and bring her ass back home where both she and Emoni belonged.

Taking a chance, I dialed Tay's number. Keys didn't have any family down here, so that was the only place she could be.

"Hello. Who's this?" Tay answered with an attitude. She sounded like she was sleeping. I knew she didn't know that it was me calling, because she wouldn't have answered the phone.

"Tay, it's me, Cash," I said, ignoring the attitude that she had.

"What do you want, Cash?" she asked, smacking her lips. It was no secret that Tay, otherwise known as Sha' Taylor, didn't like me. She was one of the many people who thought that I was no good for Keyon. To be honest, I kind of thought that too. "Do you see what time it is? What the hell are you calling me for?"

"Ma, don't play dumb. I saw you at the club earlier. Are Keys and Emoni over there?" I asked, cutting right to the chase since she was trying to play stupid.

"Look, Cash, I don't know where Keys and Emoni are, and if I knew, I wouldn't be telling you a damn thing," she replied. "I'm happy that she left your good-for-nothing ass, because my girl was way too good for a nigga like you!"

"Look, ma, honestly, what goes on between me and my lady has nothing to do with you."

"Lies! Who the fuck told you that bullshit?" she barked. "Keyon is my best friend, and Emoni is my godchild. Therefore, whatever they go through is my business."

"No, it's not. Keys ain't fucking you, nor am I. Therefore, it's none of your fucking business."

"Nigga, please! You're not the one who's there when she cries. You're not the one sitting on the phone with her for hours at a time, trying to calm her down because some bitch done called and told her about your dirty-dick ass. You weren't the one there when that crazy bitch Lele tried to run her over. I was. I was always there. You know why? Because I genuinely love her, and I don't wanna see her hurt!"

"I love her t—" I began to say, but she cut me off.

"The fuck you do. How the fuck can you love someone when you're constantly cheating on them? How the fuck can you love her when you're forever hurting her? What kind of bullshit love you think you spitting? Because that ain't no kind of love. When you love someone, you go above and beyond the call of duty to keep them happy. You don't bring her no type of happiness. For the past few years, all you've brought her was pain, heartache, and disease," she spazzed. "Talking 'bout love. Nigga, you don't know the first thing about love. You had a whole baby on her and hid that shit for a year. Now you talking about some love. That ain't love!"

"Look, bitch, like I said before, whatever me and my lady go through ain't none of ya fucking business. It's no-man-having hoes like y'all who make me sick. How the fuck is you going to judge someone when you ain't got a man first? Bitch, you don't know what love is, because don't nobody want ya slutty ass. Ain't got a fucking man, yet you all up in our business, filling her head up with all that bullshit. You pro'ly was the one who convinced her to leave me. I always knew you was a jealous bitch. You just want what we got. What ya ass don't know is that our love is forever. She's gone today, but a few days from now, watch where she'll be."

"Aww, shit, it sounds like you're mad. Tell me, though, are you big mad or little mad?" she asked, laughing. "I could never be jealous of my muthafucking friend, dumbass, because unlike you, I have love for her. I've never once filled her head up with anything. She left you because she was tired of your fucking bullshit, and I'll say it's about goddamn time. You ain't nothing but a pussy-ass nigga. How you fuck over someone who's been there for you for years, over some ho pussy? You made your bed multiple times. It's time for you to lie in it. As for me having a man, I don't want one, especially if he got to be a flea-and-tick thing like you. Now like I said earlier, I don't know where she's at, and if I did know, I wasn't going to tell your dog ass a damn thing. It's your turn to be out here looking like a damn fool. But umm, look at the time. I have to go. Good night! Oh, and don't you ever attempt to dial my fucking number again, fuck boy!"

"Bitch, look—" I started to scream at her when I heard a click sound in my ear. Pulling the phone from my ear, I saw that she had hung up on me. It was best that she did, because I was about to bless her fucking soul. I didn't know why Keys rocked with a ho like that anyway. The bitch was always in her ear about me. She never liked me, and I tried to let that shit slide since she was my girl's best friend, but fuck all that. If she wasn't going to respect me, I damn sure wasn't going to respect her ass.

Getting myself together, I was about to pull off when my phone began to ring. Rushing to grab my phone, thinking that it was Keyon calling back, I knocked it out of my hand. The pain that shot through my hand almost made me shit on myself. I made up my mind right then and there that since I wasn't going to get to talk to Keys tonight, I was at least going to go to the hospital for my damn hand.

"Hello," I said, answering the phone.

"Where are you, Cash?" said Mia.

"The question is, where are you?" I asked her. "I hope you're on your way back to Chicago, because if ya ain't, I'm going to fuck you up big time, Mia. You can ignore me if you want to."

"Cash, go on ahead with that shit. You know damn well you ain't going to do a muthafucking thing to me. So please, by all means, shut the fuck up."

"I'on know why y'all bitches insist on fucking with me, but I swear on the life of my kids that if you hoes don't fall back in line, I'm going to make y'all . . ." I said. *Fuck it. I don't care if she heard me. I'm tired of these bitches playing me as if I weren't that nigga. They must have forgotten that my name is Cash and I don't play that shit.* It was time for me to stop playing games and start showing them. Baby mamas or not, no hoes were going to run over or play with me.

"Who you calling a bitch?" she asked.

"Yo' dumb ass. Mia, I promise you, on the life of my son, that if I catch you down here, I'm going to beat some sense into you," I said, meaning every word I was telling her.

"Cash, I'm not scared of you. You must have forgotten who I am. I'm not Keys. If you put your hands on me, you're going to regret the day your mother gave birth to you," she had the audacity to say.

I pulled the phone from my ear in disbelief, because I knew for sure this bitch didn't just threaten me.

"Since you want to be big and bad all of a sudden, stay your stupid ass down here and watch what the fuck yo' ass is going to get!" I said, hanging the phone up on her. I didn't know if she thought I was playing, but let me catch her, and let her watch what would happen.

After hanging up the phone on Mia, I tried calling Keyon one more time. This time, her phone went straight to voicemail. "Fuck!" I yelled, throwing the phone on the passenger seat. I needed my woman like an hour ago. She was the only one who could calm me down when I was going through shit like this. I'd fucked up too many times to count, but I couldn't believe that this was the end of us. I just couldn't.

CHAPTER FOUR

Mia

I couldn't believe Cash had the audacity to try to play me behind some stank ho. This nigga around here was treating me as if I were a nobody, and it was all behind a piece of pussy. *Who the fuck does he think I am? I mean, I know I was the one who went behind him first, but it wasn't as if he had to take me up on my offer.* Just like any other nigga, he didn't turn me down. He was too quick to jump in this pussy, so his girl must not have been doing something right in the first place. I didn't know why he was trying to shine on me. He was a willing participant. I didn't make him lie on top of me when we were having sex, nor did I pull his dick out and stick it in myself. He was a big boy, a grown-ass man, who did that shit on his damn own. Now he was around here trying to be a victim and shit. Hollering about how I fucked up his life. *Nah, nigga, you did that shit ya damn self. No need to fault me.* The nigga was far from being a victim. In fact, he had as much responsibility, if not more, than I did in fucking up his life.

When I came down here, I had no intention of telling Keyon about Cash and me dealing with each other. Nor was I going to tell her about li'l Cash. I just wanted to show up and let the nigga know that I wasn't playing with his ass, and that he wasn't going to throw me to the side like some piece of trash as he thought he was going to do. I needed him to know that my son and I weren't going anywhere. We were here to stay, and he was going to have to manage two households instead of one.

For the past few months, Cash and I had been going through it. We'd been fussing and fighting more than a little bit. I didn't know what was going on, but something was behind all the fussing and fighting he was doing with me. I didn't know if we were really going through our rough times, or if he was just trying to get under my skin so that I would leave him. If it was the latter, he was going to be surprised, because I was in it for the long haul. I wasn't going to be his side chick forever. I just knew he wasn't going to get rid of me that easily. I was staying until I got tired, and with the way I'd been living, that wasn't going to be anytime soon.

Thanks to Cash and his money, I didn't have to work. I lived in a four-bedroom house that had three and a half baths, a two-door garage, and a swimming pool. I was comfortable, and I wasn't ready to give that up and go back to living with one of my family members. That was not what was up, nor was it on my agenda. Before I started dealing with him, I was living with one of my cousins and her three bad-ass kids in a two-bedroom apartment out in the Chi. To make matters worse, I didn't have a room. I had to sleep in the living room on a fucking sofa bed, and that shit was super uncomfortable to me. I didn't have any privacy and barely got any sleep because her kids would be up early watching TV in the living room or making noise in the kitchen. I couldn't complain because I didn't have anywhere else to go, so for a year straight, I dealt with it. That was when Cash came along, and oh, God, how I was happy.

I'd been ripping and running all day with my friend Jazz, trying to make sure that we were extra dolled up.

We wanted to make sure that we left a good impression on every man in the building, and, boy, did we. We basically had every nigga in that bitch checking for us, and every bitch was hating as usual. We didn't have to buy one drink that night, because as fast as our drinks were gone, someone was replacing them. By midnight, the club was packed, and the DJ was spinning those beats. I'd just come from the bar when I spotted him over behind the bar, talking to the bartender.

Standing at six feet five, weighing about 220 to 230 pounds, with a chocolate complexion, he sported a model's body, a headful of dreads that stopped in the middle of his back, and a killer smile. I just knew I had to have him. I didn't know if it was the liquor that I had consumed throughout the night or just me, but I walked over to the bar on a mission. I waited until he was finished doing what he was doing, and then I called him over to me.

"Say, daddy, what's your name?" I asked him.

"The name is Cash. What's yours, li'l mama?"

"It ain't li'l mama for sure," I corrected him.

"Smart-mouth, huh? I like that," he laughed. "Well, what is it?"

"Mia," I said, extending my hand.

"Nice to meet you," he said, grabbing it and placing a kiss on it.

"A gentleman, huh? I like that."

"So what are you drinking tonight?" he asked.

"Hennessy," I replied, looking into his eyes.

"Okay. Wait right here just a minute," he said, walking back behind the bar. I watched as he fixed my drink and walked back over to me. "Here," he said, handing it to me. For a moment, our hands connected, and I swore my heart skipped a beat or two.

"So I'm wondering if you're trying to leave with me tonight," I said boldly.

"Hold on. Before you even go there, I already have a girl, and I'm not leaving her," he said, catching me off guard. To say that I was disappointed would be an understatement. I just knew his ass was single and up for the taking.

"Well, where is your girl now?" I asked, still determined to get him.

"She's at our house back in Tennessee."

"Well, since she ain't here in Chicago, that means I get to have you all to myself while you're here then," I said, determined to get him. This nigga looked and smelled like money, and I wanted some of that shit. *"'What your girl don't know won't hurt her,'"* I then said, quoting SWV.

"She's persistent," he said with a smile. *"Okay, but I'm letting you know now, I don't care how good your pussy or head is. I ain't leaving my girl for no one."*

"All right. You got that," I replied. At that time, I really didn't plan to fall for him. All I really was worried about was his money. I wasn't even worrying about the dick too much. Money made me cum, so if he was spending that, then I was definitely about to cum for his ass.

"Okay, give me your number," he said, handing me his phone. I programmed my name and number in it, and then handed the phone back to him. *"I'll give you a call later."*

"Okay," I replied.

He didn't call me that night as he said he would, but he did call the next day and invited me to lunch. That same evening, we got a room, and the rest was history.

Now he had me sitting in this hotel room looking like a fool while he was out chasing after his bitch. I knew I shouldn't feel some type of way, but I did. He acted as if

I didn't matter when I should have. I was the mother of his one and only son, yet he treated me like shit while he held Keyon's fucking thot ass on a pedestal. I didn't give a fuck what his ass said. I wasn't going back to the Chi until I got some fucking answers, and they'd better be the muthafucking answers that I wanted to hear.

I sat there on the bed, thinking of a plan. I didn't know anyone down here, and I had my son back at home waiting for me. I didn't want to be away from him for too long, but as I said, Cash was our support system. He was trying to leave me, which meant that I would have to get out and get a job. He wouldn't leave his son dragging, but we still wouldn't be getting as much as we were getting now with him there, and I wasn't trying to work. I barely had a high school education. Nobody was going to hire my ass, not even McDonald's. I needed to find a way to get him back before he was gone forever. I didn't know how, but I was going to fight for my baby daddy.

I sat there for a few minutes longer before I started to get sleepy as hell. I was waiting for Cash to call me, but once I saw that it was getting late and he still hadn't called, I decided to pack it in. I took a quick shower and jumped in bed ass naked. Tonight didn't go as planned, but I was going to think of another way to get Cash. He was mad at me right now, but he wasn't going to be mad forever. He just needed some space, and I was going to give him that, but in no form, shape, or fashion was I giving up on us.

I'd been with this nigga, and all the while, he had a whole other bitch. Now that they weren't together anymore, that meant I was the next bitch in line to be the main lady. I would not stand by and watch this nigga pick some other bitch over me when I deserved to fill that number one spot. Li'l Cash, he, and I were going to be a family. In the meantime, I was making moves, trying to make sure my son and I would continue living the lifestyle that we were living even if his daddy bailed out on us.

The next morning came, and I was up early. My stomach was turning in knots. I didn't know why, but before I could think about it, I had the sudden urge to throw up. I got up off the bed and ran full speed, trying to make it to the toilet in time. Luckily, I did, and I threw up everything from the previous night, including all the bottom of my damn stomach. *God, don't let me be pregnant,* I thought as I continued to throw up. I'd missed my period for this month, but I was hoping that it was just late.

When I was finished, I flushed the toilet and walked over to the sink to splash a little bit of water on my face. I looked in the mirror, and I absolutely hated the woman staring back at me. There was nothing wrong with my appearance. It was my life that I hated. I couldn't stand living weak. I had to depend on a man and the people in my family to be able to survive. Some shit had to change, and it had to change right now.

Since I was already in the bathroom, I decided to take care of my personal hygiene. First, I hopped in the shower and took a five-minute shower before I got out, brushed my teeth, and washed my face. When I was done, I went back into the bedroom. With a towel wrapped around me, I lay down on the bed, contemplating my next move. Then it hit me. That nigga Bundy had yet to ring my line.

Grabbing my phone, I went into my contacts and found the number that I was looking for. I placed the phone to my ear, waiting for him to answer. *Let me find out this nigga is trying to play on me.*

"What's up, ma?" he answered on the first ring.

"You tell me. I've been waiting all night to hear from you," I replied. "What's good?"

"Oh, yeah, I was just about to call you."

"Yeah, I bet. Y'all do that thing I told y'all to do?" I asked, wanting to know what was up with the job I sent his bitch ass on.

"Yeah, ma. We fucked that shit up last night. I got your money right here waiting for you to get back," he replied.

"Baby, who you on the phone with?" I heard a female voice say in the background.

"Oh, no the fuck you ain't!" I yelled. I knew this nigga was not acting a fool since I wasn't there. "Bundy, you could have some bitch in my house if ya want to. Let me catch y'all, and I promise you ain't going to like it one bit, nigga."

"Mia, chill. I don't have nobody in ya house. I'm over here at the strip club," he said, sounding like he was lying.

"Yeah, be lying if ya want to, but if I catch yo' ass, I promise I'ma fuck yo' stupid ass up. Make sure you have my money when I get home," I said before I hung up the phone in his face. I didn't even know why I started fucking with that nigga. Dude was really beginning to work my last fucking nerve. I should've known better than to fuck with the help anyway. If Cash found out about the things I'd been doing behind his back, he'd kill my ass.

"Oh, well. What he don't know won't hurt him," I said. I sat there for a few minutes. I'd never been on Cash's bad side, but I'd seen it a time or two when he was taking care of his workers. I was glad that I was here when everything went down in Chicago so he wasn't going to be able to tie none of that shit to me. At least that was what I hoped.

I was brought out of my thoughts by the ringing of my phone. I looked at the screen to see Cash calling me. A smile immediately formed on my face as I hurried to answer it.

"Hello," I answered a little too excitedly, but oh, well. I was happy that he had called me.

"What you doing, ma?" he asked in that sexy-ass voice that always made my panties wet.

"Lying in bed thinking about you."

"Where are you? Are you still in Tennessee?" he then asked.

"Yeah, why?"

"Because I'm trying to see you. Tell me where you at."

I hurriedly told him where I was before he hung up. I jumped out of bed super excited. I guessed all wasn't lost after all. Noticing what I had on, I slipped into a black and pink teddy that he had gotten me from Victoria's Secret. I sprayed on my favorite Victoria's Secret perfume before I grabbed a few lavender-scented candles and lit them. I went over to my suitcase and pulled out my iPod Touch and Beats Pill speaker. I put on my slow jams playlist just as someone started knocking on the door. I walked over to the full-length mirror to make sure that I looked good before I went to open the door. I already knew that it wasn't anyone but Cash, which was why I let him wait a few seconds longer. I guessed that was too long for him before he became impatient and began banging on the door. *This dumb nigga gets on my nerves.*

"Why the hell you banging on the damn door like that?" I asked, opening the door. He paused before he looked at me from head to toe and walked in. I rolled my eyes and shut the door behind me. "If you came here to trip, you should've stayed where the fuck yo—" was all I got out before he wrapped his hand around my throat.

"Bitch, you thought I was going to let that shit you pulled slide?" he asked before he slapped me in my face.

"Cash, what are you doing?" I barely got the words out before he began squeezing tighter. He released my throat as I bent over, gasping for air. I looked at him, and the look on his face was one of a maniac's. I stood up but immediately regretted that when he punched me so hard in my stomach I started throwing up.

"I told yo' ass to keep still, but you had to test me. Now I'm about to show yo' ass a thing or two!" he hollered, wrapping his hand around my throat again. He then threw me on the bed. I tried to get up and run to the bathroom so that I could lock myself in it, but he caught me before I could get near the door. "Don't run now, bitch. You had all that heart last night. Let me see that shit again."

"Cash, don't do this," I begged him, but my pleas fell on deaf ears as he backhanded me, making me fall to the ground. I tried to scream, but seeing as the music was on so loud, I knew no one could hear my ass.

"I bet you're going to think twice before you try to play with me again!" he yelled. My eyes widened at the sight of him removing the belt from around his waist. He then wrapped it around his hand and started hitting every spot that wasn't covered.

I couldn't do anything. I was trapped and helpless. I lay there crying as he continued to beat my ass to a pulp. I prayed to God, wishing that this pain would go away, before everything went black.

CHAPTER FIVE

Keys

The next day came faster than I expected it to. I thought for sure that, when I opened my eyes, everything from the previous night would be a dream, and Cash and I would be back on good terms. Unfortunately, when I woke up in my apartment alone with Emoni, instead of in the house I once shared with Cash, I knew that yesterday was no dream. In fact, it was much more real than I wanted it to be.

Looking over to the clock that sat on the nightstand, I noticed that it was a little after nine o'clock. I wished that I could sleep in, but I needed to take Emoni to the mall to get her some clothes. Her momo would arrive to get her in a few hours for her trip. Lord knows I was glad that she was leaving, because I really needed a little alone time, and since I didn't want to be bothered with her father, I knew for sure that she wasn't going over there as of yet. I was not trying to keep his daughter from him. I wasn't that type of lady. I just needed to make him sweat, to make him wish he never fucked me over, to make him see what he had was now gone and not coming back in the way he would have liked it to.

As slowly as possible, I got out of bed, trying my hardest not to wake up Emoni. I was trying to go to the car and get our things so we could get dressed and head out, but if she woke up now, we'd be stuck inside like this all day.

I managed to get out of bed without waking Emoni up. I grabbed my keys off the nightstand, put on my slippers, and headed out of the room. I made sure that I locked the door behind me before I power walked outside to my car. First, I grabbed Emoni's things off the back seat along with my other purse. I then went around to the trunk, where my things were. It was a good thing that I only had one bag, because my hands were already full.

"Every time I see you, your hands are full," a man said behind me.

I turned to find Kane standing there in a wife beater, some black and gray basketball shorts, and a fresh pair of white and black Retro Air Jordan IXs.

"You see me, huh?" I laughed.

"Yes, I do. May I?" he asked, reaching for the bags that I had in my hand.

"Sure," I said, handing them to him, and then I closed the trunk behind me. Thank God he offered to help me, because I didn't know how I was going to make it back to my apartment in one trip with all those bags.

"So, how are you feeling today?" he asked me. "You ain't going to try to bite my head off again, huh?"

"Nah, I'm straight today, and I apologize yet again for the way that I acted toward you." I laughed, because I knew he was trying to crack a joke on me.

"Well, that's good. What do you have planned today?"

"Nothing major. I'm just going to take my daughter to the mall and chill, that's it," I said as we entered the building.

"Oh, baby girl from last night? If she looks anything like her mother, her father needs to get his gun ready for all those little niggas who'll try to get at her," he responded with a smile.

"Thank you," I said, blushing at his comment.

"What's her name, and how old is she?"

"Her name is Emoni, and she's four years old."

"Oh, how nice," he replied. "I have a four-year-old daughter myself. Her name is Ahmyri."

"Oh, yeah?" I said sadly. I should've known a nigga that fine had a few kids running around somewhere. "Well, are you and her mother still together? Because I ain't trying to be in no baby-mama drama."

"Nah. Unfortunately she died giving birth to our daughter, and I've been a single parent ever since," he replied sadly.

"Aww. I'm sorry to hear that," I said genuinely. I really felt bad for him. If I had known that his baby's mother was dead, I never would've asked him that. I was glad when we made it to the door, because things were beginning to get a bit awkward between us. "Are you okay?"

"I'm straight, li'l mama," he said, being his jolly self again. "So, what's up with you and your baby daddy?"

"Nothing really. We aren't together anymore," I said, keeping it short.

"Are you sure? I don't want to make you my lady and have you step on my heart by getting back with him," he said cockily.

I was thrown off by his comment about making me his lady. We barely held a good conversation, and he was already talking about making me his lady. We hadn't even been on a date yet. Hell, the man didn't know my first name, yet he wanted to make me his lady.

"Who said that I was going to be your lady?' I asked him. "Besides, I told you last night that me and my baby daddy weren't together anymore, and we're not getting back together either."

"Me," he replied. "Well, me and God, it seems, by the way He keeps sending me here right when you're in desperate need of help."

"Uh-huh. If that's what you say."

"Seriously though, I want to make you my lady. I know I don't know you and we've just met, but there's something about you that just draws me to you. Like I said, every time you're out being the damsel in distress, I'm always there to help you. Not to mention that you're cute as a muthafucka, you're fine, and your spirit is mind-blowing," he said, sounding as corny as a muthafucka.

"Cute is for puppies, boo. I'm beautiful," I told him. "Besides, you being there for me when I needed help them two little times wasn't nothing but a big coincidence."

"Nah, ma. I don't believe in coincidences. That's what you call faith."

"Look, I just got out of a long-term relationship with my daughter's father. I'm what you call damaged goods. I've been cheated on more times than I care to remember, and I can tell you that I'm not in the mood to be trying to get in another relationship with another man who's going to try to do the same thing to me," I said, getting tired of this bullshit. Kane was a pretty boy, and with pretty boys came ho problems—problems that I didn't need right now. I knew just by looking at him that he had about two to three hoes lying in the cut somewhere. "Thank you for helping me."

"Ma, I'm not that type of man. I don't do that to people I truly care about. Furthermore, I'm not like the rest of them niggas. I'm cut from a different cloth. I'm one of the few men left on this earth who actually appreciates a good woman when he sees one," he said, spitting that bullshit that every nigga spat. "At least let me get your number then."

I stood there, thinking whether I should actually give this man my number. I really didn't have time to be playing around with him, because as I said, I'd just gotten out of a relationship. I wasn't trying to automatically jump into a new one a day later. "Okay," I said, giving in. I was only going to give him my number. It didn't mean that I was going to actually go out with him or anything.

"A'ight cool," he said, handing me his phone. I grabbed the phone, dialed my number, and saved it. I called my number from his phone so that I could store his number, and then I handed it back to him. "Thank you."

"You're welcome," I said, grabbing my bags from his hand. "Have a nice day."

"You too," he said. I opened the door and made my way inside before he could say anything else. Once the door was closed behind me, I placed the bags on the floor and placed my back against the door. I couldn't lie. I really enjoyed being in Kane's presence. I knew what I said about jumping in a relationship too soon, and I meant that, but that didn't mean that I couldn't go out with a friend. If he called me, I was going to let him know that I wanted to take things slowly, start out as friends, and if things progressed further than that, we would cross that bridge when we got there.

I must have stood by the door for damn near five minutes before someone began knocking, scaring the shit out of me. It almost made my heart jump out of my chest. "Who is it?" I asked from behind the door.

"It's me, Tay," I heard her say.

"Damn, you scared the shit out of me," I said, opening the door for her.

"Uh-huh, I bet," she said, walking in, closing the door behind her. "I saw your slick ass."

"What are you talking about?" I asked, confused.

"I'm talking about you talking to that fine-ass nigga just a little while ago," she said, smiling.

Oh, fuck! "You talking about Kane?" I asked, still playing dumb.

"You know who I'm talking about. Don't play dumb with me, Keyon," she said, matter-of-factly.

"Girl, Kane ain't nothing but a friend. I just met him last night," I told her nosy ass. She was always in somebody else's business.

"Y'all ain't look like y'all just met last night. Let me find out you been holding out and hiding that nigga on me."

"Bitch, please. I told you I just met the dude last night. He lives in this building. Besides, you're my best friend. You don't think that if I had a man on the side, I'd tell you? Come on now," I said. I couldn't believe that she would think I'd keep something like that from her.

"Uh-huh. Okay," she said. "Where's Emoni?"

"She should be still asleep in the bedroom," I told her as I began grabbing the bags to bring them into the room.

"Your room or her room?"

"My room."

"I should've known that brat was in your room. I don't know why I even asked that question," she said as she made her way to my bedroom. Moni was still asleep. "That's a shame. That spoiled-ass child of yours."

"Girl, I don't know what she's going to do when she goes with my mother for this little month," I said, shaking my head. Moni was so spoiled that she barely liked me to go to work sometimes.

"She's going to be just fine. Besides, you know Mama C don't care if she's spoiled. She's still going to take her with her. You know she loves kids, and seeing that Moni is her only grandchild, her being spoiled ain't going to matter one way or another."

"You're right, and I bet when she comes back, she's going to be looking to leave right back again with my mother."

"And ya know it!"

"A'ight, girl, let me hop in the shower right quick," I said, heading to the bathroom. "Oh, do me a favor, please."

"Yeah, what's up?" she asked, taking a seat on the bed.

"Wake Moni up and put her hair in two big braids for me. Please," I begged, showing her my puppy-dog eyes.

"You so lucky you're my best friend and Moni's my god-daughter, because you know how much I hate braiding hair," she said, playfully rolling her eyes.

"I do, and that's why I said please, smart ass," I said, making my way back into the bathroom before she said something else smart. I turned on the water so that it could be warm enough when I got in there. I then undressed and pinned my hair up so it wouldn't get wet, because I was not trying to take all day combing it.

Before getting into the shower, I stood in the mirror and looked at myself. I was trying to see what it was about me that would make Cash really cheat on me, have another child in this world, and not tell me. I wasn't badly built, even though I had a pudge from when I had Moni. My breasts weren't small, and my ass was huge. To any other man I had it all, but to the man I had, I didn't have enough, I guessed. "Get over it already," I said to myself. I was tired of feeling sorry for myself just because of what Cash did to me.

Pushing Cash and his problems to the back of my mind, I hopped in the shower. "Fuck!" I yelled once the scalding-hot water had connected with my skin. After adjusting the water to my liking, I lathered my washcloth with that Summer's Eve lavender body wash, then began washing my body. I then rinsed off my body and repeated the process three more times before I turned the water off. Wrapping a towel around my body, I got out and headed into the bedroom.

"Good morning, Mommy," Moni said once I entered the room.

"Good morning, Mama's baby," I said, walking over to her and placing a kiss on her forehead. "You ready to go by Grandma's today?"

"Yeah, Mommy," she said, surprising the hell out of me.

"Girl, you hear that shit?" I asked Tay, who was finishing up Moni's last braid.

"Did I? I can't believe she's excited to go. I thought her little ass would've been stuck all up under your ass and not wanted to go," she said, getting up from the bed. She walked over to Moni's suitcase and removed a few outfits before she picked one. "I'm going to give her a bath, because if I wait for you to do it, we'll be here all day."

"Girl, whatever. Okay, I'm going to get dressed. I'll be ready in twenty minutes," I told her.

"Okay," she replied before she and Moni disappeared into the bathroom.

While they were in the bathroom, I went about getting dressed. I put lotion on my body before I threw on my bra and panties. I then got dressed and put my hair into a high ponytail, put a little lip gloss on my lips, threw my shoes on, and was ready to go. I walked over to the full-length mirror hanging on the door to check myself out. At the same time, Tay and Moni were coming out of the bathroom.

"You're so pretty, Mommy!" Moni said, running over to me.

"Like mother like daughter," I said, stooping down to her. "Come on, let's take a picture."

"Yay! Picture time, picture time," she said, clapping her hands together. We stood in the mirror posing for a few pics before we were done. "Let me see!"

I picked her up as I swiped my finger across the screen, showing her picture after picture. "Daddy!" she said, seeing a picture of her daddy and me. "Mommy, I want Daddy!"

"Daddy's not here, baby."

"I want to talk to Daddy," she said, pouting.

I looked back at Tay, asking her what to do with my eyes. She hunched her shoulders and mouthed, "I don't know."

"Okay, I'm going to call Daddy, but you can't be on the phone long because we have to go, Moni," I said to her. Dreadfully, I dialed Cash's number. I placed the phone on speaker as I prayed like hell that he didn't answer. My prayers were answered when the call rolled over to voicemail.

"Daddy's not answering. Do you want to leave him a message?" I asked her.

"Yes," she said, nodding her head just as the phone beeped. "Hey, Daddy, why are you not answering the phone? It's me, your princess Moni. Call me back, Daddy."

I felt bad that my child had to go through what she was going through all because of her dumb-ass daddy. I knew how much she loved him and how she loved to be around him every day. This new arrangement was going to be hard on her because she was somewhat of a daddy's girl. She was going to be all right, though, because I was there to fill in when he wasn't available.

"How 'bout we head over to the mall and go shopping?" I said, trying to brighten her mood.

"Yay, let's go shopping, Mommy," she said, returning to her normal happy self. One thing she loved besides her father and me was shopping.

"Girl, you really do have a little diva on your hands there," Tay said, butting in.

"Girl, don't I know it. What little four-year-old child do you know who loves to shop as much as a grown person?"

"Your damn daughter," she laughed. "Y'all creating a monster."

"Don't say 'y'all.' You helped create that monster also. Don't act like you don't take her to the store just as much as we do, and might I add, you buy her everything that her little bad ass wants," I said, correcting her.

"I can't help it. Whatever she wants, she gets," she said.

"Uh-huh, and when she acts up, I'm going to send her your way, you hear?" I asked, grabbing my keys and purse from the dresser. "Now let's go fuck up some commas on Cash," I laughed as we made our way out of the apartment.

So far, today started out as a good day. Cash hadn't called me, and I was really glad, because I still didn't have anything to say to him. He didn't know where I stayed, so I wasn't worried about him finding us. Moni was scheduled to leave today, and I was taking off from work the next two weeks. In those two weeks, I planned on getting myself straight and prepared to live life without Casimere.

It didn't take long for us to pull up to the mall from where my apartment was located. Thankfully, there weren't many people there, because I would've hated to be in the store all day knowing it was only going to take my mother a few hours to get here. I needed Moni to be good and rested before she got here. Luckily, I found a parking spot by the entrance door. I parked my car, got out, and went around to the trunk to grab Moni's stroller before I grabbed her out of the back seat and strapped her in. Seeing as I knew this mall and which stores had things for my daughter, I wouldn't be long. I was going to time this trip. An hour and a half was all the time I needed to shop for Moni and get a few things for myself.

"Okay," I said once we entered the mall. "An hour and a half is all the time I'm spending up in here. I'm not trying to spend all day in here and then have to rush to get Moni ready. That's not gon' work for me, and you know like I know that my mother don't do late."

"A'ight cool."

Together we headed to babyGap. I just loved that store. There were so many things in there to choose from. Not to mention that they had different pairs of sandals in all types of colors that I loved to see on Moni's feet.

"You like this?" Tay asked, walking over to me and holding a yellow and navy blue sundress with a navy blue bow around it. "It's on sale, too. And I see the pink and gray one just like it."

"Yeah, get 'em. In fact, I just saw some little shoes that would go perfectly with them."

"Okay, I'll be right back," she said, heading back to where she'd gotten the dresses.

I found a few jean dresses that I liked and picked them up. I couldn't get too much from here because she had almost everything that was here already. I did find four new 'fits, three jumpers, five pairs of sandals, and three dresses. "That should be enough from here," I said, gathering up everything I had. I headed over to the register, where the lady began ringing me up immediately.

"There you go. I thought you had done left me in here," Tay said.

"You can put them on the counter with the rest of her things," I said, waiting as the lady began ringing the last two dresses up.

"Hey, Emoni," she said, placing our things in the bag.

"Hey, Miss Lilly," Moni replied and waved at her from the stroller.

"She gets cuter by the day," she said, bagging the last of my things.

"Thank you," I said, handing her the money to pay for my items. I stepped to the side to let Tay purchase her things. When we were done, we said goodbye and headed on with our shopping trip.

It was almost noon when we were through shopping. We had to make three trips to the car in order to get all of our bags to the car. By then, I was tired, and poor Moni looked worn out. All she was good for was something to eat and a long nap.

"You got everything you need for Moni out of the store?" Tay asked once we had gotten back in the car.

"I got that and then some. Lord knows Moni ain't going to need all them clothes. Hell, she might not need any of the things I bought for her to go by my mama's. You know my mother likes to have her own things. She's going to end up taking her shopping. I bet you my last dollar that Moni's got a whole room in her house, and she hasn't even been there yet," I said, backing out of the parking lot.

"Keys, you already know how your mother is."

"Don't I."

"Mommy, I'm hungry," Moni yelled from the back seat. "I want a box."

"Okay, baby. Mommy will stop at McDonald's up the street and get you a box."

"Yay, box," she began cheering.

"She ain't nothing but a braaaaaat," Tay sang from the front seat.

"So?" I said just as my phone began to ring. I looked at the screen and noticed that it was my mother calling. "Hello," I said, answering the phone.

"Now is that how I taught you to answer the phone, Keyon Lynetta?" she asked, starting already.

"No, ma'am," I said, rolling my eyes in my head.

"And don't be rolling your eyes at me neither, little girl," she said as if she could actually see me doing it. That was why I barely called my mother on the phone. She was always ready to give me a sermon on how she raised me and how I acted now. "Now where is my granddaughter?"

"She's right there in the back seat."

"Hey, Momo's baby," she yelled out to Moni in the back seat.

"Grammy," she yelled, hearing my mother call out to her.

"What's Momo's baby doing?"

"I'm going get a box," she yelled, referring to a McDonald's Happy Meal.

"Keyon, hurry up and get my baby her box," she said, snapping.

"I'm on my way to get it now, Ma."

"Well, hurry up, because I'm about to pull up to your house any minute now," she said, shocking me.

"What do you mean? I thought you weren't coming until like five or six," I said.

"I was, but I couldn't wait to get my granddaughter. So I came a bit early," she said, sounding like a kid in a candy store. I wanted to go off on her for popping up like that, but I had to remember that she was my mother. I knew how much she loved kids.

"Okay, well let me hurry and get Emoni's food. Then I'll be right on my way to you," I said, trying to rush her off the phone.

"Oh, well, hurry, but be careful. I don't want anything to happen to you girls."

"Okay, Ma. I love you."

"I love you too, baby," she replied. I hung up before she could say anything else.

My mother really knew how to put a bitch in a sour mood. Like, really? I didn't know why she couldn't call me before she came down here. I had nothing packed. She was going to holler when she got there.

"Oh, shit, I bet she's at Cash's house, because she knows nothing about the apartment, and I want it to stay that way. If she finds out that I moved out, she's going to want to know what's going on, and right now, I really don't feel like explaining the shit to her."

"Well, all you have to do is go over to Cash's house and pretend you still live there until Emoni leaves. Then we can head back to your apartment once they're gone," Tay suggested.

"Yeah, I could do that. Lord knows I don't want to face Cash's ol' lying ass right now, but it's only going to be for a few minutes," I said, pulling into the McDonald's drive-through. "You want something to eat from here?"

"Nah, I'm straight. I don't even have an appetite right now."

"Me neither. Thinking about being around Cash made me lose my appetite," I said, feeling my stomach knotting up. I really didn't know if it was seeing Cash or seeing my mother that had me feeling this way, but either way, I wanted this day to go by just as fast as yesterday went. Lord knows I didn't have any plans to face Cash after what happened at the club, and now I had no choice but to do just that.

Deciding not to dwell on it any longer, I pushed that to the back of my mind, and I ordered Emoni's Happy Meal. Two minutes later, we were back on the road and headed to meet my mother at Cash's house. I had to say a small prayer, asking the good Lord to humble me, because if Cash said anything wrong, I was going to blow my top. I didn't care if my mother was there or not.

Cash

The next morning, I woke up wishing that everything were just a bad dream and that Keys and Emoni would be lying in the bed next to me like always. However, when I woke up to an empty bed and an even emptier house, I knew that last night wasn't a dream. I had really lost my girl, and I was more than sure I'd lost my daughter also. Every time I thought about how Mia came and showed her ass, I wanted to strangle her ass with my bare hands. She was lucky that I wasn't the man I was a few years ago, because mother of my child or not, I would've deaded her ass without a second thought. Since I'd gotten help with my anger issue and promised Keys that I would do better, I didn't. Instead of her being jealous of Keyon, she should have been thanking her. She'd have been cold as ice in a morgue with a toe tag if it weren't for her.

Dreadfully and slowly, I got out of bed. I looked at the clock that sat on my dresser and noticed that it was almost noon. I didn't know that it was that late. It must have been that medicine the nurse in the ER gave me last night for the pain in my hand. Speaking of my hand, it wasn't hurting as bad as it was earlier. When I went to the hospital, I was told that, luckily, nothing was broken, but I did bruise a few things, and it was hurting because of the swelling. They gave me some pain medicine and some other shit I couldn't pronounce. I wished Keyon were here. Seeing as she was a nurse, she would've known what to do.

I was brought out of my thoughts by the round of my phone ringing. I walked over to the nightstand, picked it up, and noticed that it was my homeboy Jamel calling.

"Sup with it," I said, answering the phone as I made my way to the bathroom.

"We need to be on a flight to Chicago by tonight," he yelled. There was something about the sound of his voice that I did not like at all.

"Man, what's going on? You don't normally just pop up out of the blue demanding that we go to Chicago.

Something's gotta be wrong, so talk to me," I replied, wanting to know why all of a sudden we had to pack up and go to Chicago without notice.

"Ya boy Bundy called me this morning. You know them ice cream shops you set up around the area?" he asked, speaking in code.

"Yeah, I know. What's wrong with it?" I said, beginning to worry my damn self.

"Well, two of them got hit last night."

"What the fuck? By who?" I asked, pacing the floor. I knew setting up shop there was going to be a huge problem.

"That's the thing. They don't know. I think something fishy is going on, because in the three years we've been there, ain't nobody had enough balls to fuck with our shit. Now all of a sudden niggas feeling froggy and shit!"

"Shit, I know that, and I agree with you. Them niggas already know what's up with it. Something ain't right with this one," I said, taking a seat on the toilet. A funny feeling began settling in the pit of my stomach. "So what are we going to do about it?"

"What you mean?" he asked. "We're going down there to get some answers. Ain't no way two shops got robbed and don't nobody know about it!"

"Yeah, man, I feel you," I said, getting up to turn the shower on. "Well, what time you want to leave?"

"Be ready around seven. I wanna do a pop-up visit. Them niggas don't even know that we're coming down there. I told him we were out of state and we weren't coming back anytime soon."

"Shake 'em up. I see where ya coming from," I said with a hint of a smile. This was why I was glad to have this nigga as my friend and business partner. Whenever I forgot to think about something, he already had it down pat. This nigga thought about everything. He made sure that we had all our i's dotted and our t's crossed. "A'ight, man. I'm about to hop in the shower right quick. Then I'ma go check on the club. I'll see you later tonight."

"A'ight, man, cool," he said and hung up.

I sat on the toilet with my head in my hand. Wasn't shit about what was going on that was adding up. We'd had our shop set up in Chicago for three whole years, and the whole time, ain't nobody thought to rob us. Now all of a sudden, our shit was getting jacked. That shit just wasn't adding up, and something most definitely wasn't right with this. I swore on the life of my kids that if I found out them niggas were trying to cross us, I'd put them and everyone else involved in a body bag.

Putting that problem on the back burner for later, I stripped down and hopped in the shower. I stepped under the showerhead and let the water run down my body. As the water began running down the drain, I wished it could wash all of my problems down the drain also. I didn't know what was happening, but I felt like God was beginning to punish me for all the things that I'd done in my life. In a matter of two days, my life was spiraling out of control, and I had this feeling that it wasn't about to get better anytime soon.

"Jesus, I know I barely pray, and I know you won't steer me wrong. So please help me out of this hell on earth," I prayed. Grabbing my towel, I squirted some body wash on it and began washing my body. The soft feel of the towel rubbing against my skin felt so good. It made me think about all the times that Keys and I showered together and she'd wash my entire body. God, how I was missing my baby dearly.

Knowing that I didn't have enough time and I had things to do, I rinsed my body off under the water and repeated the process. When I was done, I hopped out of the shower, threw a towel around my body, and went back into the bedroom. Seeing that today was going to be a chill day, I decided on a white V-neck, some blue jean shorts, and some all-white Air Max 90s. When I was finished dressing, I grabbed my phone and keys and headed down the stairs. No sooner than I made it off the last steps was someone ringing my doorbell. I started to not answer it, but since I was about to leave, I did.

I was confused and shocked when I opened the door to find Keyon's mother standing there. "Hello, Ms. Charmaine."

"Hello, Casimere. May I come in?" she asked, looking me up and down. I knew she wanted to say something, and I really hoped she wouldn't, because right now wasn't the time for her to be getting slick in the mouth.

"Well, actually, I was about to leave—" I began to say, but she interrupted me.

"Well, I was waiting for Keyon to get Emoni. They're on their way over here as we speak," she said, which totally made me want to stay now.

"Oh, okay, well, come on in then," I said, stepping to the side to let her in. I was staying only because my girls were coming. That, and I didn't want to leave her old ass in my house all by herself. Not for her to go meddling and trying to find shit, being nosy. "When did you get in?"

"Actually, I just got here a few minutes ago."

"Well, how long are you going to be staying?"

"Not long. I'm going to get Emoni, say hello to my daughter, and head back out. I'm not trying to stay on the road all day," she said, having a seat on the sofa. She placed her purse beside her as if I were going to steal it or something. I wanted to laugh and throw her old ass out, but she was my girl's mother and the grandmother of my daughter. "Lord, this is a nice little house you all have here. What did you say you do again?"

"I'm part owner of a nightclub, and I have a few rental properties I've invested some money into," I said, knowing why she'd asked me that. She always thought that her daughter was too good for me, and for a time I agreed, but I was thinking very differently now. I was a new man, and it was a completely different ball game this time around. She used to be mad when Keys was working two jobs to take care of us. She would always tell her daughter that she needed a man who could pull his own weight and bring his half to the table. She almost cost me my girl, but luckily our love was strong. She could keep her opinions to herself, because I was able to provide for both my girl and my daughter. I even tried to get Keys to quit her job, but she wasn't having that. She said she wasn't trying to depend on me and that she needed her own money. I couldn't lie. That shit pissed my ass off. That was when I first began cheating on her.

"Oh, okay. How's my daughter been doing?"

"She's been fine," I said, keeping it short. I didn't know why she was trying to be all up in our business. It'd been like that since we first got together.

"You say you own a club, huh?"

"Yes, ma'am, I do—" I began but was interrupted by the sound of the front door opening. *Saved by the bell.*

"Daddy!" Emoni said, running toward me.

"Hey, Daddy's baby, how are you doing?"

"Good. I miss you."

"Aww, li'l mama, Daddy missed you too."

No sooner than I said that had she turned to see her grandma sitting there on the sofa. "Grammy!" she yelled, fighting to get out of my arms.

"Hey, Grandma's baby," she said, getting up to get her. "How's my little glam baby doing? I love you."

"I love you too," she replied, placing a kiss on her grandma's cheek.

I smelled Keys before she came in. The scent of vanilla made it to the living room before she did. My heart began racing as my stomach started doing backflips. When she finally made it there, I wanted to grab her into a big hug and shower her with kisses. I loved it when she rocked a ponytail. It gave her all the space to show her beautiful facial features.

"Hey, Ma," she said, walking over to her mother and kissing her face, totally ignoring me. I wanted to jack her little ass up, but I didn't want to cause a scene in front of her mother. I didn't need her all up in our business. Hell, if she knew what was going on, her old ass would probably start doing backflips in the living room. She might even try talking her into moving back to Louisiana. "How was the drive?"

"Hey, baby, it was okay. How are you?"

"All is good."

"Hey, Ms. C," Tay said, walking in with both hands full of bags. She placed the bags on the table, then walked over and gave Ms. Charmaine a hug and kiss. "It's good to see you."

"Oh, my God, Sha' Taylor, is that you?" she asked, returning the gesture.

"Yes, ma'am, it's me," she replied shyly.

"Chile, I haven't seen you in a while. How have you been, baby?"

"I've been great."

"That's good. You give your mama any grandbabies yet?"

"No, ma'am, and I don't plan to anytime soon," she laughed.

"That's good. Make sure you find yourself a good man to birth children with. Don't go out picking just any old man to have kids with," she said before she glanced at me then Keyon. I knew her old ass was referring to Keys and me, but I wasn't going to give her ass a response.

"Well, Ma, how long are you staying?" Keyon asked, interrupting them. I guessed she was getting tired of her mother throwing hints at us. "I have to go upstairs and pack Emoni's bags."

"All she needs is a few nightclothes and one outfit. I will take her shopping tomorrow."

"Okay. I'll be right back," she said, leaving the room.

I stood there for a minute, feeling lost in my own house. I couldn't believe she would actually play me like that in my own house. Not thinking about it anymore, I went behind her. She was mad and all that, but fuck that shit. She was about to talk to me whether she wanted to or not.

"What the fuck is the matter with you?" I asked, busting through the door. She was pulling clothes out of the drawer and putting them in one of her suitcases. "Keyon, you don't hear me talking to you?"

"What? What the fuck do you want?" she asked, not even looking up. She just kept on doing what she was doing as if I weren't even in the room.

"Can you please just stop and talk to me? I know you're mad about what happened at the club, and, baby, if I could take it back, I would. Please believe me!"

"Well, you can't," she said, finally looking at me. I could see the tears in her eyes threatening to fall. It burned my heart and soul to know that I was the cause of her pain, and I couldn't do anything to help soothe it. "You know how bad you made me look? I looked like a fucking fool out there in front of all these people, as your baby mama went on to tell the whole damn club how you cheated on me and had a child I didn't know about! You played me like a fucking fool again. All behind some bird bitch who probably ain't got a pot to piss in or a window to throw that muthafucker out of. I've been with you for years. I was the bitch there when you ain't had nothing, not a dime. It was me working two jobs to take care of us. Hell,

I put my freedom on the line for you, and you go and fuck me over for this bitch? I thought you loved me. Well, that's what ya kept on hollering, but you don't know the first thing about love, because if ya did, you wouldn't have been doing the things that you've done to me. Hurt! Pain! Misery! Those are the words and things that you know, not love."

"Key—" I started to say, but she put her hand up to stop me.

"When were you going to tell me?" she asked.

"Tell you what?"

"Don't play dumb with me!" she yelled. "When were you going to tell me about the son you had three years after I had Emoni?"

"I don't know."

"Honestly, were you ever going to tell me?" she asked.

No, I answered in my head, but I wasn't going to tell her that.

"I thought so. You're a coward, a dog, and a typical-ass nigga. Get the fuck out of my face, Casimere."

"Ma, like I said, if I could take it all back, I would, but I can't. I do love you, ma. I love you with every breath in my body. I never meant to hurt you."

"Cash, I'm tired of hearing you say the same thing over and over again with no action. Your words mean nothing to me without action, and since I'm over you and there's nothing left, your actions mean nothing also."

"Keyon, please give me another chance. Marry me. Be my wife. I promise you this time that I will do right by you and make an honest woman out of you."

"Cash, it's too late. I'm sick and tired of your bullshit and games. You've put me through too much already. I can't and won't go for more," she said as she put the last of Emoni's clothes in the bag and began zipping it. She picked the suitcase up off the bed and began walking toward the door. Before she could place her hand on the knob to open it, I stopped her.

"You're really going to let this shit come between us after all the things we've been through together?" I asked, defeated. I kept asking her the same questions, hoping that she would change her mind. When I touched her, I felt her whole body stiffen. I knew we were practically over, but I still didn't want it to be.

"I didn't let anything come between us. You did when you started thinking with the head between ya legs instead of the other one, not giving a fuck about me." I heard a sniffle before she placed the suitcase back on the ground and turned around. "I know it's hard for you to accept it, but I'm good on you. I'll always love you because you're the father of my child and my first love, but our love has run its course. Be free, do what you want to, and be with whom you want to. I don't care anymore. I'm tired of letting you hurt me and not saying anything. I'm throwing the towel in, Cash. Like I said, I'll always love you, but I gotta love you from a distance. I really hope you can accept my wishes and leave me alone so that we can be parents to Emoni without all that extra bullshit."

I stood there staring her straight in her eyes as she told me we were done, and I didn't see a sign of regret or confusion. I wanted badly for her to just say she forgave me and for me to never hit her again, but she didn't. She just stood there without saying another word, as did I. I couldn't find a word to say. I'd said all that I could right now, but I still wasn't convinced that we were over. As I said, time was what I was going to give her, because right now she was obviously talking from her emotions.

"Is everything okay in here?" her mother said through the cracked door. She couldn't open it wider because we were standing almost right behind it.

"Yeah, Ma, everything is fine. I'll meet you downstairs in a minute," she said, still looking at me. I didn't know what she was trying to prove, but I really hoped she didn't expect me to go for anything she was saying. I was Cash. People knew I didn't listen to shit when it wasn't going my way.

She then grabbed both of my hands and held them before she stood on her tiptoes and kissed my cheeks. "When Moni gets back, we'll come up with some type of schedule for you to see her." With that said, she let go of my hands, turned around, grabbed the suitcase, and was out the door. As she was walking away, it felt like I was about to have a heart attack at any minute. That was how much my heart was hurting right now.

I thought about what she said. *Maybe I really should just let her go.* After all, she was right. I kept on doing the things that I was doing to her. It wasn't as if she were doing the shit back to me and I kept putting it on me being a man, but I really didn't know. I couldn't lie. The bitches who threw pussy at me were ridiculous, but I could still man up and tell them no. However, as she said, I was thinking with my dick. Shit, who was I kidding? I owned one of the hottest clubs in Tennessee. Being a club owner came with the pleasure of fucking beaucoup bitches, and I wanted to reap the benefits. I just didn't think that I'd get caught and my girl would leave me, but that was cool. I was going to let her get a little time to herself. It wasn't as if she was going to get another nigga, because she wasn't the type of female to rock like that. Once she had her little moment, it was going to be us again. While we were having a break, I was going to try to get all the cheating out of my system. This time I was really going to try to do right by her no matter how hard it was going to be.

After getting myself together, I headed back downstairs to say goodbye to my daughter. Lord knows I really didn't want my baby to go, but since Keys's mother drove so far and I needed to get back on her good side, I decided to let her go. When I made it downstairs, they were on their way to the door.

"Come here, Daddy's baby," I said, walking over to her. I tickled her little arms before I kissed her forehead. "I'm going to miss you, baby."

"I will miss you too, Daddy," she said, hugging me tight. "Mommy will be with you."

Even though she talked better than any normal child did at her age, she didn't understand what her mother and I were going through right now. All she really knew was that we were a family, and to her, we would always be a family.

"Okay, baby," I answered her. I placed her down on her feet and held her hand as we walked outside to the car. I half listened as Keyon, Tay, and her mother talked. I buckled Moni into her car seat, got her suitcase from her mother, and placed it in the trunk.

When I walked back over to the side of the car, Keyon was there talking to Emoni. I watched the beautiful sight before me. It warmed my heart to know that even if Keyon never wanted to see me again, my daughter had a wonderful mother who was going to always be there, no matter what, and who loved her unconditionally.

"I love you, baby," she said, making my heart skip a few beats.

"I love you, Mommy," Moni replied, waving. She then turned to me. "Love you, Daddy."

I walked over to her and kissed her on her cheek. "Daddy loves you too. Be good for Momo, okay?"

"I will. Bye." She waved. I moved back from the car, shutting the door.

"Call me when you make it home, Ma," Keyon said to her mother, who also had gotten in the car. "Be careful, and I love you."

"I will, and I love you too," she said as she started the car. "Try not to worry, okay?"

"I'll try not to," Keys replied. With that said, we watched as her mother backed out of the driveway and disappeared down the street. Poor Keyon looked like she wanted to cry a little. This was going to be strange because this was going to be her first time being away from Emoni.

"You ready to go?" she asked Tay, who I had forgotten was even here.

"Girl, yes, please," she said, taking a quick glance at me before she walked over to Keys's car and got in.

For a moment, Keys and I just stood there staring at each other. *I'd give all the money in the world just to know what she is thinking about right now.* "A penny for your thoughts," I said, breaking the silence. I wanted so badly for her just to stop playing so damn hard to get and run straight into my arms, but she didn't. She didn't even answer me. She just looked at me, shook her head, walked over to the car, and got in. When she started the car, I thought for sure that she was going to try to run me down as long as she sat there, but she didn't. Instead, she pulled off without so much as a horn blow or a wave.

I stood there in the middle of the driveway all by my lonesome. I wished I could start the past forty-eight hours over again. Hell, I wished I could start this whole week over. "God, if you're up there, please hear my cry," I said as I walked back to the house.

I went into the kitchen and grabbed my keys off the counter. I made sure that everything was locked and secured before I left. My damn day was already fucked up. I just hoped that no one fucked with me any more than this, because I was liable to go straight to jail.

One Week Later

Keys

It'd been a whole week since Cash and I broke up, and I was still in a somewhat somber mood. It wasn't that I missed him or anything. It was just that I couldn't believe I played a fool to the man for so long. As I sat there listening to Sparkle's "Be Careful," I couldn't help but think about all the things that Cash had put me through these past few years: the lying and cheating, the late-night phone calls from his bitches, the keying of my cars, the letters, many DNA tests, and more. I'd been through it all with him, and still I stayed with his ass like a damn fool while he continued to mistreat me. There wasn't that much love in the world for me to be stupid and stay with his ass, but I did. I guessed I really didn't know any better.

All I wanted was to be loved by my man, to have my thug in my life, not caring what problems it came with, but that shit was dead. If having a thug in my life meant I had to go through all of this, then I was tapping out and getting me a regular nine-to-five nigga with good credit. I wasn't by far a gold digger, but I needed a man with credit at least. I wasn't trying to pick up just anybody anymore. From now on, I was going to start doing background checks to at least know what type of nigga I was dealing with. I wasn't trying to attract a ho nigga anymore. I needed a man who was going to be all about me and me only!

Grabbing my drink off the table, I took a seat, and then puffed on a Kool cigarette. It was a good thing Emoni was with my mother, because I wouldn't have been able to throw myself a little pity party. Yes, I was having a party for myself, but only for one day. Tomorrow, I was going to begin my new journey in life. I had my hair pulled up into a ponytail, an old lady nightgown on, and my stereo system blasting. I needed this to numb the pain, the many memories, the hurt, the lies. I needed to get all of Cash out of my system so that I could begin to heal, to move on with my life. I wasn't about to take him back, not this time. I was finally laying down the law and sticking to my guns. Cash and I were over, and there was nothing he could do about it.

I remembered when I first caught Cash cheating on me. It was about five years ago. I was in my last class of the day, preparing to go home. I was just about done with school. Seeing as it was time to take our midterms, I was stressed and tired. I had texted Cash earlier in the day and told him that I was going to be late because I had to stop by the library and that he should just pick us up something to eat while he was out. He texted me back and told me that he would, for me to be careful, and to call him when I was on my way. I texted back an okay and continued to listen to my professor. Lord knows I was tired, but I had to go to the library to study or else I was going to flunk my midterms.

The minute the bell rang and class let out, I gathered my belongings, got up, and left, heading to the library around the corner. When I made it to my car, I realized that I had left the papers I needed at home. I called Cash's phone a few times, trying to get him to meet me with them, but he didn't answer. Instead of going straight to the library like I had planned, I went directly home to get the papers.

I tried calling Cash to inform him that I was on my way home, but he wasn't answering. I figured that he was maybe taking a bath or asleep and had left the phone in the living room, so I thought nothing of it. After a few minutes of not reaching him, I gave up and continued to drive home. When I pulled onto the street that we lived on, an uneasy feeling throbbed in the pit of my stomach. Shaking it off, I ignored it. Pulling up to my apartment complex, I noticed Cash's car sitting in its usual parking space along with some other car that I didn't recognize. I went ahead and parked on the street. Seeing as I was only going to grab my papers and head back out, I left the car running, only grabbing my purse. When I made it to the door, I fished out my keys to unlock it, until I noticed that it wasn't all the way closed. I pushed the door open and was about to call out Cash's name when I heard R. Kelly's *12 Play* CD playing from the sound system that was hooked up in the bedroom.

"Lord, looks like my baby is in a good mood. I might not make it to the library tonight at all," I said to myself as I made it into the living room. I placed my keys and purse on the table, and then I made my way to the bedroom. I thought I was tripping, but as I got closer to the door, I could hear the sounds of someone moaning. Again, I thought Cash maybe had a flick or something on with the TV up too loud. Once I got to the door, I slowly twisted the knob and began to open it. I had to brace myself at the sight before my eyes. I was mortified at the sight of him long stroking whoever the fuck this bitch was from the back. I couldn't lie. That bitch was taking all ten inches of that dick pretty well. For a moment, I just stood there and watched them. I didn't know if I should stop them or if I should just leave and not do anything. Hell, it was my first time being in a position like that. I didn't know what in the hell to do, but then a thought came to me. I paid damn near every bill in this apartment, and this nigga was in our bed having sex with another bitch.

I quietly closed the door and went back into the living room. I was about 22, so my mind wasn't as vicious as it was today. I just sat there on the sofa and waited for them to come out. While I was waiting, I called Tay to ask her what she thought I should do. Right off the bat she went off, naming a bunch of shit I could and should do to him.

"You know what? Fuck all that. I'm coming over. I'll be there in six minutes," she said and hung up. I sat there and waited while they were still fucking back there.

Six minutes later, Tay was ringing my phone, asking me to open the door. "They still in there?"

"Girl, yes," I replied sadly. "What should I do?"

"You should be a fucking scorned black woman and fuck they asses up, but make sure you start with your man first. He's the one who's obligated to you and your feelings, so make sure you start with him. If I'm right about the girl, she's going to run out of the room and outside, where I'll be waiting for her. Just make sure you don't take too long to come whoop her ass, okay?" she said, walking back to the door.

"Okay," I said, and walked back to the bedroom and tore Cash's ass up.

Tay and I also whooped the bitch's ass, and I never saw her again. That day, I opened my eyes to the fact that no matter how good of a woman I was, I was never going to be good enough for a man who wasn't ready. That was also the day that my attitude toward him changed and I stopped being a pushover, but it didn't stop Cash from continuing to cheat on my ass.

I was brought out of my thoughts by the ringing of my phone. Whoever was calling, their number wasn't saved in my phone, so I didn't have any idea who it was. I was a little skeptical about answering the phone. Grabbing the remote to my stereo system, I lowered the volume and answered the phone anyway.

"Hello."

"What's up with you, ma?" I heard a voice say.

"Who is this?" I asked because I didn't recognize the voice.

"Oh, that's how you doing it, shorty? It's me, Kane," he replied.

"Oh, Kane. What's up?"

"Obviously you didn't save my number," he said, sounding offended. "I thought we were at least friends."

"Don't get ya panties in a bunch. We are friends. I just forgot to save your number."

"Uh-huh. Let me find out you don't miss me as much as I miss you," he said in a sexy voice.

"Boy, quit it. You don't miss me. Why did you take so long to call me anyway?" I asked. "I gave you my number like a week ago."

"I was out of town, shorty. I just got back today."

"Out of town, huh? And I told you my name, and I'm pretty sure I didn't say it was shorty," I said in a playful tone.

"My bad, ma . . . I mean, Keys," he said, laughing. "I know that ain't ya real name either."

"Nah, that ain't my real name, just like Kane ain't yours."

"It's not. My real name is Kahreem. What's yours?

"Kahreem, huh? My real name is Keyon."

"How come both our real names and nicknames go so well together?" he asked. "Kane and Keys, and Kahreem and Keyon."

"I don't know, but they do sound good together," I said, flirting. I didn't know what it was about this man, but he had me wanting to bend all the rules I made up last week.

"So when am I going to be able to take you out to dinner . . . as friends?" he asked.

"When do you want to take me out to dinner?" I threw back at him.

"I'm asking you. I know you got your daughter, and I want to respect that," he said, which caused me to blush. Most men would run away from a woman who had a kid, but not him. He was different. I swore he was cut from a different cloth, and I liked that very much. "Okay. Well, how about tonight?" he asked.

"Tonight would be great," I blurted out. "Wait, what about your daughter?"

"She's with my mother for the rest of the summer. She won't be back until August when she starts day care. So I'm all yours."

"All mine, huh?" I said sarcastically.

"Yup. What time do you want me to pick you up?"

"Umm, it's almost one in the afternoon. So you could come around seven or seven thirty," I said nervously.

"Okay, ma."

"I told you what my name is."

"I'm sorry, Keyon. It's the way I talk. Charge it to my head, not my heart."

"Okay, you got that. See you later."

"Okay, I'll see you later, Keyon."

When he hung up the phone, I sat there smiling my ass off. It wasn't long ago that I was in a relationship, but this man here had me feeling some type of way. He had me wanting to experience life again. It wasn't like when I was with Cash. When I was with Cash, I felt like an old woman. With Kane, I wanted to be a normal 27-year-old woman.

Remembering that I looked like a dusty old woman, I jumped up and headed to my room. Using the house phone that my mother insisted I get, I dialed Tay's number. While waiting for her to answer the phone, I went into my closet to search for something I could wear tonight.

"Hello," she answered on the second ring.

"Are you busy?" I asked because it sounded like she was.

"No, I'm not, why? What's up?" she asked.

"Guess who's going on a date?" I said, barely able to contain it. "Well, it's not really a date, but going out to eat dinner at night."

"You dirty dog, with who?" she asked, sounding a bit more alert.

"I'm going with Kane. He just called and asked a few minutes ago," I said, sounding excited.

"You talking 'bout the cutie from your building?" she asked, just as excited as I was.

"Girl, yeeeeeeeeeeah!" I stretched. I was feeling too bucked right now.

"Girl, he's a cutie. You go, girl," she replied. "What are you going to wear?"

"Girl, I'm in the closet right now looking for something to put on."

"Oh, hell no, not them grandma-ass clothes you used to put on when you were with Cash's ass. We need to go shopping. It's time for Stella to get her groove back." She busted out laughing. "Besides, I got a plan."

"Bitch, fuck you. I do not wear no grandma clothes," I said, laughing with her.

"Get dressed. I'm taking you to the mall. It's my treat. I'll be there in five minutes tops."

"Well, bitch, where yo' ass at?" I asked because she didn't live anywhere near me.

"Actually, I was on my way there already."

"Girl, you so sad. You was trying to pop up on me, huh?"

"Yup, I was trying to make sure you didn't relapse and let Cash's ass back into the fold."

"Bitch, bye. I ain't thinking about Cash," I said, suddenly becoming offensive. I knew that from the past few times, it was going to be hard for her to believe that I wasn't taking Cash back, but I was serious this time. I was moving on to better things.

"I'll believe it when I see it," she then said. "Get dressed. I'm almost there."

"All right. Bye."

After hanging up the phone, I got up and got dressed. I had not long ago gotten out of the shower, so thankfully I didn't have to take one. All I had to do was brush my teeth again, throw my hair into a ponytail, and get dressed. Since I had beaucoup sundresses, I put one on with a pair of sandals. When I was done getting dressed, I threw my hair into a ponytail. *Thank God I just put in a perm.* Normally, my hair would be super thick, and it would take me about twenty minutes just to brush it into a ponytail. When I was finished, I added a little lip gloss just as Tay began knocking on the door. Grabbing my purse and keys, I went to open the door for her.

"Damn, you really ain't playing, huh? You got dressed in them five minutes. Let me find out you're crushing on dude and extremely excited about your date . . . I mean, outing tonight," she laughed, walking inside.

"Well, I won't tell you then," I said, grabbing my phone from the table.

"Go 'head with ya bad self," she said.

"You're more excited than me."

"That's because I'm happy that you left that zero and found you somebody else."

"Don't start, Tay, and for all I know, Kane could be a zero too."

"Well, we won't know until tonight, now will we? Now come on," she said, dragging me out the door.

"Girl, what am I going to do with you?"

"Love me. Now let's go. We don't have all day," she said, and with that, we were out the door. "You ready to get back to your pre-Cash-cheating self?"

"Girl, am I. I'm so ready to start living my life again."

"You ain't said nothing but a word. I got you. Trust!" she said, throwing her shades on. With that being said, we hopped in her car and were headed to the mall.

Kane

I was cruising the streets of Memphis when my phone began ringing. I looked at the caller ID and saw that it was my li'l cousin from out of state. *The fuck his ass want now?* Lord knows I really didn't want to, but I answered the phone anyway.

"Sup, nigga?" I asked.

"Yo, man, thanks again for helping me out with that thing," he spoke through the phone. "Y'all done made it home yet?"

"Yeah, and it's no problem. You don't have to keep thanking me, li'l nigga."

"Yeah, yeah, I know, but I'm just grateful that y'all niggas came through for me, man."

"We family. I'm going to always have your back, but listen here. You need not speak on the shit we did. That shit is dead for all we know, ya feel me?"

"Yeah, I feel you," he replied.

"Oh, yeah, and I meant what I said back in Chicago, son. I ain't fucking with that street shit no more. So next time y'all need someone to help y'all out, don't call me. I got too much to lose if anything goes wrong, ya feel me?" I said, stretching that shit to him again. I was through with that street life. I had my daughter to think about, and seeing that she'd already lost one parent, I wasn't trying to make her an orphan.

"I heard you the first hundred times you said it. I get it," he replied, sounding frustrated. I didn't give a fuck if I said it a million times. I needed to remind his ass because he always had a tendency to do shit the opposite way. He never fucking listened. Just as sure as I told him I wasn't fucking with that street shit anymore, his ass would probably try to call me again for something else dealing with the streets.

"A'ight, well, I'll talk to you later, fam. Be easy and stay ya hardheaded ass out of trouble, li'l nigga," I said, hanging up the phone. I had this feeling that Bundy wasn't the nigga pulling all these strings. No way had his dumb ass come up with a scheme like that. It was just too big and had too much money involved. I knew for sure that someone else was behind this shit. I really didn't care who it was, just as long as they didn't bring any heat my way. My life was running smoothly. I didn't need anything or anyone fucking it up.

I placed my phone on my lap and reached for the blunt that I had lit in the ashtray. My day wasn't going so well until I scrolled through my contacts and came across Keys's name and number. I couldn't lie. Ever since the day I met shorty, I knew I had to have her. She just had a thing about her that screamed, "I need to be loved." Baby girl was my type, and all I wanted to do was love her. Even when she was giving me all that attitude, I still wanted to make her mine. I was somewhat disappointed when she started talking about her baby daddy, but I was glad when she said they weren't together anymore. I was mad that he had hurt her, but I should have thanked him, because if he hadn't hurt her, I probably wouldn't have met her.

I hadn't been in a real relationship since the day my daughter's mother passed away three years ago. Yeah, I fucked a few bitches here and there, but I was never in a relationship with them. I wasn't a ho, but none of them seemed to spark my interest. They only made my dick hard. Once I finished getting my nut, I'd give them some money to play with, and I'd bounce. I never even cared to stay for breakfast. With Keyon, it was different. She did get my dick hard, but something about her was telling me that it was about more than catching a nut.

"Nigga, what are you over there smiling about?" my boy Ant asked, snapping me from my thoughts. We were in the car on our way to the mall.

"Man, nothing," I said, shooing him off.

"Yeah, nigga, it don't look like nothing. I haven't seen you smile hard like that since the day my sister gave birth to Ahmyri."

"Remember shorty I was telling you about last week?" I asked, trying to refresh his memory.

"Yeah, what about her?" he asked, whipping the car through the mall's parking lot. He quickly found a spot and parked.

"I'm taking her out to dinner tonight," I said, trying hard to hide my smile.

"No shit. How did you pull that off?" he asked, surprised.

"I just called her and asked her out, and she agreed. I told you she just broke up with her nigga."

"So is this going to be like all the rest of them times?" he asked with a raised eyebrow. "Because you know how you do 'em."

"No, this will not be like the rest of them times. I told you she was different. I'm not trying to treat her like the rest of them hoes," I told him as we got out of the car.

"Uh-huh, if that's what you say."

"Man, I'm serious. I don't want just a nut from her. I want more."

"And did you tell her that?" he asked as he walked through the mall door. Thankfully, it wasn't as busy as it would normally be, because I wasn't trying to spend all day in here. Besides, I needed to freshen up my haircut and shit before tonight.

"Yeah, I told her."

"And what did she say?"

"She said what any other woman who had just gotten out of a long-term relationship would say."

"And what was that?"

"That she wasn't trying to jump headfirst into a relationship, but she didn't have a problem with us starting out as friends."

"And what did you say?"

"Nigga, what's with the twenty questions?" I asked him.

"Shit, I'm just trying to get all the facts, son. Now what did you say?"

"I told her that I was cool with that. Why?" I asked. This nigga was really beginning to piss me off with all these muthafucking questions.

He stopped walking and turned to face me. He looked me in my eyes before he took a deep breath. "I was wondering when this day was going to come."

"What do you mean?" I asked, confused.

"I'm talking about the day you'd finally let my sister rest in peace and start to live your life again. I know my sister was everything to you, but damn, two years? It took you two whole years to grieve," he said, shaking his head. "It's like my sister still had your heart and mind, and she was six feet deep in the dirt. She wasn't coming back, and you put your whole life on hold."

"Man, go on with that bullshit. I don't have time to hear this speech again," I said, waving his dumb ass off. "Yes, I loved ya sister dearly, and yes, I did grieve a bit, but that don't mean anything. Yes, she's gone, but I respect her enough to move on when the time is right. Besides, I'm a father. I wasn't trying to have all them different women around my daughter, nigga."

"Uh-huh, whatever, nigga. Save that soap-opera shit for *The Young and the Restless*. My sister still got you pussy whipped, and she ain't living no more," he said, laughing.

"I swear you a dumb nigga, yeah—" I said, but the rest of my words got caught in my throat. I spotted her before she even spotted me. She was walking with her hands full of bags beside some other chick who didn't look so bad herself.

"What the fuck is you looking at?" Ant asked once he noticed I wasn't paying his ass no attention.

"You see the girl in that peach sundress with the gold sandals and ponytail in her hair?" I asked, trying to get him to see what I was looking at. He turned just as she looked up and noticed us standing there. She smiled the most beautiful smile I'd ever seen before she waved us over.

"Damn, nigga, who that is?" Ant yelled. "Shorty bad like fuck. I need them digits there."

He walked a few steps forward before I pulled him back. "No can do. That's my date for tonight," I said as I went to meet her with him following closely behind me.

"You's a lucky muthafucka, Kane, I swear," he whispered just as we made it to them.

"I thought I wasn't supposed to see you until tonight," she said, walking over to me, giving me a big hug.

"I guess fate had other plans," I replied, hugging her back.

"What are you doing in here?" she asked.

"I'm here with my boy. We 'bout to do a li'l shopping and stuff."

"Excuse me, where are my manners?" she said. "Kane, this is my best friend, Tay. Tay, this is Kane."

"Hey, how ya doing?' her friend said, shaking my hand. "Nice to meet you."

"I'm doing great, and it's nice to meet you also," I said, shaking her hand. "This is my boy, Ant. Ant, this is Keys."

"So you're Keys, huh?" he asked with a smile. "I've heard so much about you."

"All good things I hope," she replied.

"Yes, all good things," he said to her. He then turned to her friend. "How are you?"

"I'm fine and yourself?"

"Better now that I've seen you," he flirted. I wanted to smack his ass upside the head, but I didn't. He was talking about me, and here his ass was drooling over this chick.

"Well, we have to get going. I'll see you later?" Keyon asked, speaking up.

"Okay, and yeah, I'll see you later," I said. They said their goodbyes and went about their business, and we went about ours.

"Man, you ain't tell me shorty's drop-dead gorgeous. No wonder your ass wants to up and make her your old lady and shit. With a body and face like what she got, I'd make her my woman too," Ant said just as we entered the shoe store.

"Man, it's not about all that. No lie. All that is an extra bonus and all, but baby girl got this vibe to her."

"Vibe or whatever, I don't blame you for trying to wife her. I feel sorry for the nigga who had the nerve to cheat on a woman like that."

"Same thing I said when she told me that shit. Anyways, let's get what we have to and be out. I'm not trying to be in here all day."

"Ay, you think you could call her and get ol' girl to come along? We can double date. You know, how we used to do it. Well, that's if she ain't got a man and shit," he said.

"Yeah, man, I'll see," I said, pulling my phone out of my pocket and dialing her number.

"Aww, you miss me already?" she asked, answering the phone.

"I surely do," I said, blushing. Shorty really had me feeling like a little nigga in high school. "But check it out. Yo' girl, is she single?"

"You talking about Tay?"

"Yeah, I'm talking about her."

"Yeah, she's single, why?"

"Because my boy wants to know if she wanna go out with him tonight."

"Wait, let me ask her," she said. The phone went silent for a few seconds, then she came back. "Umm, hello?"

"I'm still here," I answered her.

"She asked if he was single."

"Yeah, he's single."

"I mean, with no side bitch or nothing. She said she ain't trying to get herself into no dumb shit."

"Ma, I'm telling you he's single," I stressed to her.

"Uh-huh. Well, she said she'll go out with him then."

"Okay. Tell her to be ready at seven, because we're all going together."

"All right, well, she's going to be over at my house with me."

"A'ight, well, I'll see y'all later then."

"Okay," she replied as we hung up the phone.

I went to tell Ant the news. He was happy, yet the nigga was talking about me being excited and shit. He didn't even know shorty. He only knew her name, yet he was excited about going on a date with her. I started to burst his bubble as he'd tried to do mine, but I didn't even have the time. I just let him be as we finished shopping. I was going to get his ass though, if not now, then for sure later. Right now, the only thing on my mind was getting myself straight for my date tonight. That was, if I could call it a date. Well, whatever it was, after tonight, I was going to leave such a big impression on her that she was going to be thinking about me day and night. I couldn't wait for tonight to come.

CHAPTER SIX

Keys

We spent the whole damn evening getting ready for our date tonight with Kane and Ant. We ended up going to another mall and the nail shop. It was a good thing we'd gone to the hair salon earlier, because things would've been drastic if we had to get our hair done last minute. By the time we made it home, it was almost five o'clock that evening, which left us with a little over two hours to get dressed.

"Girl, I got a good mind to call and cancel on Kane," I said, walking through the door. The first thing I did was kick my shoes off and take off my bra. When I let my girls loose, I felt a whole lot better.

"What? Why?" Tay asked, taking a seat on the sofa.

"Because I'm tired, girl. All I wanna do is crawl in my bed and catch some z's," I said, yawning.

"Bitch, please. You been sleeping in for the past week. It's time to get out and have fun. Shit, you're finally single. It's time to start acting like it instead of acting like an old grandma," she said, preaching.

I sat there for a minute, thinking about what she was saying. It was true that when I was with Cash, I barely went anywhere, and when I did go, it was probably because we had gotten into it. I'd go because I wanted to make him sweat me as much as I would sweat him.

"All right, damn, I'm going. You don't have to act like my damn mother and shit," I said, picking up my bags from by the door and bringing them in the bedroom.

"I'm glad you see things my way," she said, grabbing her bags, following me. "Girl, I haven't been on a date in so long I don't know how to feel."

"And you want to talk about me. Bitch, please, you pro'ly don't even know how to act around a nigga no more," I said, clowning her.

"Girl, whatever. I'm not even about to go there with you."

"Good. Anyways, I'm 'bout to go hop in the shower," I said, pulling out my purple lace bra and panty set that I had just bought.

"I'm so tired of seeing your ass wear purple. Put on another damn color for a change."

"Don't hate because I look good wearing purple and you don't."

"Bitch, whatever. I'll see you when I get out of the tub," she said before she left the room. I was glad that my apartment had two bathrooms. Between the both of us having to take a bath and get ready, we wouldn't be able to do it with one.

Grabbing my phone, my purple Pill speaker, and my vanilla candle, I made my way into the bathroom. I set my things on the counter before I walked over to the tub, plugged it, and started the water. I grabbed my phone off the counter and turned Pandora to its Monica station. I lit my candle before I walked over to the light switch and clicked it off. I stripped out of my clothes and got in the tub. I just prayed that I didn't fall asleep, because if I did, I would not be going out at all.

Tay

I was really happy when my girl called me earlier and told me that she was going on a date. That meant she was actually trying her best to get over her bitch-ass baby daddy. I was skeptical about this date at first, but when she told me that she was going with the cutie from her building, I was all too glad for her to be going. To be honest, I really thought she was going to relapse and take Cash's ass back like always, but she was surely proving me wrong. I was still a little bit concerned about her now, but since she agreed to go on a date and I didn't have to set it up myself, I was going to give her a pass.

Even though she said that she was really over Cash, I still had the feeling that she wasn't. Hell, they'd been together for years and years. Shit like that didn't just go away within a week. She was trying hard to hide it, but she was really torn up behind this, and I didn't blame her. If I had been in only one real relationship in my entire life, had been with one person for years and years, I wouldn't know how to act when it was time for us to call it quits. Hell, I didn't know if I would be able to call it quits at all. I would probably do the same thing she'd been doing.

That was why I was glad I didn't have a man. People thought I couldn't get a man, but the truth of the matter was I didn't want one. After the death of my fiancé, Shawn, I never wanted to get close to another man. It wasn't that I was scared to love, because I'd rather love and have love lost. I couldn't take seeing someone I'd grown to love taken away from me too early in life again. There was a difference between loving someone and losing them to another person, and loving someone and losing them to death. Knowing that I would never get to see that person again was scary and heartbreaking, and I did not wish to go through that again. Losing Shawn had cut me deep, so deep that I had gone into a state of depression. It was so bad that my mother thought I would never come out of my funk. That was why she suggested that I move out here. That was the best thing that ever happened to me.

"Tay," Keyon yelled, banging on the bathroom door. I was happy that she interrupted me when she did, because if I'd thought about Shawn a little while longer, I wouldn't be going anywhere.

"What up?" I asked, dabbing at the lone tear that had fallen from my eye. Even after all this time, Shawn was still a touchy subject for me.

"Shit, I'm trying to find out now. You've been in that bathroom forever. I'm almost done getting dressed."

"Me too. All I gotta do is put my shoes on, grab my clutch, and I'm finished," I said, opening the door for her to see me. I then spun around, giving her a full view of my whole outfit. "What do you think? How do I look? Do you like it?"

"Like it? Bitch, you're wearing the hell out of that dress. Red is really your color," she said, looking like a proud parent who was about to send their daughter to her first prom.

"Bitch, please get your mushy ass out of my face and spin around so I can get a good look at you," I said, motioning my finger in a circle. Slowly she turned around so I could look at her, and I had to say that I was very pleased with what I saw. I swore if I were a carpet muncher, I'd have been all over her ass.

"Soooooo," she said with her back facing me. "How do I look?"

I kept my mouth closed on purpose. I knew what she looked like, and my best friend was drop-dead gorgeous. I could guarantee that when Kane saw her tonight he would probably be thinking about marriage, and he hadn't even sniffed her pussy yet.

"Tay, stop playing and tell me what you think. Shit, I'm standing over here nervous as hell. The least you could do is ease my worry and tell me what you think," she whined like a child.

"Shut up, big baby," I said, poking my tongue out at her. "Honey, you look drop-dead gorgeous. I bet if Cash were to see you now, he'd regret the day he fucked up and gave another nigga a chance to win."

"You really think I look good?" she asked. I didn't know why she needed reassurance. She looked good in her nurse's uniform, so imagine how she looked now. In fact, she needed to see what I was looking at now.

Grabbing her by her hand, I led her into her room. "Close your eyes."

"Tay, what are you doing?"

"Just do what I say, Keke," I said, calling her by the nickname I gave her. She rolled her eyes before she did as I said. "And don't peek either."

"Girl, I'm not. Just hurry up, damn."

Just to make sure that she wasn't looking, I covered her eyes with my hands and then guided her over to the full-length mirror hanging from her closet door. Removing my hands, I said, "Open your eyes. What do you see?"

"I see me," she answered.

"You want me to tell you what I see?"

"Go ahead."

"I see a woman who's been through the storm and the rain but hasn't given up. A woman whose heart is made of pure gold, and she stays getting fucked over but doesn't ever lose faith. I see a winner, a star, a mother to a beautiful baby girl. I'm telling you now that you've got it going on in this dress, baby. Chile, the way you're rocking this two-piece lace dress is absolutely ridiculous. It should be a crime for a person to look this damn good," I said, smiling. She noticed a tear had fallen down her face. She wiped it before she smiled back. "Chile, when that man sees you, he won't be able to take his eyes off of you."

"Thank you for always being there for me. Through the good times and the bad."

"Girl, whatever. You're stuck with me. So either way I'm going to be here. Now come on and let's finish getting dressed. It's almost seven, and the guys will be here any minute now," I said before she could let another tear fall from her eyes. I wasn't trying to be crying up in this bitch, not when it took me a good half hour to put my face on.

CHAPTER SEVEN

Keys

It was safe to say that I was a bit nervous about going on a date with Kane. I hadn't been on an actual date in a minute, and I was a bit scared and extremely nervous. Cash was the only man I ever really dated in my whole life. I didn't even know how to be around a man anymore. How was I supposed to act or feel? I was so used to being around Cash that I really didn't know how to be around any other man. It was a good thing that Tay was going with me though, because if I were going by myself, I honestly didn't know what I would've done.

By the time we were finished getting dressed, the guys were knocking on the door. "Tay, go answer the door," I yelled from my bedroom. I stood in the mirror admiring myself. I couldn't lie. Tay had picked out the perfect outfit for me, but somehow I still felt insecure. I looked and felt like a grown woman, a woman who was worthy of being loved, but deep down I still had a problem with myself and how I looked.

"Girl, come on. You've been in that mirror for ten minutes now. I told you a million and one times before, you look great. Stop feeling unsure and come on out here. The boys are here, and we're ready to go."

"Okay, girl, damn," I said, spraying some more perfume on my body. I looked at myself one more time in the mirror before I grabbed my clutch, cut the lights off, and headed to the living room.

As I made my way to the living room, my heart was beating faster than a muthafucka. I didn't know if I was scared, nervous, or excited. All I knew was that when I entered the living room, the looks on the guys' faces were priceless.

"I told you that you looked like a goddess," Tay whispered behind me. I guessed she saw the same thing I saw. Immediately, my insecurities went away. I smiled, knowing that I actually did look good. Now I was beginning to feel good, too.

"Hello, ma," Kane stuttered, walking over to me. "You look beautiful."

"Hello, and thank you, handsome. You don't look too bad yourself," I said, blushing.

"These are for you," he said, handing me some flowers. I took them from him and then reached in and gave him a hug. "You keep looking as good as you look and I'm going to have to kidnap your fine ass," he said, flirting. He reached in and kissed my cheek, causing an electric shock that damn near jolted me out of my skin.

"Wow," I whispered to myself. I didn't know whether to run and hide. This man had me feeling all kinds of ways. He was about to say something when Tay interrupted us.

"Okay, I know my girl looks good and everything, but can we please leave before you two end up ripping each other's clothes off and head straight to the bedroom?" she said, embarrassing me. I told her about her mouth. Sometimes she just should be quiet.

"A'ight, ma," Kane said, laughing. "Come on, beautiful, let's go make this a night to remember," he said, reaching for my arm. Again, I felt that surge of energy, but this time I didn't pull back. I decided to let it flow. It was going to be what it was going to be. I just hoped and prayed that this night was going to be a great one.

Kane

When shorty came out of that back room looking like a million and one dollars, my heart skipped a beat. I wasn't supposed to be doing this this early in the game, but all I could think about was making her my wife. Baby girl looked like she belonged on the cover of a magazine. Hell, I pitied the nigga who fucked over her, because this woman was everything a man like me needed. She was well-rounded and smart, had a good head on her shoulders, and wasn't around looking for different ways to dig into the next man's pocket. Actually, I wanted to meet his ass so I could personally thank him. He just didn't know what he'd done. I was going to make sure I treated her like the queen she was so that she would never think about leaving me. I wanted to cherish and love her in a way that no other man could, and give her everything her heart desired, both her and her daughter.

Since this was a last-minute thing, I decided that we would go eat at Chili's. It was convenient, and we wouldn't have to wait almost an hour to be seated. I really didn't have time to book any reservations at a fancy place. I just hoped that they didn't look at us as being funny or anything, because a nigga wasn't cheap at all.

When we pulled up to Chili's, the place was somewhat packed, but not too packed that we couldn't get a parking spot. We were parked and seated within fifteen minutes. It wasn't until the waiter came and took down our drink orders that we really began to loosen up.

"So, how's everyone doing?" I asked, trying to spark a conversation. I hated when I went out with people and it was too silent for me. That shit was awkward and boring as hell.

"We're good," Tay said. "How about y'all fellas?"

"We straight. Still breathing, so we can't complain," Ant answered.

"Well, well, well," some bright chick said, walking up to the table. I had no idea who she was, but by the looks on Keyon's and Tay's faces, I guessed they knew her.

"Bitch, what the fuck do you want?" Keyon asked calmly from across the table.

"Where that nigga Cash at?" she asked, looking from me to Ant. "Who y'all niggas is? Let me find out little Miss Goody Two-shoes is out here thoting."

"Probably out fucking one of them crusty-ass broads like you, and why the fuck are you worrying about who they are?" Keys asked, standing along with her friend. By then they had attracted the attention of the people in the restaurant. "But if you call me a thot one more time, I'm going to come across this table and fuck you all the way up."

She began laughing before she stepped a little closer to the table. "Bitch, I didn't say you was a thot. I said you was out here thoting, but excuse me if the shoe fits."

"Whoa, shorty, you need to leave before you let your mouth overrule your ass," I said, trying to dead the issue before it started.

"Nigga, who the fuck are you to be saying anything to me?" was all she got out before Keyon reached across the table and slapped the dog shit out of her. Shorty's head turned so hard I thought for sure that she had whiplash. "You stupid bitch," she yelled, trying to charge her, but I stopped her.

"Nah, shorty. You don't want to do that," I said.

"Nigga, fuck that shit. I know you just seen this bitch slap me in my face. You think I'ma let that shit slide?" she yelled, still trying to charge Keyon.

"Nah, boo, you asked for that. I don't even know why you stopped over here. You were being messy in the first place."

"Kane, let that bitch go so I can dog walk that ho up and down Chili's," Keyon replied. I turned and noticed that Ant was holding her, which was a big mistake, because that left Tay open and gave her the perfect opportunity to flow freely. I saw her hand move, but before I could block the lick, she punched shorty in her face so hard she drew blood.

"Oh, no, fuck this shit," shorty said, holding her nose.

"Man, fuck her. Let's go, because I know damn well these people done called the fucking police, and you know how much I hate fucking with them pigs," I said to Ant, who was still holding on to Keyon. I let go of shorty and grabbed Tay. Somehow, I managed to pull a $20 bill out of my pocket and throw it on the table. I looked over at shorty, who was still standing there, holding her nose, talking shit.

Not giving a fuck about what she was saying, we grabbed the girls and headed for the exit. Once we made it to the car, we hopped in and pulled off, leaving smoke behind us. It wasn't until we were about five blocks away from the restaurant did Keyon realize what she did.

"Oh, my God, I can't believe that I just did that," she said, talking to herself.

"Ma, it's cool. Shorty had that shit coming," I said, trying to calm her down.

"But what about my job, Kane? I'm a damn nurse for crying out loud," she shouted, getting hysterical.

"Ma, the police ain't going to do anything, so don't even worry about that shit. Besides, I know a few niggas who work for the police department. It ain't nothing for me to get that shit erased," I said, trying to soothe her. She didn't say anything. She was trapped in her thoughts.

Every so often I would glance at her, and she was still in a state of shock. Then out of nowhere, she pulled her phone out and began dialing. She then placed the phone to her ear and waited for whoever it was to answer.

"Where you at?" she asked the person. She waited for their reply before she began to go in. "Well, you need to come back in state and get your bitches in check. Tell them hoes to stop playing with me behind yo' dog ass, because I'm good on you. You want to be a pimp or whatever the hell you call yourself, but you got all yo' hoes fucking up royally. The next time a bitch comes at me sideways behind you, I'm coming after you, Cash," she said, and with that she hung up.

I wanted to say something to her, but I didn't. I didn't want to say the wrong thing or come off the wrong way, so I kept quiet. Shorty looked like she was going through so much right now, and she needed badly to get it together. If things went right between us, I was going to make sure that she got the break she needed.

"Take me home," she suddenly burst out and said.

"Damn, shorty, you want to go home and end the night already?" Ant asked from the back seat.

"Who said anything about ending the night?" she asked with a determined look on her face. "Let's go have our own little party. What y'all say?"

"Shit, I'm down," Tay said. "Ain't nothing like getting fucked up in the comfort of your own home anyways."

"Shit, I guess we down," I said, looking to Ant. He nodded his head in agreement.

"I guess it's a house party then," she said, getting excited.

"You ain't said nothing but a word. I hope you amateurs are ready to party with us," I said, turning the car around, heading back to the apartment.

"Boy, we ain't no damn amateurs," she responded, playfully rolling her eyes.

"Uh-huh, whatever."

Even though our day was messed up, our night wasn't. On our way home, we stopped by the store and bought so much food and liquor you'd have thought we had a gang of people coming, but it was only us four. That night was so epic! We cooked, talked, and drank until the wee hours of the morning. We talked about everything from when we were kids growing up to our adult age. Well, we didn't talk about everything, but we talked about a lot. Some things were good and others were bad, but overall, we had a great time. We had so much of a good time that the next day it was too hard for us to get out of bed, so we didn't. We ended up spending the whole weekend at Keyon's place, and that was the start of a beautiful friendship and relationship.

Cash

"Nigga, what the fuck you mean you don't know?" I asked that nigga Bundy. I was tired of playing games with these little niggas. We'd been down there for a week, and we ain't heard shit about the niggas who robbed us yet. Like I told Jamel before, something wasn't right about this shit, and I was beginning to get impatient with all of these niggas up in here.

"Boss, I told you before that I don't know," he replied.

I got up from my chair and walked over to him. We were in the warehouse holding a meeting and trying to find out who in their right mind would try us.

"I don't believe you," I said to him. Something about the way he kept stuttering and constantly looking around had me a little skeptical about the story he was telling me.

I grabbed him by his dreads and spoke directly to him. "If I find out that you had anything to do with this, I'm going to kill you without a second thought, and this ain't a threat. It's a promise."

"Man, I'm telling you that I didn't have anything to do with this," he pleaded. I waited a few moments before I let go of his hair and walked back over to my chair.

"I don't like the way this is going. We have too many niggas on our team for us to not know anything about what went down," I said, sitting back down. I folded my arms because I was trying very hard not to get out of pocket on these niggas. They were going to make me make an example out of one of them. "I'm giving y'all a week, and if ya don't find nothing, then I'ma have to start making an example out of a few niggas. Get up. This meeting is over."

I watched closely as every man got up and walked out of the building. I didn't know if they thought I was playing, but just let them come back without something. The time for playing around was over. We took a major loss when those niggas robbed us, and I wanted that shit back, along with those niggas' lives.

"Yo, lemme holla at you for a minute," a little nigga named Lamar said. I looked at him before I got up, and we began walking toward the door. "Yo, man, I think you need to pay more attention to that nigga Bundy. Lately he's been splurging a little too much, and he's been acting funny, and I think he's fucking with ya girl Mia, too."

"Oh, yeah, how you know all this?" I asked, curious.

"Because one night I spotted them in the car together and they've been on the phone more than usual," he said, stopping to look at me.

"You know what? Since you was the one who brought this to my attention, I want you to watch him for me," I told him. "If that nigga looks like he's doing something shady, hook his ass up first. Then I want you to call me. In the meantime, I'll take care of my bitch."

"All right, man," he said before he dapped me off and let.

"So what do ya think?" Jamel asked me.

"Man, I don't know, but we're going to have to keep a close eye on Bundy. Something about the way that nigga is rolling ain't right," I informed him.

"All right, man. Let's get the fuck up out of here."

"I'm 'bout to stop by Mia's house and check on my son," I told him.

"Cool."

When I pulled up to Mia's house, her car along with another car were parked in the driveway. I had to park on the street. I told her about having people over to my house when I wasn't around. That shit drove me fucking insane. You put a bitch in a house, and she continued to disobey you. If it weren't for the fact that she had my son, I would've kicked her ass out a long time ago.

Before getting out, I grabbed the bags that I had gotten from the mall and Toys "R" Us the other day and got out. I made my way up to the door and was about to stick my key in when the door came open.

"Look who's here, CJ," she said, holding my son in one arm while pointing to me.

"Daddy," CJ said as he began reaching for me. I placed the bags that I had in my hands on the ground before I took him from her.

"Hey, Daddy's big man," I said, kissing his cheek. He smiled before he wrapped his arms around my neck and gave me the tightest hug his little arms could give.

"I love you, Daddy," he then said to me. My heart shined bright at the sound of those words. My little nigga was every bit of me, and I made sure to be active in his life even if I was living in another state.

"Daddy loves you too, li'l man," I said before I heard a female voice. I pushed past her into the house as I tried to see who the hell it was. "Yo, who is this?"

"Hello, I'm Shelly," she said, reaching out her hand for me to shake it.

"Cash," I said, checking her out.

"Nice to meet you," she replied.

"You too," I said. Baby girl was beautiful, and she was fine. Only thing she had wrong with her was that big-ass scar on her neck that led from one ear to the other. Other than that, she was a ten. Hell, she looked like she and Mia could be sisters because they kind of resembled each other. "I'm 'bout to go give him a bath. Have something to eat for us when I finish, please."

"Okay. Come on, girl, let's take this in the kitchen while I fix them something to eat," Mia replied.

I took one last look at shorty before I made my way up the stairs. I first stopped in CJ's room to get his things for his bath time. When I was done, I headed into the room where Mia and I slept. Since there was a bathroom in there, I decided that we would take a bath in there. I placed both CJ's and my things in the bathroom sink before I walked over to the tub and ran the water. I undressed CJ and was about to put him in the tub when my phone chimed. I knew it was a message, so I didn't go look at it right away. I gave CJ his bath and put his clothes on. Then I sat him down on the toilet before I went to grab my phone.

I was furious when I saw a picture of Keys walking into Chili's with some nigga. There was also a video with it. I began to watch it. I watched the whole confrontation between Keys and a chick named Candy, who I used to fuck. I ended up cutting her off because she ran her mouth too much. She was also the same bitch who Keyon had to get gangsta on before she finished school. I ended the video and dialed Keyon's number, but she didn't answer. I started to leave her a voicemail, but I decided against it. She was most likely not even going to listen to it.

"Mia," I yelled downstairs to her. I was so fucking pissed off by the picture that I had just seen. I tried calling Keyon again, but still she didn't answer the phone.

"What do you want, Cash?" Mia appeared through the door and asked.

"Get CJ for me while I take a quick shower," I told her.

"Why can't he stay in here like he always does, Cash? I'm cooking, and he's going to want me to hold him," she said, folding her arms across her chest.

"Look, just get him. I don't have to be explaining shit, and you should've thought about him always wanting you to hold him when you kept holding him as a baby," I said, picking him up. I walked over to her so that she could get him.

"Come on, Casimere," she said, calling him by his real name.

"You can be mad all you want, but you're still going to get him," I told her.

"Boy, come on," she said, jacking him from my arms.

"Bitch, if you jack him again, I'm going to make them eyes black again, I promise," I threatened her.

"Yeah, yeah, yeah," she said, leaving the room.

"I told your stupid ass about playing with me. Watch me fuck yo' stupid ass up again," I yelled behind her. I didn't understand why she constantly wanted to fuck with me. I knew she only did that because she wanted my attention, which right now was on something else. However, if she kept playing with me, I was going to show her better than I could tell her again!

I took a chance on trying to call Keys again, but this time the phone went straight to voicemail. Frustrated, I threw the phone in the bathroom sink, and then began to get undressed. Letting the water run out of the tub, I then turned on the shower and got in. As I stood under the water, letting the water beat against my skin, I silently prayed that that water could wash away my problems and I could get my girl back.

After getting out of the tub, I went downstairs to get something to eat. When I walked in the kitchen, Mia was just about done with the food. I stood there watching her as she slaved over a hot stove for me even after everything I'd put her through. I was wrong for putting my hands on her. I just didn't know how I was going to fix it. First, I had to start by apologizing to her. I walked over to her, wrapped my arms around her waist, and gave her a big kiss. It wasn't one of those weak kisses. This kiss spoke volumes, and I really wanted her to feel that.

"What was that about?" she asked after finally breaking away.

"I want to say that I'm sorry for the way that I've been acting. It's just that with the money and everything going on, I've been stressed and on edge," I said, trying to play nice. I honestly wanted to make things right between Mia and myself. Since things weren't all peaches and cream with Keys, they could be with her. Hell, I didn't need both of my kids' mothers being mad at me.

"Okay," she said, breaking away. She stood there looking intently into my eyes. I could see how much she loved me, and the truth was that I loved her too, but my heart was with and would always be with Keyon. "Come on, let's eat."

"Okay," I said. I walked over to CJ's high chair and took him out.

Mia was a good girl. If things were different, I could probably see us being together, but unfortunately they weren't, and we had to live with it. We came from different worlds and lived in two different states. I wasn't about to just pack up and move here, and besides, my daughter and her mother were in Tennessee. I did a lot of things to Keyon, but I loved her with everything in me. I just needed to get my mind and self together so that I could be the man she needed me to be. I had to do it soon before it was too late and I ended up losing her forever.

Mia

I didn't know what was going on with Cash, but I wasn't buying his little nice act one bit. After the ass whooping that he gave me, I opened my eyes to many things. I loved Cash. He was the father of my child, but he didn't love me. Otherwise, he wouldn't have put his hands on me that day in that hotel room, and for that, I was going to make him pay. I understood that his heart was with Keyon, and if I'd seen that before, I wouldn't have done what I did, but it was too late now. The deed was done, and I couldn't change that. I also couldn't change the fact that he put his hands on me, but I could do something about it. I didn't know what that was, but I was going to make him regret the day he laid his hands on me. I didn't care if he was the father of my child. He was going to pay for that shit.

I couldn't finish eating the way I wanted to because I was feeling some kind of way about Cash. I couldn't look him in the face without remembering the way that belt felt on my body. How could he be that heartless, enough that he would actually whoop my ass as if I were his child? I left him and li'l Cash in the kitchen while I went to go take a bath. I opted for soaking since my body was still a bit sore. Thankfully, my body was almost healed. It wasn't as bad as it was before. It felt great now compared to the way it was in the hotel room.

"What are you thinking about?" Cash asked, scaring the shit out of me.

I rolled my eyes because I left his ass and here he was still bothering me. "Nothing. Where's CJ?" I asked him.

"I just laid him in his bed. He's asleep," he said, walking into the bathroom. He sat beside the tub.

"Oh, okay," I said as I reached for the bath towel. I squirted some body wash on the rag and was about to wash my body when he reached toward me, causing me to jump. "What?"

"Chill, Mia. I'm not going to do anything to you," he said, taking the rag out of my hand. When he moved his hand toward my back, it made me jump again. "I told you to chill, ma."

"Okay," I said, letting out a deep breath. My heart began beating faster as he placed the rag on my back and began washing it. *It's going to be all right,* I coached myself. Cash really had me afraid to be around him. His hands moved from my back to my left side, where there was still a bruise from when he had hit me. I looked at him as his eyes softened as he rubbed the bruise.

"I'm sorry," he said again. "I don't know what I was thinking."

You weren't thinking at all. "It's okay, Cash," I lied. Nothing about being bruised up was okay. He nodded his head and began washing the rest of my body. When his hand got between my legs, he let go of the rag and began rubbing gently on my kitty cat. Lord knows I didn't want him to touch me, but when his hand gently brushed over my clit, I became weak and changed my mind. Cash's sex game was grade A, and only the good

Lord knew how much I needed to release some built-up pressure, so I decided to let him take me there.

With his finger, he first began playing with my lips. From there, he began rubbing my clitoris in a circular motion. Closing my eyes, I began biting my bottom lip as his finger began to work its magic. A minute or two later, he inserted a finger in me, which almost made me bust immediately.

"Umm," I moaned out in pleasure. I opened my eyes to find him staring at me. Something about the way he was looking at me turned me on. Usually, I would close my eyes, but this time, I opted to keep them open.

Gently and in a rhythmic motion, he moved his finger in and out of me. At first, it was one finger, but then he inserted another one. I couldn't lie. The shit was fucking awesome, and I didn't want him to stop. The minute his finger came in contact with my G-spot, I almost melted. Slowly, he began rubbing on it in a circular motion.

"My God!" I yelled out in pleasure.

"You like that?" he asked, still looking at me directly.

"Yesssssss," I moaned as he began pressing on it as if it were a button. I almost jumped out of the tub. "Oh, Cash, right there!"

"Right here?" he asked, doing it again. I could feel my nut beginning to build up, and all I wanted him to do was to continue to do just that.

"Oh, yeah, right there. Don't move, and don't stop. I'm about to cum!" I yelled out. He let his hand up but then pressed down again a little bit harder, which only drove me crazier. "Oh, shit!" I screamed as my body began to rock and shake. I was cumming, and from the way my body and legs were shaking, I was cumming hard! He didn't stop pumping his finger in and out of me until I was done, and when he removed his hand, it was soaked. I was so busy getting a good feeling that I hadn't noticed when he let the water out.

"Come on, let's take this to the bedroom," he said, standing up. He reached out his hand to help me. I was weak, but I still got up. When I got out of the tub, he took the finger covered with my juices and stuck it in my mouth. I knew how much seeing me suck my own juices turned him on. I had to admit it turned me on too. Slowly I sucked it as he grabbed his dick with his other hand. He removed his finger and replaced it with his tongue.

"Hmm," he moaned, "you taste so good."

"Let's go," I said. I needed to be fucked properly, and Cash was the only nigga who knew how to do that.

When we made it to the room, I took charge for a bit. I walked up to him and began undressing him. First, I started with his shirt, and then I moved down to his shorts and boxers. When he was completely naked, I stood up and gave him a kiss before I began trailing kisses down his chest. When I came face-to-face with his dick, I had to thank God for blessing this nigga. Nine thick inches of pure grade A dick was what he had. I had to contain myself. Just the sight of it had my mouth watering and had me wanting to take it straight to the back of my throat. *Be patient*, I told myself. Taking it into my hand, I gently squeezed it before I began moving my hand up and down. I wanted to take my time.

Slowly I used my tongue and rolled it around the head. I then took my time as I began to lick up and down his shaft, making it soaking wet. I went to the head and took only a few inches into my mouth before I pulled back and repeated the process. He thrust his hips forward, which let me know he was ready for me to take the whole thing in, and that I did. In one swift move, I had his dick in my mouth and to the back of my throat. I wasn't worrying about gagging because I didn't have any gag reflexes. That was why he loved it when I sucked his dick. I was able to deep throat it without stopping.

"Umm," he moaned as I began bobbing my head a bit faster. I reached my hand between my legs and began playing with my pussy. There was something about sucking a nigga's dick that turned me on. It was as if I needed to suck dick to make my sexual experience complete. I guessed I was taking too long, because he grabbed my head and started fucking my mouth. If I weren't a freak and didn't enjoy that, I would have been mad, but I wasn't. I folded my lips over my teeth and made sure that my mouth was super wet.

When I got enough of him holding my head, I moved his hands and took it to the back of my throat. I made sure to hum every time it hit the back of my throat because I knew that shit drove him crazy.

"Shhhhhit," he moaned, which boosted my ego. I began going to work on his dick. Up and down, I sucked his dick as if giving head were about to go out of style. From fast to slow, I made love to his dick with my mouth. The only things that could be heard were the slurping sounds of me going hard and the sound of him moaning. When I felt his vein bulge, I knew that he was almost to his peak. "Get up. I don't wanna come yet!"

Even though I didn't want to, I got up. He led me over to the bed, where he instructed me to get on all fours. *Goody, goody,* I thought as I assumed the position. He knew how much I loved being fucked from the back. There was something about pleasurable pain that drove me crazy. He placed the tip of his dick at my opening and began moving in a circular motion, playing in my wetness. He was only teasing me because I had teased him, and the shit drove me insane. I pushed back to try to catch it, but he quickly moved out of the way.

"Stop playing, Cash," I said to him. My body was on fire, and I desperately needed him to put it out.

"You want it bad, huh?" he asked as he slipped only an inch in and pulled it back out.

"Ca—" I tried to speak when, suddenly, he plugged all nine inches of hard dick deep inside of me with one thrust. "Oh, my God!" I moaned out in bliss.

At first, he started off with slow strokes, allowing me to savor the moment, but that shit wasn't kicking it. Seeing as I wasn't in the mood for that shit, I began moving with him. It took him a minute or two before he caught on. Picking up speed, he held my hips as he began to give my pussy the greatest beating of all time.

"Oh, myyyyyyyyy Goooooood," I moaned out in pleasure. The way he was making me feel had me on cloud nine, and I was ready to forget all about what went down in Tennessee.

"Tell me you love me," he said out of nowhere as he continued to fuck me unmercifully from the back. I was confused. Was this a trick question? This man whooped my ass last week, but now he wanted me to say that I loved him. Yeah, I loved him, but what was going on with him? When I didn't answer him, he flipped me over on my back and climbed on top of me.

"Say you love me, Mia," he said, entering me. Slowly he rocked in and out of me. I wanted to believe the passion that I saw in his eyes was true, but I couldn't tell.

"I love you, Cash," I said just to satisfy him, but still meaning it. Some people would call me dumb, but that was the father of my child. He was my meal ticket, and I loved him seriously.

"I love you too," he said, placing his lips over mine. Breaking the kiss, he picked up the pace. He then placed my legs on his shoulders and fucked me like there was no tomorrow. By the time we were done, my pussy was aching and I was sleepy. I didn't even bother to get up. I just rolled over and went straight to sleep, naked and all.

When I woke up the next morning, I found Cash's side of the bed empty. *I knew this was too good to be true.* I pulled back the covers and got out. The minute my foot hit the floor, my bladder hung low, so I went to relieve it first. Since I was already in the bathroom, I decided to take a quick shower before I went to look for Cash.

When I was through, I went to the bedroom and went about getting dressed. Seeing as it was too early to be going anywhere, I decided on a pajama set. I was only going to be in the house. After putting on my pajamas, I made my way downstairs. When I made it downstairs, I didn't hear the TV on, which puzzled me, because li'l Cash would always be watching cartoons at this time.

"Cash!" I yelled, calling out as I made my way to the kitchen, but they weren't there either. "Casimere," I yelled again, but still there was no answer. I went around the whole house, checking every room, and they weren't anywhere to be found.

"I don't know where the fuck this nigga is at, but he'd better look like he's wanting to bring my fucking child home," I yelled out. Then a thought came to me. I ran up the stairs to my room to get my phone, but I couldn't find it. I frantically looked around. I must have trashed my whole room before I found it. I unlocked it and dialed Cash's number.

"The fuck is wrong with you?" he said, walking through the door with CJ in his arm and a white bag in his hand.

"Oh, nothing," I said, trying to play it off. "I was looking for my earring, but I found it."

He looked at me for a minute and then took a look at the room before he shook his head and left the room, taking li'l Cash with him. "I brought you some breakfast," he yelled behind him. "You might want to come eat it while it's hot."

"Okay," I said to him. I waited a few minutes, trying to call my nerves down before I went about cleaning my room. I may have looked like a fool, but I didn't trust Cash as far as I could throw his ass. He was up to something. I just didn't know what it was. Sooner or later, I was going to find out what it was. There was no way he was being nice for nothing. He was up to something, and I was going to find out just what it was.

CHAPTER EIGHT

Keys

A Month Later

A month! I couldn't believe it'd been a month already. A whole month had gone by since I'd broken up with Cash, and I was taking it better than I expected. I didn't think about him, I didn't call him, and hell, I hadn't seen him in a month, and I was happy. Of course, I had Kane to thank for that. Ever since we went out on that date, we'd been kicking it. Not a day went by when he didn't call or text me or vice versa. I couldn't lie. I was beginning to fall for him. I knew what I said, and I didn't break any rules, because technically he came to me. He came to me the night I was having trouble carrying Emoni into the building, which also happened to be the same night I found out about Cash's son. It was funny how God works in mysterious ways. The night I got my heart broken was the same night God began to repair it.

Unfortunately, my vacation was over faster than I'd have liked it to be, and here I was, back at work. I wished I could play hooky and stay home with Kane, but I couldn't. I was still Keyon. Regardless of how a man was treating me, my money came first. Well, after my child, but you get the picture. Still and all, I wished that

I could've at least seen his face before I came to work this morning. Hell, I hadn't seen him in two days due to him being out of town on business. I surely did hope that when I got off later he'd be there.

"What are you over there thinking about?" this chick Nene I worked with at the hospital asked me.

"Girl, nothing. I was thinking about how fast the time is flying. I have a little over a month left until my twenty-eighth birthday. It's on September fifteenth, and I don't know what I'm going to do," I lied. I wasn't trying to have her ass all up in my business. She thought I didn't know that she and Cash used to kick it behind my back. They tried to hide it as if I wouldn't find out, but I did. I just never told her that I knew. It wouldn't make any sense telling her now. I wasn't even with Cash anymore, and I didn't care.

"I know yo' ass is lying. You pro'ly ain't doing shit but thinking about that nigga Cash," she had the nerve to say. I was about to chew into her sloppy ass when some dude walked up to the nurse's station holding a teddy bear, some flowers, and a gift bag. She noticed him and the gifts he was carrying before she smiled, showing those yellow-ass teeth she never seemed to brush. I knew that ho's mouth smelled like ass because it always did. "How may I help you?"

"Umm, I have a delivery for a"—he paused, looking at the pad in his hand—"Keyon Keys Miller."

"That'd be me," I answered before she could. I got up from my chair and walked over to him. He handed me everything before he gave me the clipboard and showed me where to sign it. When I was done, I handed it back to him and said, "Thank you."

"You're welcome and have a great day."

"You too," I replied, and he was gone.

I stood there admiring the flowers for a minute before I took everything and sat back in my seat. Before I could even read the card, I already knew whom those gifts were from. There was only one man who would do something as thoughtful as this for me, and it damn sure wasn't Casimere. *Come to think about it, he never even did something like this for me. Bitch-ass nigga.*

I spotted an envelope tucked into the flowers and grabbed it. I opened the card and began reading it. A smile immediately came to my face.

One card read:

I'm amazed when I look at you, not just because you're beautiful, but because everything I've ever wanted is right in front of my eyes.

I immediately became misty-eyed. Even though it was a cheesy love quote, I still admired him for trying. I pulled the other one out, and it read:

Dear Beautiful,
I hope your day is going as good as mine is. I can't wait to see you when you get off. Yup, I'll be back in town just for you. I hope the day goes by fast because I can't stop thinking about you. Stay cool and enjoy the rest of your workday, beautiful.
Love Always,
Kane XOXO

I placed the card back where it came from and then picked up the teddy bear. Before I could put it to my nose, I smelled the Gucci Guilty cologne that he loved so much. He knew I loved that shit on him. I then looked in the gift bag and saw that he had sent me some lunch. Along with my lunch was a mini box of Turtles, which were my favorite candies, some Lays plain potato chips, and a twenty-ounce Sprite. There was a note attached to the bag that said:

Lunch is on me today. Enjoy, baby girl.

I couldn't help but smile. God had really done good this time when he sent Kane my way. Lord knows I couldn't wait to see him later on today.

"I guess you took Cash back, huh?" Nene butted in.

I was so busy admiring the things that my boo had sent me that I had forgotten she was standing there. She thought I hadn't heard her suck her teeth or seen her roll her eyes, but I caught that shit. *Lord, these li'l hoes still playing with me behind Cash, and I ain't even with him no more.*

"I knew you was going to be foolish enough to take him back after everything he's done to you. You're not going to ever learn that a dog is going to always be a dog," she said. I had to look around to make sure none of the doctors and other nurses were around before I answered her. I was tired of this two-timing bitch and her funky-ass breath always worrying about me and my fucking business.

"Look, bitch, why don't you go on about your business and stay up out of mine? Cash wasn't too much of a dog when you were fucking him with ya funky-ass breath. What you need to do is go downstairs, buy a toothbrush and some toothpaste from the gift shop, and freshen up ya stank-ass mouth that's always funky," I blasted on her ass. I was tired of this stank-mouth bitch thinking she could play with me just because I barely answered her sometimes. "Oh, and for your information, this ain't from Cash. So stay the hell out of my business."

She opened her mouth to say something but closed it again. I guessed she was thinking about what I said about her breath being funky and decided not to say anything. Instead, she stood there looking at me. I waved and blew her a kiss. I wanted her to say something so bad, but unfortunately she didn't. She grabbed her patient's chart before she stomped off like a madwoman down the hall.

"It's about time you stood up to her stank-mouth ass," a white nurse whose name was Amber said. "I was getting tired of her ass thinking she could just play with you."

"Girl, you saw that, huh?" I replied. I really wasn't worrying about Nene because, just like those other broads, they didn't want to see me when I was stupid. They only knew the sweet and nice Keyon. They didn't want to get to know the fucked-up Keyon, because she was not to be played with. "I ain't worrying about that gal."

"I hope not," she said, taking a seat behind the desk with me. "Looks like someone is having a great day," she said, referring to the gifts that were sitting there.

"Girl, as of right now I am," I said, blushing. I saw the way she looked, and I couldn't help but wonder if she too thought that Cash was the one who sent it. "No, Cash didn't send this."

"Oh, good. I'm so glad you got somebody who's worthy of you," she said as she logged into the computer. "What time do you get off?"

"Girl, I don't get off until six, and trust me, I can't wait for six to get here."

"Where's Tay?" she asked.

"I'm right here," Tay said, walking up to the desk and placing her chart down. "Oh, someone got gifts. Who are they from?"

"I shouldn't even have to tell you who they're from. You should already know," I sassed.

"Trust I already know who they're from, boo," she replied. She then proceeded to go through everything.

"Why are you so nosy?" I asked her.

"Oh, my God, he even sent you lunch, I see. You sharing, right?" she asked, ignoring my question.

"Girl, yup, and no, I am not."

"Oh, greedy ass. It's cool though. I'ma let you have that," she said, removing her name tag. "Come on, let's go to lunch before I starve to death."

"And here you call me greedy," I said, grabbing all my things. "See you later, Amber."

"Okay, have a great lunch, guys."

"We will."

When we came back from our lunch break, the rest of the day flew by. Next thing I knew, it was time for me to get off, and I was happy as fuck. I damn near skipped out of the parking lot, hopped in my car, and jetted off. I was happy the hospital wasn't that far from where I lived, because it didn't take me any time at all to make it home. When I pulled up to my building, I didn't see Kane's car, which disappointed me a little bit. I was halfway expecting him to be standing outside with some flowers and a teddy bear or something. "So much for wishful thinking," I said, grabbing my things from the car and making my way inside. I hadn't had a chance to get far in the door before my phone began to ring. Knowing it was only one person, I answered on the first ring.

"Yeah, Tay, what's up?" I asked just as I made it to my door. I pulled my keys out of my purse and opened the door. Before I could get the door open, someone snuck behind me, placing their hands over my eyes. Dropping everything I had in my hands, I didn't say one word. I was too afraid.

"Walk straight and don't you try anything," he said, trying to disguise his voice. It took me a few seconds before I caught on to his voice, but I did. Since he wanted to play, I decided to play along with him. I walked through the door slowly, being careful not to bump into anything. "I'm going to let you go, but don't try to look at me."

I tried very hard to stifle my laughter, but it was becoming hard. I heard as he brought my things into the apartment behind me and then closed the door behind him.

"You know I'm very scared," I said before I busted out laughing. I turned around and got the biggest shock of my life. "Cash! What the fuck are you doing here?"

"Why do you look surprised to see me?" he asked, looking crazed. "You thought I was going to let you go that easily? Baby, we got history."

"Cash, you need to leave. I don't know why you even came here. If Tay catches you in her apartment, she's going to freak," I said, trying to play it off. I didn't want him to know where the fuck I was staying. I didn't need him trying to be all in my mix.

"Ma, don't try to play me for a fool. I already know that this is your apartment," he replied.

"Look, I don't have to try to explain anything to you. You need to be leaving because Tay is about to be here any minute now," I said, trying to push him to the door, but he wasn't having it.

"So are you going to tell me who this nigga is who you call yourself being around?" he asked, catching me off guard. I quickly tried to come up with an answer, but I was too slow. "Before you lie, think about what you're about to say before you say it."

"Look, I ain't about to go there with you. It's time for you to go on about ya business," I said, grabbing him by the arm. Instead, he pulled me down by my arm so that I was sitting on his lap. I tried to get up, but he locked his arms around my waist, forcing me to stay there.

"So you really fronting on me for another nigga?" he asked, rubbing his hand up and down my thigh. He then pulled his phone out and showed me several pictures of Kane and me together on different occasions. *This nigga is really tripping.*

"Cash, go on 'bout yo' business. You don't need to be worrying about me. Worry about your baby mama and ya son," I said, getting angry all over again. It'd been a month, but I still couldn't get over this nigga hiding a whole fucking child from me as if I wasn't going to find out.

"Nah, I'm worrying about this baby mama."

"I don't know why, because this baby mama right here is good, and she don't need you all up in her mix at all. So why don't you find whatever the fuck her name is and go stalk her ass?"

"Ma, you know you're going to always be the one for me. No matter what nigga you get, you're going to always be mine."

"Boy, please, you can save the theatrics for the movies. I'm never going to be yours again. As a matter of fact, we're not even about to go there. Now can you please get the fuck out and be gone? A bitch has things to do, and fucking around with you ain't one of them!" I said sharply just as I heard a set of keys dangling by the door. "Let go of me Cash, fuck," I said, trying to get up, but he wouldn't let me. I prayed to God that it was Tay and not Kane, because if he saw me sitting on top of Cash, no matter whether I wanted to be there or not, he probably would blow his top.

Cash knew just as well as I did that whoever was by the door could've been a nigga. That was why he wasn't trying to let me go. I didn't know why he was trying to stake his claim on something I was about to let another nigga put his name on. The man just couldn't and wouldn't understand that I was truly not about to go there with him anymore and that I was moving on.

Luckily, it was just Tay. On second thought, I wasn't so lucky, because the look on her face when she walked through the door wasn't a good one. "The fuck is this shit?" she asked, leaving the door wide open behind her.

"I promise you, it's not what it looks like. Cash was just about to leave," I said just as Kane walked through the door with a big bunch of flowers and a few other bags in his hand. He had this weird-ass look on his face, and I couldn't describe it. He walked over to the breakfast bar and placed the bags on the counter before he took a seat on one of the barstools. He sat there, calmly rubbing his hands together, as he stared at me still sitting on Cash's lap.

"Who the fuck is this nigga?" Cash asked no one in particular.

"Nah, my nigga. Who the fuck are you, and what the fuck are you doing here? And with my girl sitting on ya lap?" Kane replied. He stood up from his seat, throwing his hands behind his back, before he walked over to the living room.

Oh, shit.

"Yo' girl?" Cash asked, finally letting go of me. He looked from me to Kane before he stood up also.

"That's what I said, homeboy," Kane challenged.

"So you fuck me over for some crumb-snatching-ass nigga?" Cash directed at me.

"I ain't fuck you over. You fucked yourself over!" I told him. I couldn't believe he had the nerve to try to pin all this fuckery on me.

"That ain't give you the right to go around acting like a ho. We've only been broken up for a month. You go out—"

he said but was stopped by the hardest slap I could ever give him.

Before I knew it, his fist came crashing against my nose, making blood gush instantly. I fell to the floor and hit my head but quickly got back up. My hands immediately went up to my nose. I was stunned. I couldn't believe Cash actually put his hands on me.

I was two and a half seconds away from fucking him up when Kane hit him with the meanest right hook I'd ever seen. Next thing I knew, there was a full-on fistfight happening right in my living room. I stood back in shock as I watch them tear up everything in sight.

"Oh, my God," Tay screamed. We both stood there looking on because we didn't know what to do. "I'm going to call the police!"

"Hurry up before they kill each other," I yelled out to her. Meanwhile, I went to try to stop them, but I didn't get anywhere.

"The fuck is going on!" Ant yelled, walking through the door.

"Oh, my God, Ant, stop them please," I yelled.

The moment he saw Kane and Cash fighting, he jumped right in, and now it was two on one. I stood off in the corner, helpless. I didn't know what to do. Everything was happening so fast that my head was beginning to spin. Before I knew it, I was starting to have a panic attack, but it didn't stop there. From there, I began feeling lightheaded. The fighting didn't stop until the building security came in and broke them up. By then, the police had also shown up. They took a look at everything and immediately called for backup.

"What's going on here?" a female officer came in and asked. I tried to tell her what was going on, but my words were trapped in my throat. The last thing I remembered before I hit the ground was Tay standing around, looking on in confusion, as Kane, Cash, and Ant were placed in handcuffs.

Kane

I sat on that cold-ass bench in the holding cell in the jailhouse and thought about the events that led to me being in jail. When I pulled up to the building where I stayed, I didn't imagine myself going to jail that day. I had just bought Keyon some flowers, a card, some sexy lingerie, some food, and a few other bedroom items, if ya know what I mean. I'd just gotten back from a business meeting, and the only thing I was in the mood to do was be around my girl. Yeah, we had made it official.

I knew she had to work today, which was why I sent all those things to her job. I wanted her to know that, with me, shit was going to be different. I wanted her to know how special she was and that, no matter what happened in her previous relationship, there were still a few good men left, and I was one of them. I had planned this nice evening for just the two of us. I had called her friend over to open the door for me because I didn't want her to know I was there. I wanted to surprise her, but boy, was I the one in for a surprise.

I was shocked when I got in the apartment and saw her sitting on the lap of this nigga who I would later come to know was her baby daddy. I couldn't lie. I wanted to clown up and act a fool, but the look on her face led me to believe that something wasn't right, which was why I decided to play it cool. I just went inside, set the things that I had brought on the counter, and took a seat as I waited for her to explain. However, she wasn't the one who spoke up. It was her bitch-ass baby daddy. I couldn't help but wonder where I'd seen the nigga before, because I knew I'd seen him somewhere. I was going to mind my business and let my girl explain whatever to me, but he had to open his loud mouth. I got up off the chair because I didn't know what he was capable of. I wanted to be prepared for whatever.

To my surprise, he and Keyon began fussing. I didn't say anything. I didn't want to get into whatever dude had going on. I watched as they went back and forth for a few minutes, and then Keyon slapped him. I saw his hand, but I couldn't get to him in time to stop him from putting his hands on her. For a minute I stood there shaken because I couldn't believe the nigga had put hands on my lady. The moment her hands came down and I saw blood leaking from her nose, I lost it. I began fucking his ass up. I couldn't stand for a nigga to put his hands on a woman. That was one thing I'd never done, and I didn't have plans on doing it either. We didn't stop fighting until someone came in and broke us up. I tried to explain myself, but my pleas fell on deaf ears as Ant and I, along with Keyon's punk-ass baby daddy, were handcuffed. They were about to take us out when I heard a small thud. I turned to see Keyon lying on the living room floor, unconscious. I tried to run to her, but I couldn't. I stood there feeling helpless as the rest of the people rushed to her aid while we were being escorted out of the building and into the squad car.

As I sat on this bench feeling helpless, I was wondering how my girl was doing. I couldn't wait until they bailed me out, so I could go and check on her. No sooner did I think that than the guard came in calling our names.

"Williams and Burke," he yelled, walking over to the gate. Ant and I both got up. "Let's go. Your bail has been posted."

"It's about goddamn time," Ant yelled. "I thought we was going to be in that bitch all night."

"Who you telling!" I said as we made our way to the front of the jail.

"I wonder, who posted our bail?" he asked.

"I had that nigga Bundy send over some chick he knows," I said just as we reached the front.

"Kane?" some yellow chick who resembled Christina Milian asked.

"Yeah, that's me."

"Mia," she replied, shaking my hand. "You guys can follow me this way. My car is parked right out front."

"Lead the way," I said, following her.

I acted as if I didn't notice the way shorty was looking at me or the way she had rubbed my hand when she shook it. I didn't have time to be flirting with anyone. I needed to get to my girl and see what was going on with her.

Cash

Keyon and her little boyfriend, or whatever the fuck she wanted to call him, had me fucked up. There was no way I'd let this nigga come in and take my girl from me. That shit wasn't legal, and it wasn't going to happen at all. As I'd told her before, she was always going to be my woman, no matter if she liked it or not. We were in it together, and just because I fucked a couple of bitches didn't mean she had to leave.

So yeah, I had one of my boys follow her around. That was how I found out where she stayed. Then the bitch wanted to play it off as if it weren't her apartment and as if I were some type of dummy or something. For about three weeks, he did that. I knew where she was, whom she was with, what she had on, and what her hair looked like. That nigga was so thorough. If he could've told me what color drawers she had on, he would've told me. I would have bodied that nigga for looking that hard at my lady.

When I went over to Keyon's apartment earlier, I was in a bad mood. Just like that nigga Lamar had said, I found out about Mia and Bundy being together behind my back. Like with Keyon, I had someone following Mia around, and that was how I found out about her and Bundy. I hadn't brought it to her attention yet because I wanted to know if they had something to do with us getting robbed. If I found out that they did, I was going to kill both of them. I might just kill their asses anyway for being disloyal. Bundy crossed the line the minute he started looking at my baby mama that way. How could he fuck my baby mama and work for me? I was the nigga who made sure he and his family ate, and he wanted to bite the hand that fed him. He claimed to be a street nigga, but for a so-called street nigga, he was dumb as hell. Everyone in the streets knows that you never bite the hand that feeds you. As for Mia's ol' thoting ass, I had something for her. Slowly but surely, I was going to take everything that she loved away from her, and right when she was at her lowest point, I was going to kill her ass. Since she wanted to be dirty, I knew just how to play dirty right back with her ass. She was going to hate me after a while, but I didn't care. She never should've bitten the hand that fed her.

I was already feeling some type of way when I went to Keyon's apartment. I was going to try to talk some sense into her and try to get her to come back home, but she was on some other shit. From the look in her eyes and the way that she was talking to me, it really sounded like my girl was through with me, but still I wasn't trying to have that. She was coming home with me, even if I had to drag her out of the apartment kicking and screaming. To my surprise though, her little friend came and interrupted things. On second thought, I wasn't that surprised. I always thought that they were a couple of dykes. Shit, why else would you usually find them together? They had to be undercover carpet munchers or something. Hell, I didn't remember us spending as much time together as she and Tay did.

If I thought I was surprised when Tay walked through the door, I was even more surprised when the dude she called herself leaving me for came strolling in behind her. Yeah, I knew who the nigga was, but I wasn't going to tell them that I knew him. I kept her on my lap because I wanted that bitch-ass nigga to try to do something. He acted as if he was 'bout that life, but he wasn't, or so I thought. The nigga bucked when I asked who he was, getting up and shit. I never knew a nigga to just get up for no reason, which was why I let her ass go and got up myself.

I became pissed off when she tried to go off on me in front of that nigga. Where the fuck did she get all this heart from and shit? Then she had the nerve to put her hands on me. That was a no-no. Still and all, I didn't mean to hit her. The slap made my reflexes kick in. That was what had caught her. Before I knew what was going on, I had hit her, and it was too late to take it back. I tried to apologize, but before I could, her nigga rushed me. Baby girl must have been fucking this nigga, because a man wouldn't fight for a bitch he just met. Before I knew it, we were getting it in right there in her living room. The next thing I knew, I was being placed in handcuffs and being hauled off to jail.

It took a few hours before my bail was posted and I was out of there. My boy Jamel came to get me. Besides Keyon, he was the only person I trusted with my money.

"Yo, where Mia at?" he asked the minute we stepped out of the jailhouse.

"She's back in Chicago, why?" I asked him.

"Because I could've sworn that I just saw her walk out of here with two niggas," he replied.

"No, man. Mia ain't even down here," I said the minute we made it to his car.

"Okay," he said as we got in.

I sat there wondering if that really could've been Mia. Hell, I'd been calling her ass for a few days, and she hadn't answered me. *If I find out that bitch is down here again, I'm going to do her just as I did her before.* I told her ass about playing with me. If she knew as I knew, she wouldn't want to be.

Keyon

When I came to, I was lying in a hospital bed. I was about to push the button to call the nurse when Tay came walking into the room.

"Hey, you're up," she said, walking over to my bed.

"What's going on?" I asked her. "How did I get here?"

"You don't remember what happened?" she asked me.

"No," I told her.

"Hold on, let me get the doctor," she said before she left the room. A few minutes later, she came back with the doctor.

"Hello, Ms. Miller," he said, walking over to me. "How are you feeling?"

"Not so good. Can someone tell me how I got here?" I asked him.

"You don't remember how you got here?" he asked just as Tay did.

"No," I said, shaking my head. He looked from me to Tay and then back at me before he pulled out his little light and looked into my eyes.

"Can you sit back for me?" he asked.

"Okay," I said, doing as he told me to. I lay there as he went about poking and sticking me. I began worrying when he left the room and came back with a female doctor.

"Can I look under your gown?" she asked me. I looked at Tay before I nodded. She then raised my gown and began playing with my stomach. She paid more attention to the lower part of my stomach before she asked me to sit up. She then began touching all over my back.

"I'm going to order some blood work for you," she told me. "I need to run a few tests on you."

"Okay," I said, confused. Something was going on, but no one was telling me anything. I waited until both she and the other doctor left before I turned to Tay. "Are you going to tell me how I got here?"

"Yes," she said, taking a seat on the bed next to me. She then proceeded to tell me everything that went down. I was confused, because it only happened a few minutes ago and somehow I couldn't remember it.

A few minutes later a nurse came in and drew some blood from my arm. I was mad, because my veins were tripping, and they had to stick me a few times. I hated being poked like a fucking lab rat. Now I knew how my patients felt when we couldn't find a vein on them. Once she was finished, she wiped my arm, placed a bandage on it, and left.

"So where are Kane and Ant?" I asked her.

"I'm right here," Kane said. I didn't even hear when he came through the door. "How are you feeling?"

"I'm good, except I can't remember how I got here," I told him.

"You can remember me, but you can't remember how you got here?" he asked like I didn't just tell him that. "How is that?"

"I don't know. I'm about to take a nap because my head is beginning to hurt me really bad." I yawned.

"Okay, I'll be here when you get up."

I wasn't tired, but I told him I was going to take a nap because I didn't feel like being bothered. Although I did need to get some sleep. Besides, my head was beginning to kill me. Maybe when I woke up, I'd be able to remember something.

Two hours later, I woke up to the sound of the doctor's voice. He was in the corner talking to Sha' Taylor and Kane. I couldn't really hear too much. All I heard was when he said my pregnancy test had come back positive, but he wanted to hold off on telling me because something was going on with my blood work and they needed to run a few tests on me again. I immediately thought about when I was 16 and pregnant with Joey's baby. Here I was having all these kids, and I still didn't have Jayla with me.

I opened my mouth to say something, but my words didn't come out. I rose but regretted that decision when a pain struck my head and chest. All I heard was the sound of the machines beeping loudly before my room became flooded with nurses.

"She's seizing," the male doctor yelled. "I'm going to need you guys to leave the room please!"

My visions became blurry before I felt something cold running through my IV. The last thing I remembered thinking before the darkness took over was hoping and wishing that I wasn't about to die. I didn't know what was going on and what was wrong with me, but I needed to wake up and find out. Soon!

Tay

I was shocked when the doctor came in and told us that Keyon was pregnant again. I knew that I was going to have to call Cash and let him know about what was going on, seeing as this was most likely his baby since he was the only one Keyon had been with. Lord knows I didn't want him around her right now, but what else could I do?

"How far along is she, Doc?" Kane asked him. I looked at him wondering why he cared. It wasn't like the baby was his.

"See, there's the thing. It looks like she's pregnant with twins, but one baby looks to be three weeks old while the other one looks to be two. It's like they're growing at two different speeds," the doctor said, confusing me.

"Huh?" I asked him. "How could that be?"

"That's what we're trying to see now. Besides that, it looks as if something is extremely wrong with her heart and kidney, and we still have to send her to get a CAT scan for her head."

"So will she and our babies be all right?" Kane asked.

"Your babies?" I asked, confused. "So y'all been fucking?"

"We'll talk about that later, Tay. What's going on with my girl and kids, Doc?" he turned to the doctor and asked again.

"Right now, I honestly don't know. I'm going to find out though."

The machines began beeping behind us. I turned to see Keyon sitting up in bed, but she looked as if something was wrong with her. I quickly ran over to her.

"Are you okay?" I asked her, but she didn't say anything. She just began shaking. Next thing I knew, the room was being flooded with nurses, and we were being asked to leave. Even though I didn't want to, I left. There was nothing I could do besides let the doctors do their work.

"What do you think is wrong with her?" Kane asked me.

"I don't know." I spotted the people bringing the crash cart in the room. Tears filled my eyes as I thought about the worst. I didn't know what was going on, but I prayed like hell that my girl pulled through this.

CHAPTER NINE

Keys

If someone had told me that I would be living my life peacefully without Cash in it, I wouldn't have believed them. I was very thankful. I was now free from his two-timing, dirty-dick, "can't keep his dick to himself," "don't know how to be faithful" ass. I remembered a time when Cash was my everything. I couldn't once imagine a time when he wouldn't be in my life, but thanks to him and all his hoes, that shit was just imaginary. Back in the day, I would've done anything for him, including laying my life down. When I was 16, I killed for that man, pregnant and all, and yet he still did me wrong. He was my first love, my second-born's father, and now he was nothing but my baby's daddy. The shit was really funny and had me cracking up, because I remembered us having a conversation about chicks and their baby daddies, and I would always say that that wasn't going to be us. *Now look at us*. I was nothing to him but his baby mama, and he made us that way.

All he had to do was be the man I needed him to be, but he couldn't do that. Now I had Kane, the man I was scheduled to marry in a few days, and I couldn't be happier. He also made Emoni happy, so that was an added bonus. Cash should have really taken notes from him, but that was neither here nor there.

"What are you over there thinking about, shorty?" Kane asked, breaking me out of my thoughts. He walked over to me and placed a kiss on my forehead before he bent down and did the same thing to my stomach. Right after he did that, the babies started kicking. "See, they know when Daddy comes around."

"Boy, go sit your ass down somewhere," I told him, laughing a girlish laugh. I couldn't help it. He made me feel like a little girl in high school. That was how Cash used to make me feel before I woke up and saw the true him.

"Keyon!" he yelled a little while fingering my engagement ring.

"What? Huh?" I asked, looking at him.

"What's wrong, shorty? You've been deep in thought since I came in here. So what's up?" he asked with this worried expression on his face. See, that was the reason why I loved him, and yes, I did say love. Whenever something was wrong, he tried to fix it.

Kane wasn't your average man. He didn't take a woman for granted, cheat on her when he got the urge to, or left her hanging. Baby, he was way different, and I do mean different. I'd never met a man to just be about one woman and never look twice at a different woman. We'd been out countless times, and I hadn't seen him even bother to look at another female. What I liked about him most was that when I had a problem, he tried finding all kinds of different ways to solve it. Not to mention he was so attentive and affectionate. He cared for Emoni just like he was her real father, and I cared about his daughter the same. Most men would've run once they found out that a woman already had a kid, but not him. He took on the responsibility of being my baby's stepdad, and I had to say, they took to each other pretty well. So you see, my little family was wonderful, and once the twins arrived, things would only get better.

"I'm good, boo. I'm just sitting here thinking how lucky I am to have found you," I said sincerely. "I don't know what I would've done had I not met you, especially thinking about how heavy Emoni was."

"Nah, baby, I'm truly the lucky one. You're about to have my babies, and my daughter absolutely loves you. I didn't think that I was going to find love again after losing my wife, but I did. I thank God every day for bringing you into my life. I can't wait until the day we say, 'I do,'" he said, kissing me again.

"You'd better be grateful my pregnancy is high risk, because I'd hop on your ass so fast. You know better than to do that. I'm already hot and bothered," I told him as I began fanning myself with my hand.

"Shit, I can't wait for these last few months to pass myself. The minute your ass is cleared, I'm going to tear that ass up," he replied as he began undressing. He stripped all the way down to his boxers and then got into bed. "Come on, big mama, you know I can't sleep without my babies."

"Ha-ha, funny. I won't be big for too much longer," I said as I snuggled up closer to him. "Just wait until I drop these babies. I'm going to be fine as wine, baby."

"Uh-huh. As long as you keep that shit between us," he said, pointing to my sex. "Then we won't have a problem."

"Baby, you don't even have to worry about no shit like that. I'm a one-man kind of girl, and I'm very faithful," I told him honestly. I wasn't the type of chick to stray. If I was with you, then I was all the way with you. I didn't believe in sharing or cheating. That just wasn't my type of style.

"That's what I like to hear," he said, placing a kiss on my lips. "I love you, shorty."

"I love you too," I responded before placing a passionate kiss on his lips. I made sure to stop before it got too far though. It was probably killing him because we couldn't have sex. He didn't say it, but I knew it was. He was a man, and men had needs. I was just happy that he wasn't like Cash and didn't believe in cheating, or else shit would've been just like before. Thank God he wasn't though. *I've finally found a winner.* I felt myself getting sleepy, so I turned the lamp off and laid my head on his chest. Before long, I was sleeping like a baby.

Every morning around 2:00 am, my bladder always chose to mess with my sleep. Like the rest of those mornings, today was no different. I couldn't wait until all of this was over and done with, because I was tired of this. It was a good thing that I was on maternity leave, because if I had to work, I would've been stupid mad. Oh, hell, I'd been on maternity leave since I found out I was pregnant and at high risk. When I tried getting up one morning to go to work, Kane nipped that shit in the bud real quick. Besides, my mother made sure to call my job and let them know. It was a good thing that I was a bad-ass nurse and that my job actually loved me. My boss made sure to tell me that I could have my job back as soon as I cleared after my six weeks. So yup, I was glad about that.

I looked over to see Kane peacefully sleeping next to me. Normally, I'd wake him up to help me, but he looked too good sleeping, and I refused to wake him up. I reached over, careful not to wake him up, and placed a kiss on his lips before slowly getting my big ass up out of bed. The only thing I hated about this house since we moved in was the fact that the bathroom wasn't finished. This meant that I had to walk all the way down the hall to use the bathroom, and if anyone knows anything about being pregnant with twins, it's very much hard to walk. My belly was twice the size of two watermelons. So yes, the struggle was definitely real.

As I made my way down the hall, I stopped in to check on Emoni and Ahmyri. We had a six-bedroom house, but they just insisted on sleeping in the same room. I was happy that they got along the way they did, because things would've been complicated if they didn't. I didn't go all the way in, fearing that I would wake them up, so I just stood by the door. I looked at my daughter, who was asleep in her bed, and said a silent prayer to God for her. I didn't know what my life would've been like if He hadn't placed her into my life. I then looked over to Ahmyri, who had kicked her covers off. I would've fixed them, but she would've just kicked them off again. She had this thing like Kane. They never could sleep hot, and now that I was pregnant, I understood why. Being hot would mess up a dead man's sleep, which was why Kane had a ceiling fan installed in our room.

After peeking in on the girls, I continued down the hall. I stopped once I got to the room where little Cash lay asleep.

Don't ask me how he's here. Just continue to read the rest of the story, and you'll find out.

Once I finished peeking in on him, I headed straight to the bathroom. It was like the minute I saw the toilet, the urge to pee became stronger. I waddled myself over as fast as I could because I felt like I was about to pee on myself. Luckily, I made it there just in time or else I would've been a fat, pissy mess. Once I was finished, I washed my hands and turned the lights out. Just as I was walking out of the bedroom, I bumped straight into a hard chest.

"Damn, Kane, you scared the piss out of me. You're lucky I just finished using the bathroom or else you would've had to bathe me again," I said, laughing without looking up.

"My bad, baby. I didn't mean to scare you," said a voice that wasn't Kane's. I immediately stood still as I recognized the voice. I hadn't spoken to him in a while, but I knew that voice all too well.

"Cash?" I asked, hoping that my ears were deceiving me.

"The one and only, baby," he replied boldly.

"What are you doing here? Most importantly, how did you get in here?" I asked in a small voice. I didn't know I was scared until I felt my hands begin to shake.

"I came here to get what was mine."

"What do you mean?" I asked, confused.

"You, Emoni, and CJ, baby. Y'all are coming home with me," he said, sounding stupid.

"Cash, we're not going anywhere with you. In case you've forgotten, I'm with Kane and we're about to have kids together."

"I'm not trying to hear none of that. Go get my kids so we can go, Keyon," he said, ignoring what I just said to him.

"No, Cash, I mean it. We're not going anywhere with you. What we have is over. It's been over, truthfully. We're not a family anymore, so you might as well show yourself out." I tried to walk away, but he pulled my arm.

"Don't walk away when I'm talking to you, Keyon." He began squeezing my arm. "It's bad enough that you're sleeping with the enemy. That nigga Bundy and that bitch Mia were the ones who robbed me, and you want to be with him?"

"Cash, let go. You're hurting me. I don't know anything about you being robbed, and truthfully I don't care," I said, ignoring what he just had said. I didn't care what Kane did to him. He was no enemy of mine. He treated Emoni and me well, and that was all that mattered. "Karma got a fucked-up way of getting to people, huh? Now let me go."

"You're not going anywhere unless it's with me," he said, sounding like a madman. I didn't notice it before, but he had an unreadable look in his eyes. I hated to admit it, but for the first time in my entire life, I was completely afraid of my daughter's father.

"I already told you that I'm not going anywhere with you, Casimere. Just let me go, and leave please," I said, as a set of hot tears fell down my face.

"So you're really trying to leave me?" he asked.

"I've already left. You're the one who don't seem to understand that."

"Remember what we said after we killed Joey in that basement?" he asked.

"What are you talking about?" I asked him. That was so long ago, and Joey wasn't a memory that I was trying to bring back up.

"When we said that we were always going to be together, remember what you told me after that?" he said, inching closer to me. I wasn't a fool. I played like I didn't, but I remember that day as clear as day. What was scary was what I said to him after. "Tell me what you said after that, Keyon."

"I don't remember," I lied.

"Fuck that. You know better than to lie to me. What did you say after that, Keys?"

"I told you that I don't remember," I whined, now crying harder. I hoped he wasn't going to do what I thought he was trying to do.

"Of course you do, so tell me what it's going to be," he said, pulling a gun from behind his back. "Either you leave with me, or you leave here in a body bag. The choice is yours, baby."

"Cash, I'm begging you. Don't do this, baby," I begged, trying to plead with him.

"Fuck that. You made me do this. Now choose before I choose for you," he yelled, which scared me more. I prayed that he woke Kane up, because only the Lord knows how the next few minutes would go if he didn't.

"Cash, I can't leave with you. I don't love you anymore. I love Kane, and that's who I'm going to be with."

"I really wish you hadn't said that, but you can't be with him if you're dead," he said, removing the safety.

"Cash, please don't do this," I began begging again. I wasn't begging for my life. I was begging for the lives of my children. I didn't want them to have to suffer for the things that I'd done in life. They weren't born yet, and it looked like they weren't going to be either.

"I'm sorry, ma, but if I can't have you, he won't either," was all I heard before the gunfire.

Several Months Earlier

Keys

I'd been in the hospital for a whole damn week, and I was beyond ready to go home to my own damn bed. My ass and back were numb from lying down all day, every day, and I missed my pumpkin like crazy. Speaking of Emoni, my mother had been calling almost every day. I had yet to tell my mother where I was, because I didn't want her to worry. When she did find out, she was probably going to chew me a whole new asshole for not telling her. I was happy Emoni was there with her, because things would've been complicated, and I damn sure didn't want my baby nowhere around her dumb-ass daddy right now. I really hoped I would be released before she came back home this week, or else my mother would be staying, and that was something I couldn't deal with. I loved my mother, and she loved me and would want to help me, but she could be a bit extreme when it came to me. She always tried to treat me like a baby even though I was a grown woman.

I was engrossed in an episode of *Empire* when the room door opened. I didn't turn to see who it was, because I thought it was the nurse or doctor. A few minutes passed and no one came into view, so I turned to see who it was. Imagine my surprise when I noticed Mia standing by the door. I didn't know if God was truly whipping my ass for everything I did in the past, but I sure thought He was trying to send me to an early grave or something. The bad thing about it all was that the bitch had a vase of flowers with a single balloon in her hands.

"I don't know how or why you're here, Mia, but what I do know is that you have all of thirty seconds to get your ass up out of here, or I'm going to forget all about me being pregnant and in the hospital," I told her before she even had a chance to open her mouth.

"Keyon, ple—" she began to say, but I held my hand up to stop her.

"Whatever it is that you're about to say, save that shit for somebody who really cares, Mia."

"I can't, Keyon. I came here to say something, and I really hope that you will please allow me to say it," she begged as she walked farther into the room. I was about to get off the bed and handle her the way I should've back at the club when I noticed a little boy clinging to her leg. I didn't have to ask who he was because his face said it all. He was every bit his father. I thought Emoni was her father's twin, but the little boy looked so much like Cash, it was as if he had spit him out himself.

I felt tears rolling down my cheeks. If I didn't accept that Cash had cheated on me before, this was all the reason for me to do so now. Casimere Jr. was definitely his father's son, and I couldn't do a thing about it if I wanted to.

"I know this isn't right, and I'm truly sorry for all that I've put you through. I can honestly say that I acted on pure emotion when I rolled up on you and Cash at the club, but I've realized that this is as much my fault as it is Cash's. I didn't bring CJ here to hurt you or to cause you any more pain. I only wanted you to meet him. I don't fault you if you hate me, but I want our kids to get along because they're brother and sister," she rushed out. I barely heard a thing she had said. My eyes and attention were focused on the little boy.

"Come here, baby," I said, holding my hand out to him. He looked at me, then up to his mother. I guessed he was asking for permission or something. When she nodded, he looked at me again before he came over to me. I carefully bent over and picked him up, then sat him on my lap. "Hey, little man, what's your name?"

"I'm Casimere. What is your name?" he asked.

"My name is Keyon."

"Baby," he said, rubbing my belly, which made me laugh.

"Yes, babies," I replied, nodding my head.

"Mama, baby," he said, turning back to his mother. She didn't say anything. She only smiled and nodded her head.

"Come on. Let's see if there's some cartoons you can watch," I told him as I began flipping through the channels on the TV. It took me a few minutes, but I found the Disney Junior channel. The minute he heard Jake talking, his attention was on the TV. I made sure that he was fully into the TV before I turned back to Mia, who was still standing by the door. It was funny how she had all that mouth in the club, but now she was quiet like a church mouse.

"Now I don't know what you expect to gain from this, but know that I don't play when it comes to mine. I agree with you, and I want our children to get to know each other. It makes no sense for them to suffer just because their parents were out there being hoes and shit. Now just because I agree to this, that doesn't mean we're cool. We're not friends, and trust we're not going to be. We're only doing this for our kids. The minute I think you're trying to be sneaky or spiteful, I will shut this shit down so fast," I said to her. "I'm not the type of bitch you would want to cross. I only let you pull that shit because I work at a hospital, and me fucking you up would cause me to lose my job, but when it comes to Emoni and her safety, none of that shit matters. I will turn into the devil himself if someone even thinks of fucking with her."

"Look, I already apologized, and I feel the same way about my son. Like I said, our children are siblings, which is why I'm here. I don't have no more dealings with Cash. I'm through with him."

"I really wouldn't care if you did. Just don't cross me and we'll be good," I said just as the door opened.

"Oh, fuck no," I heard Tay say before she came into view. "What is this bitch doing here? Bitch, what the fuck do you want?"

"Keyon, please get your guard dog before we have a misunderstanding."

"Bitch, did you just call me a dog?" Tay asked, walking up to her.

"Calm down, Tay. You're going to scare the poor child," I said once I noticed him jump. He immediately got down and ran over to his mother.

"Fuck this bitch. I'll do her in front of her child," she replied, still inching toward her.

"No, you won't," I said as I attempted to get up. "Mia, give me your number, and I'll call you once Emoni gets back from her grandma's house."

"Son, you're really starting to piss me off. What the fuck do you need this bitch's number for?" Tay asked me.

"You gon' take a seat while I get the girl's number, or are you going to continue to act like a complete idiot?" I asked her.

"First of all, I'm no idiot. I'll chill out, but the minute this she-devil leaves, I want you to fill me in on what the fuck I missed." She began walking toward the chair that sat in the corner of the room.

Shaking my head, I grabbed the paper and pen on the table next to me and handed them to Mia. She grabbed them and began writing her number. When she was done, she handed them back to me and grabbed her son. She was about to walk out the door when Tay called out to her.

"Oh, Mia," she said, "for your information, I'm no one's guard dog. I'm just a true friend. Better get you one, bitch."

"You know what? I'm not even going to entertain you, li'l mama," Mia said, walking out the door.

"Bitch better leave because I was two seconds away from digging in that ass," Tay said, playing on her phone. I was glad because I didn't feel like talking to her about me and li'l Cash. At least not right now I didn't.

"Where's Kane?" I asked, changing the subject.

"I don't know. Shit, he's your baby daddy, not mine," she said smartly.

"I see you are feeling yourself today, so I'ma let you slide," I replied as I lay back in bed. I had no idea what her problem was, and I wasn't about to entertain her pettiness either.

She was about to open her mouth when my phone started to ring. Picking it up, I noticed that it was Cash calling me again. I didn't know why he kept calling when I told him not to. Just like all the previous times, I sent his call to voicemail and placed the phone back on the table.

"Please don't tell me that was Cash again," Tay said.

"Well, I won't tell you then," I replied, rubbing my temple. I could already feel a headache coming on, and I just knew that she was about to add to it.

"Fuck all that. That shit is suspect to me," she said just like I knew she would. "I mean, first she shows up, and now he's calling. What if they're trying to pull some sneaky shit on you?"

"Girl, chill out. Cash calling me and Mia coming by don't have anything to do with each other," I said, waving her off. I wasn't trying to hear that shit she was spitting. Tay had a tendency for being ignorant sometimes, and this was one of those times.

"You can be playing if you want to, but don't make me have to say I told you so," she said, rolling her eyes. "And don't forget I thought about that shit earlier. I let you rest long enough so that you can be able to tell me what went down between you and little Miss Side Piece."

"I knew you were coming sooner or later," I laughed as I sat back up. "I'm telling you now. If you say some shit I don't like or interrupt me before I'm done, I will stop, and you will leave."

"Girl, whatever. Just spill the juice," she said like she was watching a soap opera or something.

"Uh-huh," I said before I began to tell her all about what went down when Mia showed up. I made sure that I didn't leave out a thing. I also told her about her wanting Emoni and CJ to get to know each other. I didn't miss the look on her face, but I decided not to say anything. I knew she was going to have her opinions about it, and I was prepared for that. Whether she liked it or not, I was going to at least try to see where the shit went. For Mia's sake, I hoped she wasn't on no fuck shit, because like I told her before, when it came to Emoni, nothing and no one mattered. Everybody could get it, and that was a promise.

CHAPTER TEN

Kane

"So what are you going to do about this?" Ant asked for what seemed like the hundredth time already. We'd been visiting my mother when my cousin Bundy first called me. Like most times when he would call, I would let it roll over to voicemail, but by the seventh call, I knew that something had to be up, so I answered him. The minute he started talking about the shit that happened back in Chicago, I instantly had a bad feeling, and boy, those are never wrong. Now I was sitting here with my head in my hands, wondering what the fuck I was going to do and how I was going to keep whoever those niggas were from coming after me and mine.

"Man, I really don't know. Bundy didn't say everything. All he said was that the nigga he made us rob was out looking for the niggas who did it," I said, shaking my head. I shouldn't have gotten involved with that shit, but the nigga begged me so much that I ended up doing it anyway, and me being the nigga I was, I was always the one to look out for my family, so I did it. Now I was regretting the shit, because I still had no idea who the fuck the nigga even was to try to take him out first.

"Man, just let me know what you want to do. You know a nigga will be with you regardless."

"Yeah, I know. I'm just kind of fucked up with myself for even doing the shit without getting all the details and shit. I mean, don't get me wrong, I know I was robbing

somebody and shit, but I never fully got all the information I should've," I said, shaking my head. I couldn't
believe that I was actually this careless. Never in all my
years of being in the streets had I been this sloppy. "I'ma
just chill on it for a minute, make sure Keyon straight and
shit before I go ahead and pay that nigga Bundy a visit."

"All right, but you may not want to chill on this shit too
long. You never know what the fuck may happen."

"Yeah, I know. Like I said, I want to make sure that
Keyon is straight, and then I'll deal with the rest of
that shit," I said as I got up from my chair. "Come on,
man, let's go grab something to eat before we head back
over to the hospital."

"I ain't gon' argue with that," he said as he began
rubbing his stomach.

"Yeah, I bet yo' greedy ass ain't, nigga," I replied as I led
the way back up into the kitchen. I turned out the lights
and headed to where I smelled the sweet and savory
smell of soul food.

"Daddy!" I heard my daughter yell the minute I stepped
into the kitchen.

"Myri," I replied, walking over to her. I picked her up
from her seat and wrapped my arms around her small
frame.

"Ouch, you're squeezing me too tight, Daddy," she said
in between giggles.

"I'm sorry, baby. Daddy just missed you so much," I
said as I let her go.

"I missed you too."

"How's it been going? You being a good girl for
Grandma?" I asked her.

"Everything has been fun, and I've been a very good
girl," she responded as she began walking back over to
her seat.

"Oh, I can't get no love, Myri?" Ant said, sounding as
if he were hurt. When she heard his voice, she turned
around as fast as her tiny frame would allow her to.

Ignoring what my mother had told her a million times, she ran straight into his arms, almost knocking me down. I loved the bond they both shared. Ant was the only sibling that Ahmyri's mother had. So once she died, he made sure that he was very active in her life, both he and his mother. Due to her being sick, she didn't come out much, but that didn't stop her from asking for her only granddaughter.

"When did you get here?" she asked, wrapping her arms around his neck. She then placed a kiss on his cheek before he placed her back down.

"The same time your daddy came. We were chilling in the basement though, shorty. How's my favorite little niece been?"

"I've been great. Where's Amir?" she asked, referring to her little cousin.

"He's at home with his mommy. When are you coming by the house to see him and Grandma Marie?"

"When I'm done visiting Grandma Katrice," she told him.

"Okay, good. Now go back and eat the rest of your food, li'l bit."

"Okay," she responded, but not before giving both of us a quick hug.

I waited until she was seated before I eased my way over to the stove. Before I could even reach the stove, my mother stopped me.

"I know damn well you wasn't about to go playing anywhere around my pots without washing your damn hands, Kahreem," she said before she smacked me on the side of my head.

"Sorry, Ma," I said, rubbing the side of my head where she had hit me. I then walked over to the sink and proceeded to wash my hands like she told me to.

"You too, Anthony. I don't know what's gotten into you boys. Y'all ain't too big for me to go upside of y'all heads now." She continued to fuss. She then walked over to the cabinet and grabbed two plates before she began fixing both of us a plate. "It seems like the only time I get to see you boys are when y'all are hungry. Y'all gon' make me start charging y'all asses for a plate."

"Ma, we just been busy, that's all."

"Busy my ass. You're never supposed to be too busy to come and pay your mother a damn visit," she said as she placed our plates on the table. "Go on and sit y'all knucklehead asses down and eat."

"Yes, ma'am," both Anthony and I said together. We then bowed our heads and said grace before we began digging into our food. Ant had been to my house numerous times. He knew what was up with my mother.

"I see some of the things I've taught y'all haven't changed," she said, smiling like a proud parent. "Now how's everything been going with you boys?"

"We've been good, Ma," I said, keeping it short. My mother was one to pry into other folks' business. I had no problem with her wanting to know what was going on with her only child, but there were certain things that I didn't want her to know.

"Uh-huh, okay," she said, rolling her eyes. I paid her no mind as I continued to eat the rest of my food. "How's Marie, Anthony?"

"She's great, ma'am. Chemotherapy has helped her out a lot. Outside from her being tired sometimes, she's doing just fine."

"That's wonderful. You tell her I asked about her now."

"I surely will."

"Damn, y'all must have been really hungry," my mother joked as she watched us clean the rest of the food off our plates. When we were completely done, she collected them and placed them in the sink before coming back over to the table with two bottles of water. "Y'all want something to take home with y'all?"

"Yes, but fix two for me please," I told her as I opened the water and downed the whole thing.

"Don't get greedy, Kahreem, or I may not fix nothing," she joked. "You was always a heavy eater, but damn, boy, two plates?"

"Both of them aren't for me," I said with a smile. I looked at Ant, then back to her. I couldn't lie. I felt like a big kid in a candy store every time I thought of or talked about Keyon. Shorty had a nigga feeling all goofy and shit, but I loved that, and I loved her.

"Is there something I should know?" she asked, looking between Ant and me.

"Myri, go play in your room while I talk to your grandma," I told my baby girl.

"Okay, Daddy," she said, doing as I told her. I waited until she was out of my sight before I turned back to my mother, who was sitting there staring at me.

"So?" she asked impatiently.

"Okay, Ma. I met this girl a few weeks ago, and I'm really feeling her and shit."

"Oh, my God, why haven't I met her yet?" she asked, jumping straight into questioning mode.

"Well, she's in the hospital right now."

"What? Why is she in the hospital? Kahreem, tell me you didn't find one of them chickenheads."

"Nah, Ma, she's not a chickenhead. I would never even step to her if she were," I said truthfully.

"Well, what's wrong with her, and why haven't I met her yet?"

"Because I was going to wait until the right time."

"Well, now is the right time. You're going to get your daughter together while I go upstairs and get myself together, and then we are all going up to that hospital," she said in a no-nonsense tone. I opened my mouth to stop her, but she raised her hand to shut me up instead. "I don't want to hear a word from you, Kahreem. Go on and get Ahmyri ready."

"Nah, Ma. She said that she wasn't feeling too well and that she was going to sleep. I'll take y'all to see her tomorrow morning," I said, trying to nip that shit in the bud.

"You better not be lying to me, Kahreem," she said, giving me a stony look. "Have your ass back here early in the damn morning. Don't make me have to come looking for you, because you know I will."

"Man, I told you I was going to come, so chill out," I said, heading for the door. I didn't know why I turned my back to her after I just basically had an attitude with her. I should've known that she wasn't too far behind me. That was why when I felt a hard sting to the back of my head, I couldn't do anything but laugh. I didn't even open my mouth. I simply shook my head and continued out the door, because if I said something, that wouldn't be the only slap I would get. I heard Ant having a laughing fit behind me, but I kept it quiet. The only thing I was worrying about was this meeting between my mother and my girl. I really hoped everything went cool once we arrived at the hospital. My mother wasn't one to like people easily, and I really wished she'd like Keyon, because I planned to keep her around a long time.

The next morning came faster than I wanted it to. I spent the whole night thinking and playing out the many scenarios about how things could go. I barely even slept. All I kept thinking was that this was going to end badly, although I didn't want it to.

My phone started to ring, pulling me out of my thoughts. I looked at the caller ID and noticed that it was indeed my mother calling me. I then looked over at the clock on the nightstand and noticed that it was a little after eight o'clock. *I mean, she could have at least waited until maybe nine or ten, yet she's calling this early.* I didn't even answer the damn phone. Instead, I placed it back on the table and rolled out of bed. Before I could head to the bathroom to take a piss or brush my teeth, the phone was ringing again. I started not to answer it again, but I knew that it would only piss her off more, so I decided to answer it.

"What's up?" I said, answering the phone like it was all good.

"Don't 'what's up' me, boy. I know your ass saw me calling that phone. I'm not playing with your ass. You'd better be at my house in the next hour, or we're going to have a lot of problems," she said and hung up the phone.

I stood there looking at the phone in disbelief. I really couldn't believe that she did that shit, but then again, this was my mother. Anything was possible with her little ass, which meant I needed to hurry my ass up and make it to her house, or else there was going to be a problem for real.

Thirty minutes later, Ahmyri, Mom, Ant, and I were walking through the halls of the hospital. I couldn't lie. My heart was beating louder and harder than a mutha-fucker. I honestly thought my ass was about to have a panic attack or something. Hell, I had to laugh at my own damn self. I didn't know how Keyon was going to take to my mother or even how my mother was going to take to her, but like I said, I could only hope for the best. My mother was a tough cookie, and Keyon could be also.

"What room is she in?" she asked, pulling me out of my thoughts.

"Right here," I said, nodding my head at the door we were currently standing in front of. She didn't say anything as she grabbed Myri's hand and left us standing there.

"I see you over there shaking like a stripper. You must be thinking the same thing I'm thinking," Ant told me.

"Shit, if you praying to God that my mother likes Keyon and everything goes right, then yeah, we're thinking the exact same thing."

"Shit, I've been praying since we left the house. Moms can be quite feisty. I remember that time you first introduced my sister to her. Hell, I thought she was going to chew my poor sister's head off, but li'l sis held her own."

"Yeah, it was a good thing Ava held her own, or else Myri wouldn't be here."

"Shit, don't I know it? Let's get in here before we find your mother choking the girl out."

"Yeah, you're right. Come on, man," I said as I took a deep breath. Again, I said a quick prayer before I walked in the room.

When we walked through the door, we heard what sounded like laughing. I thought I was tripping, but when we rounded the corner, Ant and I were both shocked at the sight before us. Sitting on the bed by Keyon's foot was my mother. Crazy thing was, instead of her choking her out with her hands, they were both dying laughing at whatever they were talking about. When I saw Ahmyri sitting between her legs comfortably, I breathed a sigh of relief. God was really looking out for me.

"What are y'all up in here talking about?" I asked, breaking up the party.

"Well, if it ain't the damn devil himself," my mother yelled, getting up. She walked over to me and smacked me on the side of my head.

"What the hell you do that for?"

"Boy, watch your damn mouth talking to me," she responded. "Talking crazy. I should smack your ass upside your damn head again. Say that shit again, I dare you."

"Man, Ma, chill out," I said, throwing my hands up. I wasn't a fool, and I wasn't going to play like one either.

I wasn't about to disrespect my mother. I wasn't brought up like that. I knew better, and I knew there were times when I should just shut my mouth. Right now was definitely one of those times.

"That's what the hell I thought," she said, rolling her eyes and walking away. "Now I'm going to ask you one question, and I want you to answer it. Okay?"

"Man, what you want? I don't have time for you to be trying to chastise me and sh—" I began to say but stopped when she gave me one of her looks.

"And what?" she asked, inching closer to me.

"Nothing, Ma. What do you want to ask me?" I said, getting straight to the point.

"Why you ain't tell me what was going on with Ms. Keyon?"

"What do you mean? I told you that she was in the hospital already."

"You didn't tell me everything that was going on with her. Like the fact that she was pregnant and carrying twins," she said sternly.

"Man, that's what you tripping for?" I asked, not believing she was acting like this behind that.

"You damn right," she said, punching me on my arm this time.

"Ma, stop hitting on me, man. You hit hard, girl," I said, pretending like she had really hurt me.

"Yeah, you ain't felt hard yet. Now answer my question, Kahreem."

"Actually, I was going to wait to tell you because I didn't know how to. I didn't want you thinking what you're probably thinking right now."

"And what is that?"

"You're hard as hell, Ma. You remember how everything went down with Myri's mother? You almost chewed the girl's head off," I told her honestly.

"Boy, that shit was different and you know it," she said, sounding as if her feelings were hurt.

"Ma, you know I love you. You just have a way with you."

"Boy, hush. I'm just being your mother, that's all," she said, wiping away the lone tear that had escaped from her eye. "Anyways, I like Keyon. She seems good for you. I just hope everything turns out right for the both of you."

"Thanks, Ma, and I hope so too. I'm trying to be in her life for a long time. Shit, I'm already going to be there for the next eighteen years. So that's basically forever, right?" I said, trying to crack a joke to lighten the mood.

"And you're going to do right by her, too," she added.

"I will, Ma, I will," I told her.

We all talked the whole morning away until my mother said, "Okay, well, come on and take me home. Let's get on before you make me miss the noon news, boy. You know how I feel about watching the news every day and night." She began getting herself together. I picked up Ahmyri and walked over to Keyon, who looked a little sleepy, and I placed a quick peck on her cheek.

"I'll see you when I get back, baby," I told her.

"All right. I'm going to take a quick nap. These babies are killing me."

"Okay, I'll see you later. Come on, Ma," I called out.

"You can just drop me off at my house once you drop Mom Dukes off," Ant told me.

"All right, that's cool."

"See you later, shorty," he hollered to Keys as we left.

We were walking down the hallway to the elevator when my phone began ringing. I looked down to see that Bundy was calling me again. I was going to answer it, but then I thought about my mother standing right next to me. I didn't need her hearing anything she didn't need to hear, so I'd just call him back after I dropped them off. I really hoped he wasn't calling me with no bullshit, because I already had enough of that going on from his ass right now.

CHAPTER ELEVEN

Keys

I was sitting in the room watching TV when this woman I'd never seen before walked through the door. Well, I wasn't exactly watching it. It was watching me. I had just had a talk with the doctor, and he said I would be going home the day after tomorrow, and I was extremely excited. I couldn't wait until I was out of this place. I was really beginning to lose my sanity up in here. It probably wouldn't have been so bad if I weren't confined to this damn bed all day, but I was, and that was driving me crazy. Well, that and the disinfectant smell that didn't seem to go away. So like I said, I was happy to be going home.

Anyway, the woman walked in with a little girl. I couldn't help but think that they looked so familiar, like someone I'd seen before. For a minute, we stared at each other without saying a word. The shit felt kind of weird, and I was becoming a little uneasy, so I waited a few more minutes, but still there was nothing. That was when I decided to speak. The minute she told me who she was, I became a little scared. I couldn't believe I was meeting Kane's mother and under these circumstances. For a minute, I thought things were about to go downhill, but that wasn't the case at all. She was actually nice and very loving and caring. She wanted to know what was wrong with me, and why I was in the hospital, since Kane hadn't told her. I got a kick out of her when she cursed Kane out once she found everything out. Once that wore off, she was good. She was extremely happy to know that she would be welcoming two new grandbabies into this world. When she introduced Kane's daughter, I was a bit scared to talk to the girl, even though she was 4 and I was a grown-ass woman. I didn't know why, but she had that effect on me. Then, considering that I was her father's new girlfriend and what had happened to her mother, I was treading lightly. That quickly subsided when she hopped up on the bed and began rubbing my belly. All she knew was there were babies in my stomach, and that made her happy. So everything was good from there on out.

Kane, his mother, his daughter, Ant, and I ended up having a wonderful time. We laughed at everything. It was almost like I knew his mother and daughter already. We chatted like we were old friends. When Kane came in and his mother chewed into him like he was a piece of meat, I thought it was cute to see them squabble, and it kind of made me want to call my own mother up. After they left, I took a nap, but when I woke up, I dialed her number.

As I waited for her to answer the phone, my heart was pounding away in my chest. I already knew that she was going to get me once I told her everything, and I was prepared for that.

"Hello," she said, answering the phone.

"Hey, Ma, what's going on?" I asked, sounding cheerful.

"Oh, nothing much. Just living and trying to keep up with my grandbaby," she replied. I could hear the joy in her voice, and it almost made me want to change my mind.

"Ma, I have something to tell you," I said, taking a deep breath.

"What's wrong, Keyon?" she quickly asked.

"Don't get all worried and alarmed, but I'm in the hospital. In fact, I've been here for a few days. Well, a whole week to be exact, but I'm going home the day after tomorrow," I said.

I sat there waiting for her to scream at me, but it didn't come. In fact, the line was so quiet that I had to pull the phone from my ear to see if she was still on the line. I was shocked to see that she had hung up on me. I didn't even hear when she had hung up. I quickly tried to redial her phone number, but all I got was the voicemail. I hung up and tried again but received the same thing. I placed the phone on the table next to the bed and was about to push the button to call the nurse when the door opened. Figuring that it was her, I sat back.

I received the shock of a lifetime when a little child came running over to the bed. When I looked closer, I noticed that it was Emoni. *Oh, shit,* I thought as she got up onto the bed and started hugging and kissing me. I gave her a hug back before my eyes went straight to the door. I wanted to disappear when my mother walked through the door.

"What are you doing here?" I found myself saying.

"I'm coming to check on my only child. Am I allowed to do that?" she replied sarcastically. She walked over to me and gave me a hug and kiss before she took a seat in the chair next to the bed. I didn't say anything. I only nodded my head as I put my head down. The way she was looking at me let me know I was in big trouble and there was no way out of it. I kind of felt like a teenager all over again.

"So . . ." she said, breaking the silence that fell upon us. I looked at her, still refusing to say a thing. "Are you going to tell me what is wrong with you, or are you going to continue to sit there and look like a helpless teenager?"

"Ma, please don't start that," I told her.

"I'm not starting anything. I'm just trying to figure out why you didn't call me to let me know that you were in the hospital, Keyon," she said, giving me a stern look.

"Because I didn't want you to worry. I knew you were going to come running down here, and I didn't want to interrupt your time with Emoni since you barely get to see her. I mean, we do live hundreds of miles away, you know."

"Cut the bullshit, Keyon," she said. I sat up because I knew for sure that she was mad. I mean, anytime she cursed, which she barely did, that meant she was really mad. "How in the hell could you not want me to worry when you're my only child, my baby? Anything involving you, especially a situation like this, will make me worry."

"Ma, I'm really sorry. I will never do that again, please forgive me," I said, batting my eyes at her like I used to do when I was a little girl.

"Uh-huh. I'm going to let it slide this time, but don't let there be a next time. When something is wrong with you, you pick up the phone right then and there and call me. Remember, just because you're grown don't mean a thing. I can still take my belt and whoop your grown ass," she said, getting up from the chair. She came and sat on the bed and began rubbing my leg. I didn't know why, but I felt kind of scared, so I pulled the blanket over me so that she wouldn't be able to see my belly.

"I don't know what you're trying to hide. If I didn't see it when I first walked in the door, the machine that you're hooked up to monitoring the baby was a dead giveaway. So how far along are you?"

"Well, the doctor says that I'm three and a half weeks," I answered her.

"What do you mean?" she asked, looking just as confused as I was when they first explained that shit to me.

"Same thing I said when the doctor told me that," I said, shaking my head. I sat there telling her everything about what the doctor told me about the babies. I then began to tell her all about my pressure, heart, and kidney problems. It was no big deal to me, but to her, it was. She immediately said that she was going to stay a few weeks until I could get back on my feet. I knew she didn't just decide that, but I wasn't going to put up much of a fight. A mother was going to do what a mother was going to do regardless, and there was no way of stopping my mother.

"So has Cash been by to see you and the babies yet?" she asked, making me scrunch up my face. Just the mention of his name gave me a bad taste in my mouth. Lord knows how I would feel if I were to see his ass again. "What's that face for?"

"Well, I'm not with Cash anymore," I told her.

She didn't say anything at first. She actually kind of looked relieved when I said that. "Well, then, will he be there to take care of your babies and Emoni?" she then asked.

"Emoni yes, but the situation with the babies is different," I said, trying my best to explain my situation.

"How different? What, he's denying them or something?" she asked with a little bass in her voice. My mother wasn't too fond of Cash. She hadn't liked him since day one. It was no secret.

"Ma, Cash isn't the father of these babies. I was seeing someone else, and like I said before, I'm not with Cash anymore. In fact, I haven't been with him in a while, and I don't plan on going back to him at all."

"Well, that's good. Now tell me, who is the man who fathered my new grandbabies?" she said.

I opened my mouth to tell her all about Kane when the door opened. In walked Kane again, this time with a handful of gifts, and right behind him was Ahmyri.

"Hey, baby," he said, walking over to me. He placed the gifts on the little tray table, then leaned over and placed a kiss on my forehead.

"Hey, you." I smiled at him. Before he could respond, Emoni pushed herself in between us. Just noticing her, he smiled and waved. She waved back before pressing her face in my chest. He then turned and noticed my mother. Clearing his throat, he stood up straight. "I'm sorry, ma'am. I'm Kahreem. You must be Keyon's mother."

"Yes, I am, and you must be her children's father," she said, standing. She sized him up before doing a once-over. I silently prayed that she didn't act the way she did when she first met Cash.

"Yes, I am," he said, smiling. I noticed his eyes light up when he said that.

"It's a pleasure to meet you," she said, reaching out her hand for him to shake it. He looked at her hand, then back up to her before he pulled her in for a hug.

"The pleasure is all mine," he replied before he let her go.

"I'm just so happy that she's not with that loser Casimere anymore," she said a little too happily. "I thought I was going to have to let my daughter get married to that buzzard."

"No, ma'am. If she's going to be marrying anyone, it's going to be me," he told her.

"Well, hopefully, you treat her right, and that just might happen."

"I intend to."

"Okay now, Keyon. Since you're no longer with Emoni's father, where do you live?" my mother then asked me.

"Umm, I have an apartment that we live in. I sold the house that I used to have," I told her.

"Okay, well, call up Sha'Taylor so that she can bring me over there. Emoni needs to rest, and I need to prepare the place for when you're released."

"If you don't mind, I'll take you. I mean, if that's okay with you and Keyon," Kane said, looking at us both. My eyes immediately traveled to my mother, whose eyes were trained on me. I knew that look all too well. Only she and I knew that look meant she was asking me if I trusted Kane enough for them to leave with him. Now, I know what y'all may think: why not? Shit, this was a whole different ball game though. I was about to let this man leave with both my mother and my daughter. Did I actually trust him that much? Let me stop playing. Kane hadn't given me one reason not to trust him. So of course, I trusted him with them.

"Yes," I told her.

"Okay, then let's get up out of here," my mother finally said. She walked over to me and placed a kiss on my forehead. "I'll see you tomorrow. Get some rest, darling."

"All right, see you all later," I replied as Kane walked over to the bed and picked up a sleeping Emoni.

"Good night, shawty," he said, flashing me a smile before giving me a kiss on my lips. "I'll see you in the morning, big mama."

"Okay, big poppa," I replied.

I watched as my mother gathered their things and headed for the door. She waved before she followed Kane out the door. Once again, I found myself alone. I picked up my phone and found myself scrolling through the many messages that Cash sent to me in the past few weeks. He just didn't seem to get it. Like, I didn't know what it was going to have to take for him to understand that we were no more. I was never going back to his ass, so he needed to get that through his thick skull. Hopefully, he and Mia could become one, or he could find someone else and leave me the fuck alone. Until then, I'd be getting a new number.

CHAPTER TWELVE

Mia

I honestly didn't have any bad intentions when I went to see Keyon in the hospital. I actually wanted us to get along, even though I knew that wasn't going to happen, but I guessed I'd have to settle for the next best thing. That was our kids getting to know each other. They were innocent in this whole thing, and them knowing each other was very important. I kind of thought that she was going to shut my ass all the way down, but she didn't. As much as I hated to admit it, she was a much better woman than I thought she was. She wasn't on some bull-shit, and she let it be known that she wasn't going to take any behind her daughter, and I applauded her for that. I would've acted the same way had I been in her shoes.

"What are you over there thinking about?" my cousin Brittney asked me. We were sitting in the kitchen at my house chopping it up. I didn't know I had zoned out until she spoke.

"Nothing, I'm just thinking about life and where I want it to take me in the next few years," I lied. She had no idea that I even went to see Keyon yesterday. If she did, she would've asked me a million and one questions, and I didn't have time to answer her.

"Oh, well, what's going on between you and Cash? Does he still come over here and shit?" she asked, and just like that, it all had begun.

"Nothing is going on between me and Cash. He comes over every now and again, but that's only so he can spend a little time with CJ. Most of the time, he's out there running the streets and shit, so it's like he's never here," I said, telling her half the truth. She didn't really need to know what went on in my household. One thing was for sure—there was nothing going on between Cash and me. That I made sure of. I wasn't trying to feed into or be bothered with all the drama and headaches that came along with him. After that shit that I pulled on Keyon, and Cash whooping my ass after, I learned a lot of things about him. One was that he wasn't the man I thought he was, and another was that no matter how hard I tried, how many kids I had for him, or how much good sex we had, Cash would never let go of Keyon.

"Well, at least he spends time with his son. I can't say the same thing about my no-good-ass baby daddy," she said, singing a tune I was all too familiar with. I was about to open my mouth to tell her that when someone rang the doorbell. *Saved by the fucking bell,* I thought as I quickly got up to go and answer the door.

"What are you doing here?" I asked the minute I noticed Bundy standing on my doorstep.

"Why haven't you been answering the phone?" he asked, walking in without me telling him to.

"I've been busy trying to get myself together, Bundy. That's why I haven't been answering the phone," I said, instantly catching an attitude. Bundy had been calling my phone for the past few days, and I hadn't been answering because either Cash was around me at the time, or I just didn't want to be bothered.

After everything went down, and the shit with Cash looking for the ones who robbed him, I'd been trying to keep some distance between us. Not that I would turn on him, because turning on him meant that I'd be turning on myself. But I wasn't trying to draw attention to us. I didn't want Cash or anyone on his team getting suspicious about Bundy and me or about what really happened. I'd been trying to tell his ass this, but it was obvious that he wasn't trying to hear me. I wondered if he bothered the niggas who helped him as much as he'd been bothering me.

"Come on, Mia, right now is not the time to get an attitude and shit," he said, rolling his eyes at me. I didn't care what the fuck he said. All I wanted him to do was get his ass up out of here before Cash pulled one of his surprise visits.

"What do you want, Bundy?" I asked him finally.

"You didn't read any of the messages that I sent to you?" he asked, confused.

"Nah, I told you that I've been busy. Plus, Cash has been here, and I don't want him catching on to anything. So I barely even cut my phone on when he's around," I responded. The minute I said that, the nigga started getting agitated. When he started looking around, I knew that something wasn't right. "What's up? Why you shaking like a stripper on a stripper pole?"

"Yeah, yeah, funny. That nigga knows about us," he replied in a low tone.

"What do you mean?" I asked, trying to comprehend what he was talking about.

"You know what I mean. The other night when I was out handling business, I noticed this car following me. I thought I was tripping and that I was just being paranoid, but everywhere I went, that car followed. I mean, they tried to be incognito, but I picked up on that shit after a while. Then I thought it was just the police, but I know the po-po, and that car wasn't one of them. I'm telling you the man knows, and it's only a matter of time before he comes for us."

"Man, get the fuck out of here. You a trap nigga. That could've been anybody following you, trying to come up on some shit. I've been out a couple of times and not once did I notice anyone following me," I told him straight up. I knew from the beginning that I should've never trusted that nigga to handle some shit like that, and now I wished that I had listened to myself. He was one of them wannabe gangstas. You know, the kind who acts hard and talks all that gangsta shit, but once things start to get tight, they start singing a different tune. "Looks to me like you need to start carrying more heat and being aware of your surroundings, Bundy."

"Bitch, you think this shit is a game?" he asked, suddenly grabbing me, which instantly pissed me off.

"Nigga, get your fucking hands off of me," I yelled at him.

"Bitch, if I go down, then we all go down. I didn't plan this shit. You did. Therefore, I'm not about to take the blame by my damn self," he screamed in my face. Right then and there I started to worry. Now I knew the nigga wasn't at all gangsta, but I never expected the nigga to be a fucking snitch, too.

"Is there a problem?" my cousin asked, walking up on us. He instantly released me before looking at her, then back at me.

"Bundy, you need to leave and stop calling me. I don't have any more to say to you. You got everything you wanted and needed. Therefore, I don't owe you a damn thing," I told him. He gave me a "Bitch, what did you just say?" look but didn't move. I didn't have time to play with him, so I decided to help him. Walking over to the door, I swung it open. I almost fainted when I saw Cash standing there.

"Fuck you doing over here, nigga?" he immediately walked in and asked Bundy. It was so quiet you could've heard a pin drop on the muthafucking floor in this bitch. Thinking quickly, I did the only thing that I could've done in a situation like this. I lied.

"He's over here with Brittney. You know they been see-ing each other for a while now," I said, looking at Brittney, who had this confused look on her face. I begged with my eyes for her to go along with the plan, because if she didn't, I would be in for a rude awakening. I was not up for feeling Cash's belt or hand against my skin. I almost pissed on myself thinking about it.

"Yes, we're about to go out to eat. We were actually stopping by to see if you and Mia would like to join us," Brittney added. If I could've, I would've kissed that bitch's feet right now.

"Yeah," Bundy said, looking at me.

"Nah, I'm tired. I'm 'bouta take a bath and head to bed," Cash said, heading for the stairs. "Mia, where's CJ?"

"He's in his room asleep," I told him.

"All right, I'm about to head to the shower. Fix a nigga something to eat."

"All right," I replied. I waited until he was all the way up the stairs and I heard the bathroom door close before I turned to Brittney and Bundy.

"You owe me, bitch," she said as she walked back into the kitchen. She returned with her phone, her keys, and her purse.

"I gotcha, bitch. Thanks for saving me, baby," I told her.

"Call me when you can," she said before she left.

"Remember what I said. If I go down, we're all going down," Bundy whispered before he left right behind her. I didn't waste a second closing the door behind his back. I almost closed his ass in the door, but I really didn't care about that shit.

Turning away from the door, I made my way into the kitchen. Since I had cooked mashed potatoes, meatloaf, and green beans early, I decided to heat Cash up a plate. I then grabbed a beer out of the refrigerator and headed upstairs. As I was entering the room, I heard the shower cut off. I placed Cash's plate along with his beer on the dresser and went to sit on the bed. A few seconds later, he was walking in the room with a dry towel on. I didn't mean to, but I watched as he walked over to the dresser and grabbed his underclothes. He looked so good, and I was so horny, but I really didn't want to go there with him. So instead, I tried focusing on the TV. Again, I found myself looking at Cash as he began dressing. I bit my lips when he dropped the towel from around his waist and his dick was exposed. I found myself thinking about the last time we actually had sex, and boy, was it amazing. I licked my lips as I thought about how his dick felt in my mouth. I missed the shit out of that. Before I could think more about how I felt, Cash's hands were around my throat.

"Don't say a damn thing. I'm the one who's going to be doing all the talking, you got that?" he asked, looking me in my eyes. I nodded my head as I tried desperately to hold on to the little air that I could breathe in.

"What the fuck was that nigga Bundy doing over here today?" he asked through gritted teeth. He squeezed my throat a bit tighter before he let me go. I spent the first few seconds sucking in air before I could speak.

"I already told you what he was doing here. He was here for Brittney," I said, sticking to the lie that I had already formed. He lunged for my throat again, but I managed to back up.

"What are you doing?"

"Bitch, I know you're lying. That's all your ho ass does," he said, grabbing me by my shoulders. "Now tell me what the fuck that nigga was doing over here, and don't fucking lie to me."

"Cash, stop it. I already told you what he was doing here," I said as tears fell down my face. He stopped shaking me and stood up straight. He looked me in my eyes before he pointed his finger at me.

"Bitch, you can act like you're crazy, but you haven't met crazy yet. Let me find out that you're lying, and I'll fuck clean over your stupid ass," he said. He walked over to his plate on the dresser and grabbed it. "My food's cold. Go warm it before I fuck you up."

He didn't have to tell me twice. I'd seen what this nigga looked like when he was mad, and I wasn't trying to make him mad right now. I got my ass up from the floor, grabbed his plate, and hauled ass straight to the kitchen. I popped his food in the microwave and stood there waiting for it to finish. Once the microwave dinged, I grabbed another beer out of the refrigerator, grabbed the food, and headed back up the stairs. The only thing I could think about as I walked up those stairs was how I put myself into this fucked-up predicament. If I hadn't approached Keyon—hell, if I hadn't fucked with Cash at all—then I wouldn't be in this bullshit right now. I wasn't about to become a woman who got beat on all the time. If nothing else, I was going to end this. One way or another, I was getting the fuck away from Cash's woman-beating ass.

CHAPTER THIRTEEN

Keyon

I was up bright and early, ready to get my ass up out of that hospital. There was no way I could stay in the bitch a whole other day. I really was on the verge of losing my damn mind. Lord knows I didn't need that to happen. When the doctor came and told me that they were preparing my paperwork, the first person I called was Tay. I needed to get my ass home.

"What's up, baby girl?" she said, sounding like she was still asleep. I looked at the clock and noticed that it was almost ten o'clock. I guessed she was tired or something.

"I need a ride from the hospital. Can you come and get me?"

"So they released you already?" she asked me.

"Not exactly. He just came in and told me that they were preparing my paperwork and stuff. He said that I should be ready to go within the next hour or so though."

"Okay, give me a few to get myself together, and I'll be right there."

"Okay, thanks. I really do owe you big time," I told her.

"Girl, bye," she said, laughing before she hung up. That was her way of saying that I actually didn't owe her, but I did. I couldn't wait until I was able to show her just how much I appreciated her for being by my side constantly.

***

"Thank God I'm finally out of that damn hospital," I said as Tay wheeled me to her car. "I thought them bitches were going to try to keep my ass in that bitch forever."

"Sit your overly dramatic ass down somewhere," Tay told me.

"Umm, I already am," I said, referring to the wheelchair I was sitting in.

"You know what I'm trying to say," she said, rolling her eyes. "You've been complaining about being in the hospital ever since you got here. You should thank the Lord up above that you're still here, you and your children, so stop with all that shit, Miss Lady."

"Okay, Mom, I'm sorry," I said before I busted out laughing. I knew she was serious, but that still didn't stop me from laughing.

"Come on, let's go before I leave your ass right here," she said as we reached the car. She unlocked and opened the door, then came back over to me.

"I wish you would," I replied as she helped me up out of the wheelchair and into the car. She then walked the chair back to the hospital entrance before doing a slight jog to the car and getting in. Once in the car, she started it up and we were on our way.

"You want to stop and get something to eat?" she asked after we had been silent for a few minutes or so.

"Nah, I'm good. My mother will probably cook for me later. Right now all I want to do is take a hot bath and jump under the covers," I said, yawning. Even though I had practically never left my hospital bed, I was still tired. That was because whenever I would find sleep, someone would walk in, interrupting me, or if I moved my body the wrong way, the machines would start beeping. That happened quite often, so as I said, I didn't get much sleep.

"Yeah, you're right," she replied with a sneaky grin.

"Why are you grinning like that?" I asked her. She shook her head but kept her eyes trained on the road. That was when I noticed that we weren't headed in the direction of my apartment. In fact, we were going in the direction where all the Richie Rich people stay.

"This isn't the direction of my apartment. Where are we going?"

"I just have a quick stop to make. I promise that it's going to be fast. I won't be no longer than five minutes, I promise."

"Uh-huh," I said, waving her off. "You better not be long, or I promise I'm going to leave you in your own damn car."

"Okay," she said as she pulled up in the driveway of a house I could only hope to own one day. "Five minutes," she said before she exited the car.

I sat in the car as I looked around at the house before me. Whoever lived here was most definitely blessed. I didn't know how many bedrooms it had, but it was beautiful. It had to be a mini mansion or something. Everything from the lawn on up was perfect. The door opened, so I turned to see who was coming out of it. I was shocked when I noticed Tay followed by Kane with both Emoni and Ahmyri, his mother, my mother, and Ant all coming from inside the house. I rolled the window down while side-eyeing them all.

"What y'all doing here?" I asked once they got to me. Not one of them opened their mouth. They all stood there with sneaky grins on their faces.

"Come on, get out of the car, big mama," Kane said. He opened the door and then reached for my hand. Y'all already know how I reacted. I wasn't going anywhere until someone told me what was going on.

"No, thank you," I said as I attempted to close the door, but he stood in the way.

"Chill out and stop acting like that," he said. "Come on and get out, girl."

"You might as well stop wasting your time," I responded as I folded my arms across my chest.

"We're not about to have your little stubborn ass spoiling the moment. So get your ass up out of the car," my mother yelled, stepping closer to the car. I looked at her and rolled my eyes as I continued to sit my ass right there. She walked all the way over to where I was before she stood right in front of the door and placed her hands on her hips. "You must have forgotten who I am and who you are. I don't care if you're grown. You not too grown for me to go upside your damn head. Now get the hell up out of the car now, Keyon."

I know what y'all is thinking, but my big ass, as fast as I could, got out of that car. I knew better than to challenge her when it already seemed like she was pissed. I held on to Kane's shoulder as we stood around, looking at each other.

"Well?" I said, getting a little agitated.

"Girl, shut all that damn whining up and walk your ass up to the damn door," my mother said, walking by me. I didn't know why, but somehow I felt like I was being ungrateful, and that shit made me want to cry, but I held it in.

"Don't sweat it, big mama," Kane whispered in my ear. I gave him a smile as I made my way into the house. I wanted to slap my own damn self in the face once I saw what they had done. There was a big banner that read, WELCOME HOME, KEYON. There were also a bunch of balloons and streamers. They had this big cake and a table full of all my favorite foods. I immediately became teary-eyed as I apologized to everyone. Of course, they accepted it and blamed it on my hormones. Once all of that was out of the way, the party was in full swing. My mother, of course, waited on me hand and foot, but I couldn't complain. I was enjoying this.

Two hours passed when Kane walked over to me. Of course, he had Emoni and Ahmyri alongside him. I had to smile at how close the girls had come within two days. They were practically inseparable. Wherever one went, the other one was two steps behind.

"I have something for you," Kane said, handing me two small gift boxes and a long box. I opened one and there was a tennis bracelet. It was so pretty that it left me speechless. The other one had the chain to match, while the third had a single key. He placed the key into my hand, then looked at me and smiled.

"What's this?" I asked.

"I know we haven't been together that long, but I don't want to spend another day apart from you, and I don't want you to spend another day without me. Even though I only just met her, I'm in love with your daughter. She has this certain spunk about her that make people want to love her and just like her. I don't want to spend a day without her being around me, and I don't think that Ahmyri wants to either," he said, chuckling a bit. "Anyway, what I'm trying to say is welcome home, shorty. I bought this house for me, but I never stayed in it. I want us to both stay here with our girls, but if you don't want me to stay, I can always go back to my apartment. I just didn't want you to be there, seeing as you know what happened the last time. Now that I know that you're pregnant, my top priority, other than the girls, is to keep you and the babies safe."

"I love you," I said, jumping my big ass into his arms. I didn't know I could move that fast until I was there. I couldn't believe that he was actually doing all of this for little old me. I kind of felt special.

"I love you too," he replied. "But there's one more thing I have for you. Sit down and close your eyes."

I removed myself from his arms as I took my seat. Even though I didn't want to, I placed my hands over my eyes because I didn't want to ruin the moment. I heard when he got up. I wanted so badly to open my eyes, and yet I didn't. I really hoped that he'd hurry his ass up, because surprises were something that I really hated.

"Okay, you can open your eyes now," he said. My hands went straight to my mouth when I saw him down on one knee. I sat there in silence as tears rolled down my face.

"Don't get quiet on me now."

"Yeah, don't go getting quiet now. When we needed you to be quiet, you talked," my mother butted in. I looked at her and rolled my eyes before turning back to Kane.

"You're lucky this is supposed to be a happy time, or else I would've slapped your behind for rolling your eyes," Mom fussed at me.

"Okay, you two," Kane said to us. "Keyon, from the first moment I met you, I told you that you were going to be my lady. Something about you stood out and made me want to love you. I'm glad that you gave me a chance. Now will you please do me the honor of becoming my wife?"

"Yes!" I shouted with no hesitation.

"Well, damn, why wait, huh, Keys?" Tay asked, laughing.

"Be quiet or else I won't let you be my maid of honor," I threw back at her.

"Yeah, right. If I don't be the maid of honor, then I'm shutting that mug down," she replied.

"Go sit down somewhere," I said as Kane pulled me up and wrapped his arms around me.

"You know, I don't want to wait. I want to marry you before you have our babies," he had the nerve to say.

"Are you serious?" I asked him.

"Dead ass. If I could marry you tomorrow, I would, but I don't want to do you like that. Seeing as this will be your first and only marriage, I want to do you up right."

"Boy, you know doggone well that I can't marry you that fast. I can barely get around now. How do you expect me to plan the wedding?" I asked him seriously. This pregnancy was already beating my ass. How did he expect me to plan a wedding?

"We already got all of that covered," Tay said from behind me. "Remember that girl's night we had when we discussed how our weddings would be and how they would look?"

"Yes," I said, remembering exactly what she was talking about.

"Well, ya girl is going to make that happen for you," she replied with a smile. "With the help of your fiancé, his mother, and your mother of course."

"Really?" I asked, beaming. I couldn't believe that she would actually take on that kind of responsibility for me.

"Yes, really. Of course almost everything I find or do will not be finalized without your approval, but most of the hard stuff will be left up to us."

"Awww. Thanks, y'all," I said, getting teary-eyed.

"Oh, Lord, please don't start with that crying shit, girl," Ant threw in.

"Don't you start with her. It's her moment, and she can cry if she wants to," Tay said, punching him in his arm.

"You gon' stop hitting me, girl. You hit hard as hell," he replied, rubbing his arm.

"That's what you get, punk," I said, poking my tongue out at him.

"Well, it's settled then," Kane said, pulling me into his arms. "Moms, mother-in-law, and your maid of honor will handle all the preparations for us. I can't wait until we say I do."

"Me neither," I said, giving him a passionate kiss on his lips. He returned the kiss with just as much passion.

"Umm, y'all need to stop all of that," Kane's mother said.

"Okay, that's why she's pregnant now. G'on somewhere with that shit. We ain't trying to see y'all swapping spit and shit," my mother said, agreeing with her.

"Y'all just some haters," he said, poking out his tongue at them.

"That's right, baby. They just hating," I concurred.

"Lord, give me strength," my mother then said.

"Me too," his mother added. "Come on and let's go enjoy the rest of the day before y'all send us home with that shit."

"I knew I liked you," my mother told Kane's mother.

"I like you too," she replied before they high-fived each other.

The rest of the evening was a hit. We ate and partied like we were a big happy family. The girls ended up tiring themselves out, so they fell asleep in the midst of everything. The night was just coming to an end when I received a call from the last person I expected to hear from. Well, the second-to-last person I expected to hear from.

"Hello," I said, answering the phone.

"Keyon?" the person asked.

"Yeah, what's up? Who's this?"

"It's Mia."

"Mia?" I asked to be sure I heard her right.

"Yes," she replied.

"Oh, what's up?" I asked. I wasn't too thrilled that she had called, and I made sure that she knew that.

"Umm, I was calling about the stuff we discussed in the hospital," she then said.

"What about it?" I asked, hoping that she would get straight to the point.

"Well, I'm on my way down there now, and I was hoping that the kids could meet tomorrow."

"Umm, I don't know," I told her. I knew we had talked about this, but I didn't think that this would happen so soon. "First of all, what does Cash have to say about this?"

"What do you mean?" she asked.

"Just what I asked. What does Cash have to say about you being down here and bringing your baby to meet his sister?"

"He doesn't know about any of this," she replied just like I knew she would.

"Look, Mia, I'm all for our kids meeting and all that, but I don't want to be bothered with Cash. What do you think he is going to do once he finds out that we're meeting up and shit?"

"With all due respect, Keys, CJ is my son. I'm his mother. Cash doesn't have a thing to say about who I let my child meet. You swear that I'm letting him meet a complete stranger. This is his sister we're talking about. I wouldn't put my child in any danger if I thought that he was going to be. Let me ask you something though, Keyon."

"Go 'head," I said, ready for this conversation to be over and done with already.

"If you were in my shoes, would you ask or think about asking Cash for his permission, as you're assuming I have to get, to be able to allow your daughter to see her sibling?" she asked me.

"First of all, I wouldn't be in your shoes, but I get where you're coming from," I said, letting her know that I wasn't that type of female. "I don't see a problem, but I don't want Cash to become a problem. So you better make sure that you have your business in order. I'll call you tomorrow if I have time to meet up with you though."

"Okay," she replied sadly.

I didn't even say good night or give her a chance to speak another word. I hung up the phone before either could come out. Like I said, I didn't want to be bothered with Cash. If he found out we were meeting, he would definitely try to be there just to get to me, and I wasn't having that. I did mean what I said though. I was going to call her if I had the time, though that was a big "if."

CHAPTER FOURTEEN

Mia

I didn't know why I felt like Keyon was trying to play me, but it felt like she was. I didn't need Cash's permission to tell me who I could bring my child around because he wasn't my father. He was just my baby's father. I didn't have to answer to him. CJ did.

After hanging up the phone with Keyon, I placed it back on the car charger and sat there thinking. I still had about three hours until I reached Tennessee, but it felt like forever. I was tired, and I was pretty sure that CJ was tired also. So I was going to find a little quick hotel to check into until the morning. As I was about to pull off, my phone began ringing. Cash's name, along with a picture of him and CJ, flashed on the screen. I was more than sure that he was back at the house and noticed that neither CJ nor I nor most of our things were there. Sending his call to voicemail, I immediately began panicking as I looked around. Something about him was beginning to scare me. I hadn't seen it at first, but Cash was a man I didn't know any longer. I thought that I loved him and he loved me, but I guessed I was wrong.

The night he choked me for Bundy being at the house was when I finally decided that I had enough. I waited until the next morning, when he left, to pack both my and my son's things. Since my son was at my cousin's house, I had to wait until that evening to leave. Once he came home, I placed him in his car seat and hauled ass. It was a good thing that I had previously packed all our things into the car, because that would've put us behind schedule. Like always, I didn't expect him to come to the house until later that night, and he didn't. That gave me all the opportunity I needed to leave. I knew he was going to call, and I never intended to answer him.

I was about to place my phone on the seat when it beeped, indicating that I had a new alert. I went to my messages and noticed that Cash had sent me a message. Opening it, I was glad that I wasn't anywhere near him. I was pretty sure that he would've beaten me again, but it was a good thing he couldn't. Once I was finished reading the message, I powered my phone off. Tomorrow I was going to buy another phone. I had plans on starting over, so why not start there first?

Knowing that Cash knew I wasn't home made me change my mind about rest. I was now on a mission to get to Tennessee. I couldn't have him finding me and whooping my ass all the way back to Chicago. Hopefully, once I got to Tennessee, I would be able to stay under the radar.

I didn't know if it was me trying to stay away from Cash or the thought of sleep that got to me, but I made it to Tennessee in the next two hours. Since it was still early, I decided to get a room so that CJ and I could get some rest, but first, I had to stop to get us something to eat. Since McDonald's was the first place that I saw, I opted to go there. Like I said before, I wanted to stay under the radar, so I drove through the drive-through instead of getting out. After I ordered and received our food, I left. A few miles down the road, I spotted a Days Inn, so I pulled in. Getting both my son and my purse out of the car, I headed inside. I managed to book us a room for a few days, thanks to the money that Bundy gave me from the lick he got from Cash.

Speaking of Bundy, I had been meaning to call him back. I wanted to let him know that I had left Chicago, and in order for him to remain safe, I wanted him to do the same. Well, that and I didn't want the chance of Cash finding out, or Bundy spilling his guts about my part in the whole ordeal. I needed his ass as far away from Chicago and Cash as possible. That was going to have to wait though. Right now, I had to focus on getting CJ in the room and letting him eat his food. Maybe after that, then I would give him a call.

I made sure that I parked all the way in the back of the hotel. I didn't want anyone who knew Cash spotting my car and telling him where I was. That was why I also made plans to trade my car in and get another one. My car would be the fastest way for Cash to find me, and I couldn't let that happen. *Maybe I should just go to another state,* I thought as I parked. I grabbed CJ and headed to my assigned room. Since I didn't want the hassle of carrying bags back and forth, I grabbed only a night bag for CJ and myself. Besides, this wasn't going to be our home, so I didn't see any need in taking everything out of the car. Once I had the little things I need, I went back for the food, my phone, and my purse. Making sure that I locked everything, I headed back to the room.

CJ was on the bed watching cartoons, where I had left him. I stood by the door, looking at my son. I had to be honest. I hadn't been half the mother my son needed me to be to him. I was too busy chasing behind his daddy, trying to make him commit to me, making him buy me whatever I wanted and sex me. I neglected him from the beginning. I thanked God for my family, but it was my turn to do what I should've been doing from the beginning, and now that Cash and I were no longer together, I was going to do just that.

Shaking out of my thoughts, I grabbed the McDonald's bag and headed over to the bed. Sitting on the bed, I pulled CJ onto my lap and placed a kiss on his forehead. I then grabbed the bag and removed our food. Placing him back on the bed, I gave him his breakfast, and right away, he started eating. Before I began eating my food, I reached for my phone and powered it on. Immediately my phone began buzzing with a lot of notifications. A few of them were from Bundy, but the majority were from Cash. When I saw a message from my cousin Brittney, asking me where I was because Cash was looking all over for me, I laughed. *His ass got it now,* I thought as I pulled up Bundy's number. I took a deep breath before I called him.

I really hated talking on the phone with Bundy because he was plain ignorant and stupid. Like, if I told his stupid ass that he did something stupid, he would try to turn the shit around and make like I was the fucked-up one. I only started fucking with Bundy because Cash was always gone, and I needed someone to be there for me. It was a win-win situation when I came up with the plot to rob Cash, and Bundy was there. I had that nigga eating out of the palm of my hand, and he didn't even notice it, which was good for me.

"Where the fuck you been? I've been calling for hours now," he said the minute he answered the phone.

"Look, don't start that shit with me. I'm not in the mood," I said before he could continue. "I only called to let you know that I was out of Chicago."

"You're what?" he all but yelled.

"I left Chicago. Things with Cash have gone to the left, and I couldn't stay there any longer," I told him.

"Why the fuck you ain't tell me that shit before you left?"

"Because I was in a rush."

"In a rush? I already told you that nigga was getting close, and you go and pull some shit like this? Leaving me to take the heat by my damn self, huh?"

"Nigga, I didn't leave because of that shit. I left because I got tired of that nigga putting his motherfucking hands on me. That's why I left, and I told you about speaking on that shit over the phone, idiot," I said, reminding his ass. Bundy was a special kind of stupid, and it took a real patient person to deal with him. Too bad I wasn't that person.

"Yeah, spit that bullshit if you want to. I already know what's up. You just remember what the fuck I told you. I ain't going down by myself," he yelled in the phone before I heard the dial tone. I sat there looking at the phone like it had a disease on it. Bundy really had me all the way fucked up if he thought for once that I was going to play with him like that.

I sat there thinking about what had just transpired. One thing was for sure—I really had to put a stop to Bundy before he fucked up and outed me to Cash. I now realized how dumb it was of me to go along with this, well, with the nigga I chose. I had to come up with a plan before Cash had Bundy's body and mine stinking somewhere.

Putting him and that bullshit to the back of my mind, I placed my focus on CJ, who had made a slight mess. I didn't even have an appetite anymore, so I placed my food right in the trashcan. I then proceeded to clean up the mess that CJ had made. Once I was finished, I went to the bathroom and grabbed a soapy towel to wash him up, changed his diaper, and placed him in a little T-shirt. After that, I stripped out of my clothes and hopped in the bed. The world was going to have to wait a few hours for me, because I was beyond tired. Hopefully when I woke up, things would fix themselves. Since that wasn't likely going to happen, I'd just brainstorm and put a plan together. As of now, sleep was calling me.

CHAPTER FIFTEEN

Cash

I didn't know where that stupid bitch Mia was, and what the fuck she thought she was doing by taking my son with her, but the bitch had me fucked up. It was already bad that she had me questioning her character after I found that fuck nigga Bundy at the house, but now she went and pulled some shit like that. She must really have wanted me to put my hands on her in the worst way, like she didn't learn from the first few times. Then the bitch had the nerve to not even answer the phone. That was okay though, because sooner or later, I would find her. When I did, she was going to really regret the day she started fucking with me.

"What's up, nigga?" Jamel asked me.

"Nothing. Over here thinking about some shit," I said as I took a toke of the blunt that I was smoking.

"Man, she still hasn't answered the phone?" he asked me.

"Nah, but I got something for her stupid ass once I see her."

"Shit, I already know you in a bad mood, but Big Man called with some information on Keyon," he said, taking a seat across from me. I watched the look on his face, which was unreadable. So I knew what he was about to say wasn't going to be good.

"Spit it out, nigga," I told him as I sat up straight in my seat.

"Well, son told me that sis is pregnant with twins," he said, which made my heart drop.

"Man, you gotta be fucking with me. There's no way that my Keyon is pregnant by another nigga," I said, hoping that he was wrong.

"Nah, I'm not fucking with you," he responded, shaking his head. "And that's not the killer part about it."

"Man, ain't shit else you can say that's more fucked up than that," I said, lighting my blunt back up.

"Yeah, well, she and dude are engaged to be married," he said, dropping the biggest bomb of them all.

"Nah, fuck all that," I yelled, jumping up. "Nigga must have gotten his facts wrong. Keyon can't be about to marry no nigga who ain't me."

"I thought so too. That was when I looked up ya girl Tay's Facebook, and sure enough, she's getting married," he said, showing me a picture of Keyon and dude. The caption read, My bestie is getting married. Knocking the phone out of his hand, I grabbed my phone and hauled ass outside.

I pulled my phone out and dialed Keyon's number. I wasn't surprised when the call went straight to voicemail without so much as one ring. I knew she had to have me on the block list, but that was cool. I marched right back into the house. I was going to get in contact with her one way or another.

"Lemme use ya phone, man," I said to Jamel.

"Nah, I don't need you breaking my shit. Use ya own damn phone," he replied, now puffing on the blunt that I previously had.

"Man, I ain't going to break ya damn phone. All I want to do is use it to call somebody."

"Yeah, all right, but if ya break my shit, you're going to buy me another one, bitch," he said, handing me the phone. I didn't have time to even answer him. I walked out the door that quick.

Trying to get myself to calm down, I began walking up the sidewalk. I waited until I was a few yards away from the house to dial Keyon's number again. This time, the phone began ringing, which I was glad about. I stopped walking as I waited for her to answer.

"Hello," her sweet voice came through the phone.

"Tell me that what I'm hearing ain't true," I said, getting straight to the point.

"Cash?" she asked.

She still remembers my voice, I thought. "Yeah, it's me," I said, answering her.

"What do you want?" she asked in a sour tone.

"Like I said when you first answered the phone, tell me that what I'm hearing ain't true," I said, repeating myself. I really wished all that shit was just one big-ass joke to get my attention or something.

"What are you talking about, Cash?"

"I'm talking about you and dude getting married," I answered, upset.

"Why do you care?"

"Because you're my woman, Keyon. That's why I care."

"Cash, I'm not your woman, and I haven't been for a while, but to answer your question, yes."

"Yes what?"

"Kane and I are getting married."

"No, the fuck y'all ain't," I said, all the way mad. "It's bad enough that you're pregnant by that nigga. Now you're trying to get married and shit? You think I'ma let that shit happen, especially with my daughter? What, I'm supposed to let y'all live together like one big happy family or something?"

"You're not going to let me do a damn thing. In case you've forgotten, I'm grown and you're not my damn daddy. As for Emoni, I'm her mother, so I decide who she can be around, and for your information, she loves Kane," she said, which only pissed me off more, knowing that my daughter and this fuck nigga had already met.

"Keyon, you can play with me if ya want. I will fuck your whole world up. What we have is right. No one can come in between that."

"What we had was over when you let Mia and CJ in."

"We ain't over until I say we over, Keyon."

"Cash, all that bullshit you spitting right now I'm not trying to hear. Like I told you before, try to work things out with Mia, because we're no more. I have my own man, and in a few months, we're getting married. If you don't like that, then that's on you, but I'm happy with my life now that you're no longer a part of it. Find happiness, Cash, but it won't be with me," she said.

I was about to light in her ass again when I heard the phone beep in my ear. I looked at the screen to see that the call had ended, which meant that she had hung up on me. I tried dialing her number again, but the phone went to voicemail. I tried a few more times after that before I realized that she had blocked Jamel's number as well. Frustrated, I wanted to throw the phone as far as I could. I had something better in mind though.

As I walked back toward the house, I got on the phone and dialed up my travel agent. I needed to be on the first thing smoking out of here. Since Keyon wanted to play with me over the phone, I wanted to see her do that shit in person. I was going to fuck her up, pregnant or not, and I wished her punk-ass nigga tried to do something so I could light his bitch ass up too.

"What's up, nigga? You finish begging and pleading yet?" Jamel asked once I entered the house. I gave him a look that shut him up instantly.

"I'll be back in a few days," I said, handing him his phone back.

"Where are you going, man?" he asked, jumping out of his seat.

"I'm about to head back to Tennessee," I said, turning to head back out the door.

"What? Why? What are you going to do about our situation?" he asked, following me.

"Right now, that shit really don't matter to me. My family does, and I'm trying to get that back right now."

"Cash, you're my nigga and everything, but you need to really wake up," Jamel began saying. I was almost to the car but turned all the way around to see what he had to say.

"Speak ya piece or be the fuck quiet, Mel," I said, walking a few steps back in his direction.

"I'ma be honest with you, man. Whether you be cool or blow your top, you really need to hear this."

"Speak, nigga," I yelled, ready for him to say what the hell he needed to say.

"You need to let Keyon go, man. It's quite obvious that she's moved on with her life, and now it's time for you to do the same," he said.

I shook my head because I wasn't trying to hear that shit right there.

"Man, I'm just saying. I'm your boy, and it's my job to let you know when you're fucking up or are about to fuck up. What do you honestly think is going to happen when you get back to Tennessee? I'm pretty sure that Keyon was the one you used my phone to call. By the way you came in the house and hollered that you was going back there, it lets me know that she said some shit that you didn't like. What was more shocking was that you, of all people, are willing to say fuck the niggas who robbed us and shit. Now correct me if I'm wrong, but I've never seen you act like this, not even when you and Keyon were an item. Now I know that you still love li'l sis, but I'm really trying to see why you don't want to see her happy. If I'm not mistaken, you was the one who fucked up what y'all had, and you know why—because she allowed you to. You fucked the girl over more times than I care to remember, and like the loving and caring person she was, she took you back, which she shouldn't have repeatedly done. You pushed her away because you thought that she would never leave you. She really surprised you this time, and now you're feeling played, but like I said, you brought that on yourself. If you hadn't fucked her over, then y'all probably would've been married. But you did, and now you made ya bed, so ya have to lie in it," he said before he took one final look at me and walked back in the house.

I stood there thinking about all the things he had just said to me. The shit was true, but I didn't want to hear that shit. To me, I had every right to be mad about Keyon moving on with the next nigga. Yeah, I knew I may have sounded super selfish, but fuck all that. This girl and I had been through a lot, yet we'd overcome all that shit. So this wasn't anything that we couldn't fix.

But you haven't seen or heard from her in months, a little voice in the back of my head said to me. I stood there thinking maybe it was time for us to move on, maybe she did deserve someone other than me, and maybe I was the reason that she wasn't with me. The question was, could I accept the shit and move on peacefully?

Thinking with a clear head, I decided not to focus on Keyon. I still had to find Mia and figure out what the fuck was going on with her. Then there was this shit with Bundy. My mind was telling me that the nigga was behind the shit that went on with my money. Some may have said that I was being a little too hard, but my guts never steered me wrong. Hopefully, this time they would. I'd known that nigga Bundy since I first came down this bitch, and it would really hurt me to find out that I was fucking with a snake the whole time.

Pulling out my phone, I decided to call him. I didn't know whether he was guilty or not, so I was just going to meet up and talk to him. They say a guilty person will tell on himself. So this one-on-one time was probably just the answer to what I needed to know.

"Hello," he answered the phone.

"Yo, Bundy, what's up, man?" I asked as I began walking back to the house.

"Ain't shit, nigga. What's up with it?"

"Nothing. We need to meet up soon. There's something that I need to talk to you about," I told him, getting straight to the point of why I was calling him.

"Meet? For what?" he asked. I didn't know if he was busy, but I could've sworn that I detected a little nervousness in his voice.

"Man, you know I'on speak about shit over the phone, nigga. Where you at?"

"I'm over here by this li'l broad's house, man. I can't meet you right now," he had the nerve to say. I pulled the phone away from my ear and looked at it as if I were looking at Bundy himself.

"Nigga, I'on give a fuck if you was with ya mommy. Have your ass at the trap in an hour," I yelled into the phone before I hung up.

"Who was that?" Jamel asked, scaring the shit out of me.

"Man, don't be scaring me like that, shit. I didn't know that your ass was even standing there. Make some damn noise when you're walking behind a nigga before you fuck around and get accidently shot or fucked up," I told him as I took a seat on the steps.

"My bad, man," he said, laughing that li'l goofy-ass laugh he always had.

"Yeah. That was that nigga Bundy, though. I don't know why, but my gut is telling me that that nigga was behind that shit," I said seriously. With everything that had been going on with him and Mia, I just couldn't put that shit past him. "Shit, that bitch Mia pro'ly got something to do with that shit too."

"Nigga, you must be tripping. You really think that ya baby mama would do some shit like that to you?" he asked.

"Shit, the way this bitch done pulled this little disappearing act on me, I wouldn't be surprised if she did."

"Man, no," he said, shaking his head. While he was shaking his head, I was serious. If it wasn't that, I thought it was definitely that nigga Bundy. I couldn't go after him until I had proof. So right now, I was just going to keep playing that nigga close. If I found out that he had something to do with that shit, his mama had better get her black dress ready, because there was going to be some flower bringing and sad-song singing. That went for that bitch Mia too.

An hour later, I found myself thinking about one thing or another, mainly thinking about my life. If my mother were still alive, she would probably be whooping my ass for all the things that I'd done. She and my grandmother were probably turning over in their graves right now. My life hadn't been the same without my main ladies, and now that Keyon was gone, I didn't think it was going to get much better.

I was brought out of my thoughts by the alarm beeping, indicating that someone had come in. Getting up, I placed my hand on my strap as I waited for whoever it was to come into view.

"Sup, man?" Bundy asked, looking a little rugged. I couldn't tell the last time dude had a haircut, or a good night of rest, for that matter. He had bags under his eyes, and it looked like that nigga was doing some heavy drugs or something.

"It's 'bout time your ass showed up. I thought I was going to have to come and look for you," I told him, taking a seat. I made sure that my hand stayed where it was. I didn't know if that nigga was on one, so I had to be prepared for anything right now.

"Nah, I wouldn't have you doing all that," he said, standing up.

"Nigga, take a seat. I'm not going to bite ya ass," I told him, gesturing to the seat across from me. The nigga looked like he was scared to take one or something. A few seconds later, he did, but then he began tapping his leg. "Is something wrong or something?"

"Nah, man, everything is straight," he said, noticing that I was still looking at him tapping his hand, so he stopped. "So, what's up?"

"Bundy, you already know that I think of you as being one of my niggas, and you know how I don't appreciate a snake, a phony, or a pig," I started off. I noticed how his eyes got a little big and one of his hands began to shake. "Now instead of me beating around the bush, because you know I hate that shit, I'm going to just come out and ask. Did you have anything to do with the two shops getting hit?"

"What?" he yelled. His eyes grew bigger than they already were as his hand began shaking a little faster.

Fuck that. Something ain't right with this dude.

"Man, you already know that we're family, so what I don't understand is why you would even think some shit like that."

"I know all that, but I'm not sure you do. So, I'm going to ask you again, and the best thing you can do right now is to be completely honest with me. Not only do I hate a snake, a phony, and a pig, but I also hate a fucking liar."

"Man, fuck no," he said, jumping to his feet. Stuttering, he continued, "I didn't have a damn thing to do with what happened. When that shit went down, I was over by my girl Shandrell's house. Cash, you know I wouldn't do you know shit like that, man."

"Uh-huh," was all I said because now I knew the nigga was lying, and getting the truth out of him was going to give me a headache, so I decided to play it cool. "All right, well, what's this I'm hearing about you and Mia fucking around? The streets told me that they've seen you and her around multiple times together. Plus you remember that day I caught you over at the house?"

"Man, come on, man. I feel like you brought me over here to try to set me up. You already know why I was over there at the house. Ya girl already told you, and as for me and her being seen around, that shit is a fucking lie," he said, stuttering a bit. What the nigga didn't know was that I had a few pictures of them that people sent to me, but I wasn't going to show him. All I wanted him to do was what he was doing now, and that was lying.

"All right, man. I'll catch you later," I said, standing. My face was stone cold on the outside, but I was smiling on the inside. This nigga Bundy's days were numbered, and he just didn't know it.

"All right, fam," he replied, making my stomach churn. My hand inched closer to my gun. I wanted so badly to shoot him for saying that word. Family was one of the most important things to me, and I considered all the niggas who worked for me to be just that, but Bundy wasn't. I was starting to think that the nigga never was either. How could he consider himself family when he went around fucking my baby mama and possibly robbing me? That ain't family. That's a snake, and that was what I hated.

"I'll see you around."

"Bet," he said, reaching his hand out for me to dap him off. I wanted to slap the shit out of it, but I played it cool. So I dapped him off and watched as he headed for the door. The nigga was so nervous that he was shaking like a stripper on a fucking pole.

"So what do you think?" Jamel asked once Bundy was gone.

"Nigga, what do you think?" I replied. "That nigga was lying through his yellow muthafucking teeth. He thinks everything is cool, when in all actuality everything just got bad for him. Have Young tail that nigga. One thing I learned in life is that what's done in the dark will come to the light."

"What are you going to do about Mia, though?"

"Like I said before, when I find that bitch, I'm going to make her wish she never laid eyes on me."

"Man, you wild, yeah," he said, laughing as we headed for the door.

"You're going to see just how wild I can get in a few weeks, maybe days," I replied as I placed my shades over my eyes. He hadn't seen wild until he witnessed one of my episodes, and I wasn't talking about the one where I just busted my guns. I was talking about the one where I took my time torching muthafuckers. Mia saw a glimpse of that, but she was going to see the full thing the minute I found her stupid ass.

CHAPTER SIXTEEN

Mia

I honestly didn't remember lying down, let alone falling asleep, but I did. I must have really been tired, because we checked into the room around 9:00 this morning. Here I was waking up at almost 4:00 in the afternoon. I guessed being away from Cash and his unpredictable behavior allowed me to finally get some rest. I was glad for that, because my body really needed it.

Rolling over to my side, I noticed that CJ was already up, watching the cartoon channel that I had left on earlier. I smiled, knowing that I had such a handsome and well-behaved child. Any other child would've woken their mother up, but not my son. As long as he had something to eat and cartoons in front of him, he was good. Speaking of eating, I was pretty sure that my baby was hungry because the only thing he ate was breakfast, and that was much earlier. *I guess I'll get up and go get us something to eat.*

Getting off the bed, I grabbed my phone and headed to the bathroom to handle my hygiene. Then a thought came to me. Instead of going to get something to eat, I was just going to order some take-out. That way, I wouldn't have to go out and risk the chance of someone finding me. Looking on the internet, I located this Chinese restaurant not too far from the hotel, which was perfect. I was about to get their number and call when my phone began ringing, flashing Keyon's name at the top. Wondering why she was calling me, I answered.

"Hello."

"Mia?" she asked like she hadn't just called my phone.

"Yeah, this is me. What's up, Keyon?"

"I was calling to see if you were busy or something. I was about to take the girls to the mall, and I was wondering if you wanted to bring CJ," she said, shocking me. I thought for sure that she wasn't going to call at all, but I guessed she was another one full of surprises.

"Yes, I am," I said as I headed back into the room.

"Well, can you meet us at the Hickory Ridge Mall in an hour? I don't know where in Tennessee you're located, but the mall is down here in Memphis," she said, which made my heart drop. Memphis was Cash's stomping grounds. I was pretty sure that he knew most of the people out here, and the minute any one of them saw me, he'd know about it. So I really had to think about it. I really wanted my child to meet his sister, but I didn't want Cash finding me. Then again, Cash wasn't my damn daddy. So why was I scared? Yes, he would beat my ass, and I was foolish enough to come to his hometown, but in my mind, it would be the last place that he would think to find me.

"Okay, cool," I said, coming to my senses. I was just going to have to be really careful.

"All right, cool. I'll see you in an hour," she said, hanging up the phone.

"Come on, CJ," I said, picking up my son. I had to get us both ready, and I didn't have a minute to wait. My stomach started talking to me, but that was going to have to wait. I would just get something to eat in the mall.

I stood there for a minute with my heart in my ass. I couldn't believe that this thing was actually about to happen. I just prayed that everything went well and as planned.

An hour later, we were pulling up to Hickory Ridge Mall. My stomach started doing backflips as I hopped out of the car. I went around the back to get CJ from his car seat before I placed him in his stroller and headed inside. I felt like a teenager who was going to meet her boyfriend's parents for the first time. It was like I was scared or something. I just remembered how I acted with Keyon at the club and then Cash whopping my ass for doing that. I then remembered her telling me all those things in the hospital when I first went to her about this. Now almost a week later, it was finally happening.

Walking through the mall's door, I pulled out my phone and sent her a text that I was there. I was about to put my phone away when Bundy's name came through, flashing at the top. Not wanting him to spoil my mood, I sent him to voicemail and kept it pushing. Not even a few seconds later, he was ringing my phone line again. Just like before, I ignored it. I thought he would get the hint, but then he started texting me. I opened one message, and when I read it, it made me call him back ASAP.

"What the fuck are you talking about, Bundy?" I asked the minute he answered the phone.

"Look, man, I'm not even in the mood to be playing with you right now. I just came from seeing that nigga, and I can almost bet my last dollar that you told that nigga something. That's why your ho ass got ghost. You're trying to let me take the fall by myself," he said, sounding like he was about to cry.

"That's insane, Bundy. Why the fuck would I tell Cash about that lick, nigga? That would mean that I'm telling on my damn self, and I already told your paranoid ass to stop talking about that shit over the phone, nigga. You really trying to get us busted, huh?"

"Fuck all that. The question that nigga was asking me was suspect. It was like that nigga already knew the answer but wanted me to tell him. Then he gon' ask me if I was fucking with you, bringing up that shit that happened at the house and shit," he said. This dude was really beginning to annoy the fuck out of me.

"Bundy, you gon' make me slap the fuck out of you, for real. Cash is just baiting you, and like a fucking dummy, you're falling for everything. You're cracking under pressure, and it's only a matter of time before you tell on your damn self. So here's what I want you to do," I told him, trying to get in control of the situation.

"Fuck that. I ain't listening to nothing else you're saying. It's your fault that a nigga is up in this predicament now, bitch," he yelled, which made my left eye jump. I bit the inside of my cheek to keep from going off on his bitch ass.

"Bundy, you got one more fucking time to call me out of my name," I told him. "Now this is what your bitch ass is going to do. You're going to pack some shit and get the fuck out of Dodge. Get as far away from Chicago as possible before you have us both in the fucking river somewhere. You have twenty-four hours to leave. I'll call you back in twenty-four hours, and if you're still in Chicago, I'm going to come up there and kill you my damn self."

"Where you at? Why can't I just come to you?" he all but whined like a fucking child.

"Bundy, get real. If you and I are caught together, we're dead for sure," I told him as I noticed Keyon and two little girls walking in my direction.

"Man, fuck all that shit. Tell me where the fuck you're at," he yelled again.

"Twenty-four hours, Bundy. I'm going to call you back in twenty-four hours," I repeated before I hung up. I powered my phone off, because I knew that he was going to try to call me again.

"Are you okay?" Keyon asked once she reached me. "I wasn't trying to be nosy or anything. It's just that you looked stressed and you were screaming a little."

"Everything's fine. That was just one of my cousins asking me to do something for them, and I told them no," I said, coming up with the first lie I could think of. "Are you ready?"

"Sure, come on. Oh, let me introduce you to the girls," she said, turning around again. I already knew who her daughter was. She looked like a mixture of her and Cash. The other little girl kind of looked familiar. "This is my daughter, Emoni, and this is my fiancé's daughter, Ahmyri."

"Your fiancé?" I asked, trying to be sure I heard her right.

"That's right," she said, wiggling her left hand in the air. I noticed the ring, but that wasn't all that I noticed. Something told me to look at the purse on her shoulder. I was only looking because I thought it was cute, but what I saw was a bottle of prenatal vitamins. I wanted to ask her about it, but I didn't want to come off as nosy. Besides, she'd probably think I was trying to get information for Cash and end the day before it even started. I decided not to bring that subject up.

Smiling, I pulled my eyes from the bottle and looked back up to her. It was a good thing that she was paying attention to the girls or else she would've known what I was staring at. "Congratulations, boo," I said happily. Knowing the things I was going through with Cash and not knowing if she had experienced them too, I was actually happy for her.

"Thanks, boo," she said as we began walking again.

"So when's the wedding?" I asked.

"Actually, it's in a couple of months. Kahreem wants us to get married before I have the babies," she said, smiling so hard my cheeks were hurting for her. "Oh, yeah, I'm pregnant with twins also."

"Well, congrats again," I said, shocked once again. I knew she was pregnant, from seeing the prenatal vitamins, but I wouldn't have ever guessed her to be pregnant with twins. *Lord, I'm sure when Cash finds that out, he's going to probably flip the fuck out behind that shit.*

"But enough about me. Come on and let's let the kids have a great time together. The bounce house is a couple of stores down to our left," she said, changing the subject. I didn't want her to, because I wanted to know everything, including who her fiancé, the babies' father, was.

When I looked down to check on CJ, I noticed Emoni had made her way next to him. I couldn't stop smiling when I noticed her holding his tiny little hand as we walked. This was all I wanted, and I honestly could say that I made a great choice visiting Keyon in the hospital that day.

CHAPTER SEVENTEEN

Keyon

I honestly didn't think that hanging out with Mia would even go good or that I would like it, but I was wrong. After Mia showed up at the mall and we talked for a few minutes, we took the children to the bounce house, where they had a ball. I never imagined Moni being happy about having a brother, but she was. In her words, she had a brother and a sister. Since I couldn't play with them, I decided to take a seat at a table close enough for me to watch them. Mia joined me, and from there, we sparked up a conversation.

I didn't know how or why Cash's name even came up, but what she told me about Cash scared my ass to death. I had no idea that I was living with, let alone in love with, a monster. She asked me if I ever went through that, and I told her no, which seemed to sadden her. I guessed she figured if he was doing it to her, then he probably had been doing it to me, but hell no. If he had even tried to put his hands on me, his mother would've known where to find his ass every All Saints Day. I never played that shit with Cash, so his putting his hands on me was out of the question. I was kind of glad that she came in between what we had. I was sorry she was going through that, but I was happy it wasn't my ass. Who knew? He probably would've tried that shit with me. But unlike her, I wouldn't have stood for it.

We must have stayed there talking and watching the kids play for three hours until they came over saying that they were hungry. Since there was a McDonald's not too far from the mall, we decided to go there. It was just our luck that the McDonald's had a damn playground. Once we ordered their food, they were off to play once again. Poor CJ was so little and his legs were so short that he had a hard time keeping up with the girls, but once they saw him lingering too far behind, they'd stop and wait for him. I'd been watching Emoni in the mall and now here. Not one time did she go anywhere without CJ by her side. I now saw why it was so important for them to meet. Emoni instantly became that big sister CJ didn't have, and he became the little sibling she always wanted. Now in no way did that sheer her thoughts of Ahmyri, because she was always included too. It was just that CJ was her blood. They were bonded because of their father, and that was a huge difference.

"You all right?" Mia asked, waving her hands in front of me. I was so busy watching the kids enjoy themselves that I had completely zoned out.

"I'm sorry, girl. I was just watching Emoni with CJ, and I must admit, this was really a good idea. Seeing her that way with him makes me happy about the twins. Like at first, I thought she was going to be one of those kids who would act out and always want my attention, but I was wrong," I said, smiling. I was truly happy.

"I know, and CJ seems so happy. I've never seen him with this much energy before. Thank you again for doing this," she replied. I nodded my head as I continued to watch the kids play. "Can I ask you something?"

"Go ahead."

"With everything that I've told you about my dealings with Cash, you know his violent side. Do you think it's really safe for me to be out here? I mean, this is his domain. He knows these streets like the back of his hand. I know it won't be long before he finds me here," she said, looking a little worried. She started looking around, which made me do the same. I used to hate her, but my heart really went out to the girl. Cash had her so scared that she didn't want to be seen in public.

"Honestly, I don't know. Yes, Cash knows Memphis, but I'm pretty sure that he doesn't know the whole state. Maybe you shouldn't be here in Memphis, but I don't think you should leave the state. As a matter of fact, tomorrow if you'd like, I can drop the girls off at my fiancé's mother's house. And then we can take a little trip to Brownsville, which is an hour away from Memphis," I said, honestly trying my best to help her out in her situation.

"Are you sure? I mean, will you be comfortable enough riding an hour away in your condition?" she asked, referring to my pregnancy.

"I can't fly or anything like that, but I'm pretty sure that an hour's drive won't kill me," I said with a light chuckle.

"Okay, well, yeah. I'd be so thankful if you did that for me," she said, getting up from her seat. She walked around the table to me and gave me a hug. Yeah, I know what y'all must be saying about me, but I was kind of happy that she and Cash had a thing. If they hadn't gotten together, I wouldn't have met Kane.

"You're welcome," I said as the kids came running back to the table.

"Mommy, we're sleepy," Emoni said, rubbing her eyes. I knew what time it was.

"Looks like CJ is too," Mia said.

"Well, I guess we know what time it is," I said as I began putting everything on the tray to throw it in the trash. Even though the kids barely ate anything, I wasn't trying to haul any of that home.

"It's okay. I got that," Mia told me. She got up and quickly cleaned the table before walking over to the trash and dumping everything in it.

"Thanks," I said once she came back to the table.

"No problem," she said, picking CJ up. "Thanks again for doing this. I . . . well, we had a blast."

"No problem. Text or call me when y'all make it to the hotel," I said as I began walking away.

"I will," she replied before we both went our own ways. Once I made it outside to the car, I placed the girls in their car seats and got in. I then cranked up the car and began the forty-minute drive it took me to get home.

Since I hadn't heard from Kane since this morning, I decided to give him a call. Placing my phone on the Bluetooth speaker like he always told me to, I dialed his number.

"Sup, beautiful," he said, answering the phone on the first ring.

"Damn, you must be missing me, huh?" I said, laughing at how fast he answered the phone.

"Ya damn right I am. Hold up, you in the car?" he asked.

"Yeah, why?"

"Are you using the hands-free thingy like I told you to?"

"Yes, I am, Daddy," I said, faking like I was annoyed.

"Stop all that. I'm just trying to make sure y'all stay safe. Where are my favorite girls at?"

"We're on our way home. I took the girls to the bounce house at the mall, and they're knocked out in the back seat," I said, taking a quick glance at Emoni and Ahmyri.

"They had fun?"

"Shit, you don't hear a peep. So what ya think?" I replied. Normally the girls would be in the back seat chatting about this or that, but it was quiet. "Where you at though?"

"I just pulled up to the house actually. I'm about to hop in the shower before y'all get here. I'm tired as hell too. Just honk the horn when you pull up so I can come and get the girls," he said, yawning, which made me yawn.

"All right, I'll see you in a few," I said, about to hang up the phone.

"Ay, shorty," he said, stopping me.

"What's up?"

"I love you," he sang into the phone, causing me to blush hard.

"I love you too, zaddy," I sang back.

"All right, I'll see you in a minute for my kiss."

"Boy, bye," I said, hanging up the phone. I was smiling harder than a fag with a bag of dicks. Kane made me so happy. I couldn't believe that I hadn't met him sooner.

I was placing my phone back on its little mount thing when Mia sent me a message saying that they had arrived at their destination. I quickly sent back an okay before I placed the thing back where it belonged. A few seconds later, she was calling my phone.

"What's up?" I asked.

"Cash is calling me again," she replied, sounding scared again.

"I told you not to answer it. Let him keep calling. Shit, you need to get rid of that damn phone anyway," I said truthfully.

"I know. I was supposed to do it today, but I forgot."

"Well, tomorrow we'll handle that first thing in the morning. In the meantime, don't answer his calls or texts. Let it roll over straight to voicemail," I said, hoping that would calm her down a bit.

"Okay, thank you, Keyon. I know you don't have to be doing this for me, but I'm glad that you are."

"It's okay, Mia. What you're going through I wouldn't wish on my worst enemy," I said as I pulled up in my driveway. "I'll see you tomorrow. Get some rest, boo."

"Okay. Good night," she replied.

I hung up the phone and sat there thinking. I honestly didn't know that I would be helping Mia, let alone have her calling me, after what she did, but I couldn't just sit there knowing what I knew and not doing anything to help the girl. Tay was going to have a fit tomorrow when I dragged her ass along for the ride, but she was just going to have to understand. No, Mia and I were not friends, and yes, she did pull that stunt on me at the club a few months ago, but that was in the past. Right now, I was trying to help an innocent child keep his mother, even if that child belonged to my daughter's father.

"Why didn't you beep the horn like I told you to?" Kane asked, scaring the shit out of me. I hadn't noticed when he walked up, or opened the door, for that matter. "Let me guess, you didn't know I was standing here, huh?"

"No," I said, shaking my head.

"You're going to have to do better than that, ma. I always tell you to be aware of your surroundings, especially when the girls are with you," he said, shaking his head. He left me sitting there as he opened the door and grabbed each of the girls in one of his arms. I never understood how his ass did that. Emoni and Ahmyri both had a little weight on them, so they were heavy.

"I'm sorry," I said, grabbing my phone and purse and getting out of the car. I hit the alarm as I followed him into the house. Once we were inside, I locked the door and set the alarm before following him up the stairs. Since the girls insisted on sleeping in the same room, even though they had rooms of their own, he placed them in the room he'd decorated for times like these. He then removed their shoes before placing their covers over them.

"I know you hate that, but they're exhausted. They can take a bath in the morning. Right now, let them sleep," he said before I could even let a word out of my mouth. He knew me all too well, and I hated when they had to bathe in the morning, but he was right. They were tired, so I guessed I could give them a pass for right now. "Come on, big mama. I already ran you a bath."

"Now that's what I'm talking about," I said, stealing a kiss from his lips as I wobbled my ass down the hallway and into the bathroom. I hated that the bathroom off our room wasn't finished, but that wasn't important right now. My body was beginning to ache, and that hot tub of water was calling my name.

Once I made it in the bathroom, I immediately stripped out of my clothes and hopped in the water.

"Damn, shorty, you couldn't wait for me?" he asked as he started stripping out of his clothes.

"Hey, I thought you took a shower already," I said, pouting.

"I did," he said, entering the tub. I moved up so he could sit behind me. That way, I could lay my head on his chest.

"Well, why are you invading my space then?" I asked, leaning my head back on his chest like I wanted to. I closed my eyes as I enjoyed the feeling.

"Girl, go 'head somewhere. You know you want me in here anyway."

"I don't know why you're laughing, because that ain't true," I said, trying to burst his bubble.

"All right, then move and let me get out," he said, trying to get up.

I opened my eyes and turned around, facing him. "Hold up, where are you trying to go?" I asked.

"I'm getting out since you don't want me in here," he said, attempting to move again.

"Nah, you good," I said, pushing him back down. I then placed my head back on his chest and closed my eyes once more. Yawning, I said, "You don't have to leave, baby. You can stay in here as long as you want."

"That's what I thought," he said, laughing. "Nah, but since you're tired and falling asleep and shit, let me give you a bath and get you into bed, baby."

"Sounds good to me," I replied, yawning. I scooted up a little as I sat there and waited for him to bathe me. Yup, Kane had me spoiled rotten. The man did almost everything for me as y'all can tell.

Once I was finished and he had cleaned every inch of my body, he got out and handed me a towel, letting me dry off before him. When I was done, I handed him that same towel, threw on my robe, and headed to our room. I didn't know whether I wanted to put on clothes or sleep naked, since I was always overheated. I figured I better at least put on some clothes since I was sleeping beside a man, and men can't take it when a woman is completely naked.

Opting for just a T-shirt and some boy shorts, I threw the robe on the dresser and hopped into bed. A minute later, Kane entered the room. He turned off the lights and then hopped into bed beside me, pulling me close to him.

"I love you," he said, kissing the back of my neck.

"I love you too," I said, yawning once more. "Oh, I have something to tell you."

"Oh, yeah, what's that?"

"I'll just tell you in the morning. Right now, I'm too tired to even stay up," I told him. I turned and gave him a kiss on the lips before assuming our lovely spoon position. Before I knew it, I was out like a light.

CHAPTER EIGHTEEN

Mia

The next morning I was up bright and early, ready to get my day started and my life back from Cash. Plus, Keyon had called me and told me to meet her back at the mall, where I would be parking my car and riding with her. I was so ready to move on with my life and leave Cash in the past. Besides that, last night dude sent me so many threatening messages, talking about what he was going to do to me once he found me, that I was really scared. I really didn't know what I could do, so I did something that I hadn't done in a long time. I prayed.

I prayed to God, asking Him for strength for one, and then I prayed and asked Him for forgiveness for what I had Bundy do to Cash. My day would come, but I needed a little peace before it did. My mother always told me that no problem was too big for God to handle, and that was where I messed up in my life. The minute I stopped praying was the minute I started dealing with everything under the sun. Cash was the devil himself. I just didn't see it at the time. Although I loved my son to the highest, I felt that if I hadn't strayed from God, I probably wouldn't have met Cash, and I wouldn't have been in the situation I was in now.

I took a minute to really think about Keyon as I sat there in the parking lot waiting for her to come. Cash must really have been an idiot for cheating on her, even though it was with me and a lot of other females. I thought that because, unlike most females, Keyon was different. She could've said to hell with me after the shit I'd said and done to her, and she could have let Cash do just what he was doing to me. Looking back at the past, I wished I had never done that shit. It wasn't because Cash whopped my ass, but because Keyon didn't deserve the shit she was going through. Well, then again, God probably saw it best to do that. In a funny way, He gave both of us a wakeup call. He wanted us to see the type of man Cash was, and even though He hadn't blessed me with a man yet, He did send Keyon hers. Knowing what Cash really was, I could say I was actually happy about that, too.

"Oh, look, she's right there," I said as her 2016 gray Lexus pulled up. Grabbing my purse, I got out and headed to the back of the car to grab CJ and his car seat. Once she pulled up beside me, I opened the back door and placed the seat in. I almost lost it when I saw her friend in the front seat, but I kept my mouth closed. Instead, I continued to buckle my child in his seat. When I was done, I made sure that my car doors were locked, and then I hopped in the car.

"What's up, boo?" she asked once we were on the highway.

"Nothing much. I'm good. What's up with y'all?" I asked them.

"Not a thing. We're just chilling," she answered, but her friend never did. I didn't blame her though. She was only looking out for her friend.

"I want to thank you again for doing this for me, Keyon."

"I told you that you don't have to keep on thanking me," she said, taking a quick glance at me. "Just sit back and enjoy the ride. Oh, but let's stop over at the store and get you a phone first."

"Okay, cool," I said as she stopped at a Sprint store.

She thought it would be wise if I'd give up my old phone number and got a whole other one. That way, Cash wouldn't be able to track my whereabouts and find me. Since I didn't care for the phone, or the number, for that matter, I was happy to give it up. Only thing was I decided to use a Florida area code. That way, if he did get ahold of my number, he'd think I was there.

Once I was squared away and had everything, we were back on the road. Keyon's friend still hadn't said a thing to me, but I wasn't the least bit worried about that. As long as she stayed that way and didn't say anything out of the way, I was fine. We didn't have to speak today, or for the rest of our lives, for that matter. As long as she gave me respect, then I was going to respect her.

"So what do you think?" Keyon asked me. She had contacted a real estate agent and had her rack up a couple of houses to show us. Now people always told me never to go with the first thing you see, which was why I said no to the first two houses, but this house? This house was actually the one for me. It was absolutely beautiful, with three bedrooms, two full bathrooms, a dining room, a living room, and a garage. The best part about the whole thing was that it was in a gated community. I had the choice of renting or buying it. Of course, I chose to buy it, since the rent was sky high and I had the money to buy it.

"I like it," I finally said. "It's small and comfortable, but big enough for me and CJ. There's a yard that he can play in, plus I can be as far away from Memphis as possible."

"So that means you'll take it?" the Realtor asked. She was probably hoping for me to say yes so that she didn't have to show us another house. I wouldn't blame her. I didn't know how she did it.

"Yes, I'll take it," I said, bouncing CJ from one leg to the other.

"Thank God," Tay finally spoke after being quiet all day. "Girl, this house is great. If you weren't going to take it, I would've considered moving here, shit."

"Okay, so do you want to rent or buy it? Now I'll tell you that the asking price is a bit much, but the owners are finalizing their divorce, which means that they want to close this as soon as possible. So I'm thinking that you can offer them a lower price, and they'll most likely take it. I know the wife. All she wants is her cut and to be free of her husband," she said, laughing.

"Okay, cool. Take a few thousand off the asking price and see what they have to say about it."

"Hold on, I'm one step ahead of you," she said, placing her phone to her ear. "I'll be right back."

"So do you really like the house?" Keyon asked once the lady was gone.

"Actually I do. Like I said before, it's quiet and small. I doubt Cash will look for us here, so I feel safe taking this one. Besides, the other two weren't my style, but this one is."

"Okay, cool. I hope the woman accepts the price that you offer," she said just as the woman walked back into the room.

"Good news. She was all too happy to take your price. Once I'm through here, I'll go back to my office and draw up the paperwork. We should close on this in a few weeks," she said, sounding happier than I was. I guessed she was also happy to get her cut also.

"Why so fast?" Keyon asked her, taking the words right out of my mouth.

"Because like I told you, she and her husband are getting a divorce. Let's just say she can't stand the sight of him, so the sooner she sells the house, the faster she completely gets rid of him."

"Okay, cool," I said happily. I was about to be a home-owner. This was the first good thing besides my son that had ever happened in my life.

"I'll call you later on this week to get the money. In the meantime, let me get out of here so that I can get to it. Thank you very much, and I'm glad that you like the house," she said as we all headed to the front door.

"I think y'all will enjoy this," Keyon said, heading toward the car.

"Me too," I said, taking one last look at the house before getting in the car. I was so happy that I almost called my cousin Brittney. Then I remembered that I couldn't contact her. I got a little sad, but if I wanted to remain safe, this was what I had to do. I could still contact her on Facebook. I just couldn't tell her where I was. Then again, maybe it was probably best if I just stayed away and kept out of contact with everyone. I really hoped that everything was going to work. I honestly want to contact my family, but I knew Cash. He would get my location out of them with no hesitation, and that couldn't happen.

"All right, y'all," Keyon said, starting up the car. "Let's grab something to eat and head back to Memphis."

"Thank the good Lord, because I'm starving," Tay concurred.

"Me three," I said. "Oh, Keyon?"

"What's up?"

"I need to trade my car in and get a new one. Can you help me with that also?"

"I can't, but my girl Tay can," she said, looking between the two of us.

"Stop looking at me like that," she told Keyon. "It may be hard for me to trust her, but I'll help her get a car, dammit."

"Thanks, Tay," I sang playfully. Now I was all the way good. If Cash was going to look for me, I was going to make it damn hard for him to find me.

CHAPTER NINETEEN

Keyon

Three Months Later

I was now almost four months pregnant, and I had
to say that I was actually enjoying life. Thanks to Kane
and my mother, who'd moved up here with us until I
had the babies, everything was going smoothly. I went
to all my doctor's visits on time. The doctor even told me
that I was somewhat out of the woods, which meant that
I didn't have to be cautious all the time. Even though I
said it would never happen, and by God, I didn't know
how it did, Mia and I had become good friends. Yes, I
did say friends. She and Tay had also become closer than
they were a few months ago. Well, once Tay saw that Mia
wasn't on any bullshit, she decided to give her a try. By
no means did I forget about the things she and Cash did.
I just decided to put all of that behind me. It didn't make
any sense for me to harbor feelings for a man I was no
longer involved or in love with, so I said to hell with it.
Kane was my man now, and I was pretty damn sure that
Mia would never get her hands on him.

Anyways, we kept on doing like we agreed to do. Every
other weekend, we would take the kids somewhere so
they could build a bond as brother and sister. I had to

admit that it was going very well. Sometimes I wouldn't even go with them because I'd be sick. So Mia would come get the girls and have them back at a decent hour. Yes, the first few times I was actually going crazy thinking that she wouldn't come back with them or something, but that never happened. Each time, she would bring them back, and they'd be worn out from all the fun they had. Of course, Kane had no idea that I was even doing this, but that was okay. He had yet to meet Mia, but I planned to change that real soon.

"Girl, look at these flowers," Tay entered the room practically screaming. With no help from me, and a lot from Kane's mother and mine, the wedding planning was just about done, and it was scheduled to take place in six weeks. I thought about it and decided that I wanted something simple. So we decided that it would be best for us to have the wedding in the back yard of our house. It would really save money, which we could use toward the twins. It would also limit the amount of people who would be there. Since the yard was pretty huge, we decided to do a maximum of 150 guests total.

"Would you quit all of that damn screaming?" I said as I looked down at the iPad she had in her hands. I had to admit that the girl really did have taste and she was one hell of a wedding coordinator, despite her not really being one. The theme of the wedding was going to be a winter wonderland, since we were going to get married in December. The colors were going to be red, white, and silver.

Kane's mother suggested that we rent out this huge, tall white octagonal party tent, with little white lights all over the ceiling. Tay suggested we go with red roses to pop the color. The tablecloths were going to be white with silver trimmings. They had this cute idea, that every table would have a cute little glass centerpiece that would hold a white candle.

"Oh, but these are really cute," I said, agreeing with her, because they actually were.

"Uh-huh, and they're talking about I can get a discount on them if I order them now. So!"

"Here," I replied, reaching into my purse and pulling out the card that Kane gave me. Yup, dude had given me a card to his account, and I was loving it. I wasn't money hungry, and I didn't need it. It was just that he even thought enough to give me the card and told me that I could do whatever with it. I didn't know what type of money he had, but he had to have a lot to be doing all of this.

"Great, I can't wait until the wedding comes," she yelled excitedly as she walked back into the living room.

"Me neither," I said, shaking my head. I picked up the phone and dialed Kane's number as I finally decided to bring him and Mia together so that I could introduce them to each other.

"What's up, big mama?" he asked, answering the phone in that sexy tone I loved to hear.

"Where are you, big poppa?" I replied playfully.

"I'm actually about to walk into the house. Give me a minute, though."

"Okay," I said, hanging up the phone. I sat in the kitchen as I waited for him to appear.

"Keyon, where you at, baby?" I heard him ask from somewhere.

"I'm in the kitchen," I told him. A few seconds later, he came walking in the kitchen with his arms full of shit.

"What's all this?" I asked, trying to get up.

"No, you don't have to get up. Stay there," he said before I could move. He walked over to the table and placed the gift on it. "Hold on, wait. I've got a few more in the car. I'll be right back."

I waited until he was gone before I tried to peek at what he had gotten. I saw a few things for the girls and some onesies. I tried peeking at the other stuff, but I heard him coming through the door.

"What are you doing over there?" he said, catching me in the act. "I know you ain't in here peeking in my bags, huh?"

"No, I ain't peeking in nothing," I said, lying.

"I know you're lying, but here," he said, handing me this big-ass gift bag. The shit was so big that I could fit in it. Well, without my belly and shit though.

I opened the bag to find a small bag from Tiffany's that held three boxes: two small ones and a rectangular one. I opened the long one first, which contained a Paloma Picasso Loving Heart pendant. The other two were the matching bracelet and earrings.

"Aww, baby, thank you so much," I said, trying to get up again, but he stopped me.

"Don't thank me just yet. Look in the rest of the bags. There's way more in there," he said, smiling.

"Okay," I said, dancing around in my seat. I went through the bag and almost fainted when I saw a gift card to Saks along with two purses and some shoes. "Really, babe?" I asked, smiling so hard my cheeks were hurting.

"You know you're my favorite girl," he said, walking over to me. He handed me another bag, which had a teddy bear, some candies, flowers, and a card with $300 in it. "I brought y'all some food from my mom's house, too."

"Oh, bitch, I wanna be just like you when I grow up," Tay said, coming back into the kitchen, looking at everything that Kane had bought for me.

"Girl, I ain't trying to be like nobody but my damn self," Ant said, walking in with a few bags of his own. He handed Tay a bag that was almost as big as mine was, which had her ass cheesing bigger than I was. She poked her tongue out before giving him a sloppy kiss.

"Why don't y'all go on with that shit? Ain't nobody wanna see y'all slobbering and shit," Kane said, making us all laugh.

"Stop all that damn hating," she said, hitting him on his arm. "Come on, bae. Let's go in the living room so I can see what you bought me."

"Girl, bye," I said, waving her off. Ever since she and Ant started seeing each other, she'd been too happy. More like a high school girl who was dating her boy crush. Hopefully they'd last, because I would hate to have to fuck Ant up behind my sister.

"Babe, we need to talk," I told Kane once they were gone.

"About what?" he asked, taking a seat next to me.

"Well, I wanted to talk to you about Mia."

"Who's Mia?" he asked. He was probably going to blow his top when I told him, but I needed to, since the girls were spending so much time around her.

"Remember the girl I told you about who came to the club when Cash asked me to marry him? His baby mama from Chicago?" I said, trying to jog his memory.

"Yeah, what about her?"

"Well, she's been living down here for a few months," I said, giving him information slowly. "And well, I've been meeting up with her and stuff."

"What the fuck would you be meeting with her for?" he asked, shocking me.

"Well, because our kids are siblings. We thought it would be best if they got to know each other. So for the past few months, since I got home from the hospital, we've been getting together. So the kids could have some type of bond." I was kind of scared of what he might say next.

"Past few months and you're just now coming to me with that shit?" he asked, heated. "Why the fuck . . . Wait, let me stop cursing at you, because that's not the type of relationship that I want. But why would you even allow something like that to happen? I mean, she could be setting you up for all you know, and you're falling for it."

"Kane, come on, I'm not even that type of chick. You really think that I would even put my child, let alone your child, in a position like that?" I asked, baffled. I couldn't believe that he would really think of me as being so careless.

"Wait, so Ahmyri's been going with y'all too?" he asked. I could see his jaws clenching, so I knew he had to be really mad.

"Yes, but I was with them when she would go," I lied. I couldn't tell the man that I was sending his daughter off with a complete stranger.

"Come on, man," he said, getting to his feet.

"Look, you can calm down. The girls weren't in danger at all, and the only reason I kept in contact and continued to do this was that the girl was going through a lot with Cash. He was beating on her and threatening to kill her. I couldn't just sit there and let the girl get killed. I promise that I don't put myself or the kids in any harm. I only helped her find somewhere to stay and a job so that she could get on her feet," I said, lying again. I did more than that for her, but again, he didn't need to know that.

"Look, I'm going to be honest with you and keep it pushing. You were dead-ass wrong for not coming to me earlier with this shit, especially when you brought my daughter into the fold. Like I said, that girl could've been setting you up, but thank God she wasn't, because I would've been on her ass as well as yours. It's all good that you wanted to help her out, but why would you after what she and Cash did to you? I guess your heart is as big as mine is, huh?" he said, laughing a little, but not much.

"I don't know, maybe it is," I said, laughing along with him. "I want you to meet her though."

"Meet who?" he asked, playing dumb. "I'm not trying to meet nobody, man."

"Please! I kind of need you to before the wedding because I was actually thinking about putting her in it."

"Whoa, you're kind of jumping a little too far there, aren't ya? I'll meet her, but in no way, shape, or form will she be in our wedding, and that there is final," he replied. I had no choice but to respect his wish, but at least he agreed to meet with her.

"Okay, cool. She won't be in the wedding, but I'm glad you agreed to meet her, because I want to invite her to dinner tonight."

"Dinner where?" he asked, turning his head so fast I thought he was about to break his neck. "Nah, baby. You might trust her, but I don't. We'll invite her to dinner, but it won't be here. I still have my apartment, so you can either do it there or pick a restaurant. Whichever is up to you, but she won't be stepping one foot in here. I don't really trust people too much. I have to get a feel for them, and from all the things you've told me, I don't think that's going to be easy in her case."

"Really, Kane?" I asked in disbelief. I couldn't believe he was acting like this.

"Ya damn right. Just because you're quick to forgive and forget doesn't mean that I would allow a snake in my house," he said. I looked at him and noticed how serious the look on his face was and decided to leave it be. I didn't know why I would even try to pull some shit like that on him when I already knew how he rolled.

"Okay, but you can scratch the apartment out. I really don't feel like cooking, no way. So we can eat out, and since Applebee's isn't that far from here, that's where we'll be going," I told him.

"That's cool with me," he said, getting up. "And that shit is a thirty- to forty-minute drive from here."

"I don't care how long it is. I'm not cooking a damn thing today. So that's where we'll be going. Now where are you going?" I asked, getting up behind him.

"To go check on the girls. Then I'm going to take a nap before I meet your best friend," he said sarcastically.

"Stop playing with me. You already know who my one and only best friend is," I said, rolling my eyes. "But can you help me take all of this up to the room?"

"I knew you were going to do that. That was why I was trying to leave before you asked," he said, laughing as he began helping me with the things he had bought. "You're nothing but a spoiled brat anyways."

"That's because you made me that way, baby," I replied before walking over and placing a kiss on his lips. "And I love you for that."

"Uh-huh. I'm no dummy, but I love you too," he replied, leaving the room.

I stood there watching him as a smile appeared on my face. I was so in love with that man that nothing anyone could say would make me leave him. He had my whole heart, and I couldn't wait until it was time for us to say, "I do." We were going to be together for the rest of our lives.

CHAPTER TWENTY

Mia

The last three months had been the best of my life. I hadn't heard a word from Cash, nor had I heard a word from Bundy, and I'd been living in nothing but peace since then. CJ and I had been great, also. He'd been in day care for the past two months, and I'd been working. Yup, that's right. I went and got a job. I also went and got my GED. So that was a huge accomplishment for me. Just to be in this peaceful place and to be able to support my son on my own felt so awesome. Even though I was used to Cash giving me money, I was independent now, and I had Keyon to thank for giving me all the advice and wisdom that I so desperately needed. Speaking of her, she was now calling my phone.

"Hello," I answered happily. I didn't know why, and people might have said I was foolish, but talking to Keyon was actually a good feeling for me. I always waited for her to give things to me straight, no chaser.

"What are you doing? Do you have work today?"

"Nah, I'm off today and tomorrow. What's up?" I asked.

"I'm calling to see if you wanna do dinner with me and my family at Applebee's tonight."

"Oh, so I finally get to meet your fiancé, huh?" I asked, surprised that she was even about to allow that to happen.

"Yes, and even though I know that my man absolutely loves me, I don't wanna catch you looking at him all funny, because I will cut you behind that one," she said, but laughed. I laughed too, but I could also hear the seriousness in her voice.

"Man, I'm not even on that shit no more, and I've apologized to you a million times already. So make this a million and one. I'm sorry for messing with Cash and causing you so much trouble," I said seriously, even though I was tired of saying it.

"Girl, go ahead somewhere with all of that. Cash was and will forever be a nobody. So fuck him," she said, and I agreed. "Where's my baby at?"

"He's right there sleeping. Girl, it feels so good to be able to relax and shit without him crying for this or that all the damn time."

"I know you're going to leave him alone. That child doesn't bother you that damn much," she said, laughing again.

"Girl, whatever. You'll see when I be shipping his ass off to stay with you and your damn family," I told her.

"And I'll be happy to take him too, but I gotta go. See you later, boo."

"All right. See you all later," I said before we hung up.

I sat there as my heart began racing. I couldn't believe that Keyon was finally allowing me to meet her fiancé. I was quite surprised that she was allowing to meet him after everything that went on with Cash. I wouldn't do her like that again because we'd become a little close, and I didn't want to jeopardize any of that this time. But I was pretty sure they'd talked about me and everything that went down with Cash and me, which meant that he already had an opinion about who I was. He probably thought I was all kind of thots and whatnot, which was what I desperately wished to change. If Keyon could really forgive me, he could too.

"I'm on my way out the door right now," I told Keyon as I grabbed CJ's car seat with him in it and headed to the garage. Opening the car door and placing him inside, I ran back in the house to get my purse and lock up. When I was done, I went back to the garage and got in the car. Opening the garage door, I started the car and backed out. When I made it to the end of the driveway, I closed the garage door. I almost had a heart attack when I thought I saw someone standing a few feet away from the house, but when I shined the bright lights on the spot, no one was there. Figuring that I was just tripping, I pressed the button to close the garage door and continued out of the driveway and pulled off. Keyon already had sent a message and said that they were leaving the house, so I had forty-five minutes to make it there in time to meet them. So I really had to hurry my ass if I wanted to get there.

As I drove down the highway, I decided to call my cousin Brittney. Since she was the only family I had, I wanted her to know that I was all right. She was probably worrying her little head off, so this was the least I could do to put her mind at ease.

"Hello," she said, answering the phone on the fourth ring.

"Girl, you sound so different," I said, shocked. "What the fuck have you been getting into?"

"Mia?" she asked, catching on to my voice.

"Yeah, it's me," I replied, smiling from ear to ear. It felt so good to be able to hear her voice.

"Oh, my God, girl, where the hell are you?" she asked.

"I'm living," I simply said, knowing that I couldn't tell her exactly where I was. "How's everything been going in Chicago?"

"Everything's been the same. Except them niggas Bundy and Cash been by here looking for your ass like clockwork. I don't know what you did to them niggas, but they surely been by here a lot."

"When was the last time they came over there?" I asked, hoping that she wouldn't say anytime lately.

"Cash ain't been here in a minute, but that nigga Bundy was just over here about a week ago looking for you. Looking all bad and shit. I ain't seen his ass since then though."

"What the fuck did Bundy want?" I asked her. I hadn't been talking to his ass, so I wondered what he could want.

"He been looking for you like every fucking body else been doing," she replied, laughing as if the shit were funny. "I don't know what the hell you did to that boy, but he looks so damn bad. I think his ass is on some type of drug or something."

"I didn't do one damn thing to his ass, and if he's on drugs, then that's his own damn business, not mine," I said.

"Shit, could've fooled me, but seriously, where the hell are you, and when the hell are you coming back home?"

"Girl, I'm never coming back home. I done found myself a little spot, and I'm very much content."

"What?" she yelled. "You're not coming back to Chicago? Never?"

"Never, bitch. I'm not coming back to that hellhole. I done got myself a job, I done got my GED, bought a beautiful home, and me and my son are doing just fine."

"You go, girl," she said, making me smile hard. "When will you let me and your little cousin come and visit you? You know he's been asking about you, and you know I miss your ass. Plus, you're talking about not coming back to Chicago. Just tell me where you're at so that I can come and visit you."

"If I tell you, you better not tell no damn body either," I said as serious as a heart attack.

"Bitch, you know me better than that," she replied, which caused me to stop and think. Not one time did she ever cross me or rat me out. She'd been in my corner since forever and a day, and yet here I was questioning if I should really tell her where I was or just lie like I did about everything else. "Come on, Mia, we really miss you all."

"All right," I said just as my phone began to beep. Pulling the phone from my ear, I looked at it to see Keyon calling. "Hold on, Brittney, let me call you right back."

"Wait. Are you goi—" she began to say, but I was already hanging up.

"Sup, Keyon?" I asked her.

"Girl, where are you? We just got here, but we're waiting to be seated," she said, sounding like she was whispering.

"Actually, I just pulled into the parking lot," I said once I realized exactly where I was. I guessed Brittney and I were on the phone talking so much that I hadn't noticed. It was either that or I was really speeding. Either way, I was here, and I was nervous as hell, too.

"All right, I'm about to come out and get you."

"Okay, cool," I said before I hung up. I was thankful that the place wasn't packed and that I was able to find a parking spot quickly. After parking, I turned off the car, got out, and grabbed CJ from the back seat just in time to see Keyon wobbling our way.

"Girl, you're huge," I said, looking at her already-big belly. She wasn't even at five months. I didn't care what she said. She was going to end up going into labor super early.

"I don't want to hear that shit. Let me see my baby," she said as CJ reached for her. She grabbed him and began walking back toward the restaurant.

"Come on, Keyon, let me hold him. I don't want him causing you any pain. You know he's heavy."

"Girl, the boy barely weighs a good twenty-five pounds, and he's two," she said, laughing. Yes, my son was small and didn't gain any weight, as much as he ate. Even though that may have been true, I still didn't want her holding him. Her doctor recently said that her pregnancy was coming along fine. I didn't need anything backtracking that. "He won't hurt me no type of way."

"All right now, but don't have no one fussing at me because you decided to be hardheaded," I said once we entered through the doors.

"Oh, it looks like they've already been seated," she said, turning.

"Keyon, we're this way," Tay yelled as she waved us toward their table. "Come on, girl," she said as we began walking toward her.

From where I was, I noticed a man sitting at the table, but his back was turned toward us. I wasn't anywhere near him, and the man couldn't even see me, yet I was nervous, as if he were watching me walk toward the table the whole damn time.

I closed my eyes as I tried to get my breathing under control and the pounding of my heart to slow down a little. I didn't know why, but somehow it seemed like we'd been walking for an hour when it had only been seconds. I really couldn't believe that meeting Keyon's fiancé would make me this nervous. Finally we reached the table. I almost shit in my pants when I saw who he really was: the same nigga Bundy had recruited for the lick with Cash. The very same dude I had to bail out of jail a few months ago.

"Mia, meet Kane. Kane, meet Mia," she said, introducing us. Just like me, he was surprised as hell.

"Nice to meet you," I said, reaching out my hand for him to shake. Looking around at the few people sitting at the table, which included Tay and Ant, he cleared his throat and shook my hand.

"Nice to meet you too, Mia," he replied, smiling. There was something about the way he said my name and the look in his eyes that really had me scared.

"Okay, well, let's have a seat, shall we?" Keyon said, sounding happy. I was guessing that she actually missed the look Kane gave me, because there was really no reason to be happy at all right now.

"Okay, but let me go ahead and run to the bathroom right quick. Order me a Sprite if they come over for the drinks and I'm not there," I told her as I set CJ's bag in my seat and almost ran my ass to the bathroom.

I guessed it was true when people said that the world was in fact smaller than we all thought it was. There was no damn way my luck could be that damn bad, so I was pretty sure that this was one big coincidence. It was either that or God was really trying to send me a sign that I wasn't able to read. Whatever the case was, there was no way that I could stay my ass here. I had to come up with a reason to leave, but then again, I couldn't. Keyon was happy about this little meeting, and I didn't want to disappoint her.

Once I entered the bathroom, I made sure that no one was in there before I pulled out my phone and dialed Bundy's number. Placing the phone to my ear, I silently prayed that he would answer seeing that I had a Florida telephone number and he didn't answer the phone for numbers he didn't know.

"Who are you calling?" I heard a voice say behind me. I turned around and almost shit in my pants when I saw Kane standing there.

"Nobody," I stuttered, lying. He gave me that "Yeah, bitch, all right" face before he came walking over to me. Taking the phone out of my hand, he looked at it then back up at me.

"See, I thought I was tripping when I saw you and I knew for damn sure that I knew your face. I just couldn't believe that of all the girls in Chicago, you had to be that Mia who came down here," he began to say. "I thought when that shit happened with Bundy a few months ago that I wouldn't have to deal with y'all no more. Now he's blowing me up, and your ass pops up out of nowhere. Tell me what the fuck I need to know, because you coming in here and calling Bundy looks hella suspicious right now."

"Okay, damn, but it's not what you think."

"Not what I think? See, what I'm thinking is that y'all trying to bring some drama to my front door, and I'm not having that. Now tell me that is not what I think," he said, stepping a few feet closer to me.

"Like I said, it's not what you think," I said, taking a step back so that we weren't that close together. "I only came down here because I wanted the kids to get to know each other."

"That's bullshit and you know it," he said, grabbing ahold of my shoulder. He didn't squeeze it or anything like that. He just held it. "Tell me the real reason you're here, and don't play with me, shawty."

"Okay, damn. I came here because I got tired of Cash beating on me. Yes, that nigga is a woman beater, and he's been whooping my ass ever since I showed up and did what I did to him and Keyon at the club. I know I deserved the shit after the club, but I'm not anyone's punching bag. Cash isn't my father. He's my child's father, and that was what I tried to tell him, but I couldn't get that through his head," I said as my eyes got a little watery. Thinking about the shit I used to go through always made me feel down and upset. "Look, I'm not trying to bring no drama to y'all. I'm just trying to let my son get to know his big sister, that's all."

"Look, I'm sorry about that nigga beating on you and shit, but you come with too much shit attached to you. How do we know that if he does find you and if you do happen to be with Keyon, he won't attack her too? I mean, from what I'm hearing, the nigga is a loose cannon. Makes me wonder if he ever hit on Keyon," he said, looking away at the wall.

"No, he hasn't. We already had that conversation, and she said no."

"Well, I'm happy about that, but we still have a problem on our hands."

"And what's that?" I asked, because as far as I was concerned, there wasn't a problem.

"You know what I did, and Bundy's a loose cannon right now, which means that I can't have none of that around my girls."

"I haven't told Keyon a damn thing, and I promise I won't. As for Bundy, I haven't talked to him in three months, and he's not answering the phone for me now."

"Hold up, let me call him up right now," he said, grabbing his phone and dialing Bundy's number. He placed the phone to his ear, but instantly put it back down. "His phone is going straight to voicemail."

"Same thing it did when I called him a few minutes ago," I told him.

"Yo, I think we need to go up there and see what is going on with him. The nigga called me last week and said that he thinks the nigga knows about what he did."

"I told him that Cash doesn't know a thing. He's just so paranoid he's going to give us up."

"Shit, that's if he hasn't done so already," Kane said, shaking his head. "Since Keyon trusts you, you can just leave your son with her and say that you have to go back and check on your people. Ask her at the table so that I can encourage her to do so."

"Okay."

"All right now, good. Go back out there to the table before she or Tay starts to get suspicious. I'll be out there in a few minutes. I'll try to call my aunt up to see if she's seen Bundy."

"All right, cool," I said, leaving the restroom. I made it back to the table in probably twenty seconds flat.

"Damn, you must've really had to use the restroom, huh?" Keyon said, laughing.

"Uh-huh," I said, grabbing CJ from her lap. "Did everyone order yet?"

"Nah, we were waiting for you and Kane to get back," she said just as he sat back down in his seat. He spared me a few seconds' glance before turning his attention back to Keyon.

"Umm, Keyon, I have to talk to you," I told her. I looked around as I noticed everyone at the table was now looking at us. "But it can wait until later."

"Are you sure?" she said, turning toward me.

"Yes, I'm sure," I said, never bothering to look up at Kane because I was more than sure that he had a mug on his face.

"Okay," she said, flagging down a waiter who came and took our orders.

As we all sat there waiting for the food, we decided to get to know each other. Or rather, they all thought it was a good idea to jump on me, asking question after question. I answered most of them, but when they started to ask about my parents, I began to get a little uncomfortable. It was a good thing the waiter had come back with our food, because I could feel myself about to have a mental breakdown if I said anything about my family.

It wasn't until dinner was almost over and we were about to leave when I asked Keyon about keeping CJ. Like I already knew, she had no problem keeping him. Knowing that Cash was back in Chicago, she wanted me to be safe. She didn't have to worry about that, because I wasn't going anywhere around Cash. I was only going with Kane, and that was because he was basically making me. Once we found out where Bundy was, or what happened to him, then we were out. Well, I would be for sure. Kane could've done whatever he wanted to. Shit, that wasn't on me. The only thing I had on my mind was making it back to Tennessee to my son, that was it.

CHAPTER TWENTY-ONE

Kane

When I agreed to meet Keyon's little buddy, who also happened to be Cash's other baby mama, I had no idea that the chick would be the same person who hooked Bundy and me up with the lick a few months ago. I also didn't know that the bitch was Cash's baby mama. Why the hell would you try to set up your own baby daddy to get robbed by a couple of niggas in the first place? I guessed the shit was finally catching up to her now, but like I told her, I wasn't trying to bring all that bullshit to my front door. Bundy was starting to be a big problem for me, and as much as I hated to admit it, I needed to eliminate him before he became an even bigger problem. Thing was, no one could find him, which was why me and ol' girl would be taking a trip there. That nigga didn't just up and disappear without anyone knowing where the fuck he was. Someone knew something, and I was going to find out. I just had to wait until tomorrow to do so, but right now, I was 'bout to spend some much-needed time with my girl.

The next morning came faster than I expected it to, and just like that, it was back to business. Since I already hipped Ant up to the game last night, he was up also, and yes, he was going with us. Since I still had the apartment, we decided to meet up there once Mia dropped her son off to Keyon. The minute she showed up, we'd be hitting the road and heading to Chicago. We would've taken a flight, but just in case something popped off, we didn't want anything being traced back to us.

"You sure homegirl will show?" Ant asked as we sat in the living room, waiting for Mia to get there. We already had run a few errands, and shorty was still late. She was supposed to be there at nine, and it was almost eleven.

"Man, I don't know. I've called and texted her phone, but she's not answering. If her crib weren't too far out of the way, we could've taken that ride out there," I said just as someone started knocking on the door. I spotted Ant reaching for his strap as I went to answer the door. "Nigga, what the fuck is you doing? You know damn well that ain't nobody but ol' girl."

"Nigga, I don't give a fuck. I'm just trying to be safe in case it ain't her," he said, making me shake my head.

"Nigga, you wild and you know it," I said, opening the door to see Mia standing there with her bags in her hand. "It's 'bout time. I thought we were going to have to leave without ya ass."

"Y'all ain't going to believe me, but I'm pretty damn sure that someone was following me."

"Oh, shit, why the fuck you led them over here?" Ant asked, walking over to the door.

"Fuck bringing them over here. What about my girl? Were they following you when she met you to get your son?" I asked, wishing that she was going to say no.

"Chill out. I'm no dummy to this. I took them niggas on a tour around the city, and then I lost them. That's when I met up with Keyon. Kane, I already told you that I wasn't trying to bring drama nowhere near you or ya family," she replied.

"Good, now let's go. I've tried calling that nigga Bundy a few times this morning, and just like last night, he ain't answering the phone. So the faster we get to Chicago, the better chance we have of finding him," I said, grabbing my bags and heading out the door. They followed me as we headed outside to the Tahoe I had rented. We loaded the truck up and got in. Ant and I were in the front while Mia got comfortable in the back as we started our long journey to Chicago. Hopefully, we could find Bundy and put this shit to rest.

We arrived in Chicago a little after seven that evening. Of course, we were all tired, but I didn't have time to be sleeping. We went straight to the hotel, where we dropped everything off, and headed straight to my aunt's, who also happened to be Bundy's mother. If anyone knew where Bundy was, it was sure to be her.

Pulling up to my aunt's house, we parked the car on the side of the street and got out. Making our way up the driveway to the door, I noticed that damn near all the lights were off. Since I didn't call to let her know that I was coming, I was hoping that she was still up. I would hate to have to wake her up if she wasn't.

"You think she's still up?" Mia asked as I began knocking on the door.

"I don't know. I hope she is though," I replied, knocking again.

"I'm coming," I heard her yell from inside. A few moments later, we heard the sound of the locks clicking followed by her opening the door. "Oh, God, Kahreem! What are you doing here?"

"Hey, Auntie Norma Lee, how are you doing?" I asked, giving her a hug.

"I'm fine, baby. Come on in here," she said, stepping to the side to allow us in. "Hey there, Anthony," she said once she saw Ant. She gave him a hug as well.

"Hey, Miss Norma. I'm so happy to see you."

"And who might this young lady be?"

"My name is Mia. I'm a friend of theirs. How are you doing, ma'am?" Mia answered before I could.

"Oh, nice to meet you, dear. Y'all hungry?" she said. "Follow me into the kitchen."

We followed her into the kitchen, where she went straight to the cabinet and grabbed a few plates. She then washed her hands, went straight over to the stove, and began fixing each of us some food. Once we were all settled at the table, she went back to fix us some good ol' lemonade. After bringing the drinks to the table, she took a seat next to me.

"Now, I know you don't come around here much, and when you do, there's always a reason. So why are you here? And ya better not lie to me," she said without looking at me. What some people didn't know was that my aunt Norma Lee was once a savage. Truth be told, she still was. She was the only one in our family who actually knew what Bundy and I were into, and she didn't judge us for it because she once did the shit herself.

"I'm not coming here to hurt nobody. I'm actually coming here for Bundy," I said, which got her attention. "Do you know where he is?"

"What did he do? And no, I don't know where he's at," she said, standing.

"Bundy's been a loose cannon after the whole incident that involved us three, and I'm just trying to find him before the people who we robbed find him. I need to make sure that he's straight before I actually kill the niggas before they kill us. Word on the street is they know about who robbed them, but the only person who can actually tell them the truth is missing. Now like I said, I'm not going to hurt him. To be honest, I only want to hide him until all of this is over. The minute it is, he can go about his business."

"I trust that you won't hurt him, but I haven't seen or heard from Bundy in about two weeks. I've been calling him, but his phone always goes straight to voicemail," she said, getting up from her seat. She walked over to one of her little cabinets, opened it, and removed her rooster cookie jar. Walking back over to the table, she placed the rooster on the table, opened it, and removed a key.

"If I weren't sick, I would've gone over there myself. Since I can't drive, there was no way for me to go," she said, handing the key to me. "I'm praying that when you get over there, there won't be any bad news."

"He's probably all right. He probably just doesn't want to be bothered," I said, trying to make light of the situation. I didn't need her worrying her mind about something that she couldn't change if it did happen.

"Find him. Leave the dishes in the sink when y'all are done. I'll see y'all tomorrow," she said before she left the kitchen.

We all sat at the table looking at each other. I already knew what she meant, but they didn't. "Find him" meant either find Bundy or find the man who killed him. Like I said before, she already knew everything that we were involved in because she'd been through the shit her damn self. Norma Lee was an OG, one most people wished to be like.

Once we were finished eating, I emptied everything off the plates and set them in the sink. I made sure to wipe off the table and pushed the chairs back under it. Turning the lights out, we left the house en route to Bundy's house. I silently prayed that there wouldn't be any bad news when we got there.

CHAPTER TWENTY-TWO

Cash

"Oh, right there. Don't stop. Oh, don't stop," shorty moaned as I pounded her from behind. Yeah, I knew I wasn't supposed to be doing all this, but a nigga was backed up, and with everything that'd been going on, I needed the release. She was just in the right place at the right time.

"You gon' swallow this nut?" I asked, picking up the pace. I'd already been here too long, and I didn't get what I came for yet.

"Uh-huh," she said, bucking. She was just about ready to blow. I could feel her muscles tightening around my dick. So I sped up the pace even more, making sure that each stroke was filled with pleasurable pain. A few seconds later, she began nutting. Knowing I was right behind her, I pulled out of her and beat my dick until she turned around and started sucking it. She knew I loved it when she took my dick straight to the back of her throat. Something about that warm feeling drove my dick insane. A minute or two later, I was shooting my seeds all the way to the back of her throat.

"Open ya mouth," I told her. She rolled her eyes but did just as I told her to. I didn't care if she was mad. I was making sure that she swallowed that shit. "Good girl."

"So are you going to stay the night?" she asked, smiling. I looked at her and laughed softly before shaking my head. I didn't know when and why this bitch became attached to me, but what she didn't understand was that nothing was going to come of this besides a good nut. That was it.

"Now you know I can't spend the night. I have to be on the first thing smoking out of here in the morning. In case you've forgotten, I'm still looking for your bitch-ass, thieving-ass, conniving-ass cousin. That bitch and Bundy fucked with the wrong nigga. Speaking of Bundy, that nigga better be glad I sent him out painless."

"You killed him?" she asked, sounding shocked.

"What the fuck you think? And I'm going to do the same thing when I find your stupid-ass cousin," I said. "Did she tell you where she was?"

"So you're just going to kill the mother of your child?" she asked, ignoring my question.

"The fuck you think? She could've been my mother and I would've killed her. She shouldn't have stolen from my son and me. Now she has to pay for that with her life," I said without cutting one corner. Since she stole from me like any other bitch-ass nigga, I was going to have to treat her like any other bitch-ass nigga. "Now did she tell you where she was?"

"No. She was supposed to, but she said someone was calling her," she said, which was not what I wanted to hear at all.

"The fuck you mean, bitch?" I asked, madder than a muthafucker. "Well, what the fuck did she say then?"

"Like I said, she was supposed to tell me, but then someone beeped her line. Shit, for all I know, she's in Florida."

"How the fuck you know that shit?" I asked her.

"Because . . ." she said before she walked over to her purse. She came back with her phone in her hand.

Scrolling through her phone, she then turned it to me. "She called me from this number. So I Googled it, and it showed up as a Florida number."

"Let me see that shit right quick," I said, grabbing the phone out of her hand. Pulling my phone out, I copied the number and saved it in my contacts. I then handed the phone back to her. Walking over to the bed, I bent down and began putting my clothes on. Pulling my wallet out of my back pocket, I tossed her a few $100 bills before I made my way to the door. "Thanks for everything, Brittney. I gotta go."

"Will I see you next week?" she had the nerve to ask. Since I still needed her, I decided to play nice.

"Yes, I'll call you when I get back. See ya later," I said, walking down the stairs and out the door. Closing the door, I made a mental note to take care of her the minute I was done with Mia. I didn't need her running her mouth and telling nobody shit. That was why I was going to play it cool until everything was over and done with.

"Man, you won't even believe this shit," I said, walking into the house where Jamel and I had been staying for the past couple of months.

"Nigga, what the fuck is wrong with you?" he asked, walking into the living room. "You been too damn happy for me, shit."

"Man, shut the fuck up and listen," I said, taking a seat on the sofa. He stood there for a few seconds before taking a seat himself. "Now you know how I been looking for the bitch Mia and shit, right? Well, today, her cousin told me that the bitch was most likely in Florida."

"And what makes you think that?" he asked like I was tripping or something.

"Because she said she called her today, and the number she called her from was from a Florida area code."

"What makes you think that what ol' girl said is true?" he asked, kind of pissing me off.

He knew I hated when he questioned me, and right now was not the time for him to be questioning me. He knew better than I did how bad I wanted to find this bitch and fuck her up for doing us so dirty. I lost my family over this bitch, and come to fucking find out that this bitch was a fucking snake and shit. That shit made me feel fucked up in the head, and now because of my stupid-ass mistake, my girl was pregnant and about to marry another nigga. I was getting angry again thinking about that shit, and the only person I wanted to take it out on was Mia's stupid ass.

"I'm just saying, they're family, right? And even though you're occasionally fucking Brittney, what makes you think that what she's saying about her own damn cousin is true? For all you know, that number could be bogus and she could be telling homegirl all about your plans right now."

"Man, shut the fuck up and hand me that burner that's sitting on the table," I told him. I then reached into my pocket and pulled the phone out.

"Nigga, don't be mad at me, because I do what you don't do," he said, handing me the phone.

"Man, shut the fuck up with all of that shit," I said, as I began dialing the number that I had saved in my phone. Hitting the call button, I then put the phone on speaker. We then sat there waiting as the phone began ringing.

"Hello," a voice said.

"Hello, may I speak with Martha please?" I asked, changing my voice so she wouldn't realize who it was.

"I'm sorry, you have the wrong number," a voice that sounded like Mia's said.

"You believe me now?" I asked Jamel as I threw the phone back on the table.

"I have no choice but to when I just heard her voice, huh?" he replied sarcastically.

"Uh-huh. Now what was all the shit you was just popping?"

"Man, get the fuck out with that childish shit," he said, getting up. "So what are you going to do about that? You don't know where she is in Florida. So if you go looking for her, that's like searching for a needle in a haystack."

"I know. That's why I want you to call Li'l Bit and get her to put a trace on the phone."

"Okay, cool."

"And tell her that I want to hear something by tomorrow. Shit, I pay her too much for her not to be doing her job," I said, getting up from the sofa. Stretching and yawning, I began walking out of the room. "I'll catch you tomorrow. Don't make no babies tonight, nigga."

"How do you know I had someone over?"

"Nigga, I'm Cash, and I'm also your best friend. I know you," I said, laughing. "I'll talk to you tomorrow. I'm more tired than a muthafucker right now."

"All right, man."

Leaving the room, I headed straight to the bathroom. A nigga was tired, but I still had to take a shower. It wasn't going to be a long one, but I needed to wash the smell of sex and sweat off me. Once I was cleaned up, I headed to the room, where I threw on a pair of boxers and hopped into bed. I needed all the rest that I could get, because tomorrow I was going to find Mia and bring her ass back to Chicago, where I was going to end her miserable-ass life.

"Yo, you got what I asked you for?" I asked Young as I cruised through the city of Chicago. My flight to Tennessee wasn't scheduled until later on this evening.

So I decided to take care of a few last-minute things before then. I had already checked on all the shops but one, which was where I was heading now.

"Man, I got it and then some, but I'm not about to tell you the shit over the phone," he replied, making my heart skip a beat.

"Is it good news or bad news?" I asked, trying to get a heads-up on what he had to tell me.

"The best news you'll want to hear."

"All right, man, let me go check on these traps. I'll see you later on tonight," I told him as I pulled up to the last trap.

"A'ight, bet," he said, hanging up. Before getting out of the car, I made sure that I looked around. I had to be sure that there was no one around to clock or lock me up. Once I was sure that everything was okay, I got out and headed inside.

"What's up, boss?" some little dude name Bryant said as I walked up. When I reached the porch, he got up and gave me a dap, followed by the rest of the ones sitting on the porch.

"Where them bags at?" I asked him, getting straight to the point.

"Yeah. Let me get it for you right quick," he said before he disappeared into the house. A few minutes later, he came back outside with two black duffle bags.

"Everything's all right, huh?" I asked before I even reached for anything.

"Man, you know me better than that, boss. Everything is always good, and you know it," he said, handing the bags to me.

"All right, man. I'll see y'all next week. I'll be out of the state, so keep shit on lock for me, nigga," I said, taking the bags from him.

"You know I got you, man. See you when ya get back," he said before we pounded our fists together. I then said goodbye to the rest of the fellas before I headed back to the car, where I threw the bags in the trunk, got in, and headed back to the house.

Since the house wasn't too far away from the trap, it didn't take long for me to get there. When I got there, I spotted Mel's car sitting on the side of the road. Hitting the horn twice before pulling into the driveway, I got out without cutting the car off, grabbed the bags, and headed inside.

"What you out here beeping the horn for like that?" he asked, walking onto the porch. I raised the bags without speaking a word, which caused him to nod his head.

"This came from that li'l dude Bryant. You already know there's no need to count it. So put it up and holler at me later," I said, handing him both bags before I turned around and began heading back to the car.

"Where you going?" he asked.

"I'm about to head out. I'll see you when I see you," I replied, throwing up the deuces. I got in the car and backed out. I honked the horn before I pulled off, heading straight for the mall.

As I was driving, my phone began ringing. Looking at the phone, I noticed that it was Brittney calling. Shaking my head, I just placed the phone down and decided to let it roll to voicemail. I didn't have any more use for her, so I didn't see why she was even calling me in the first place. There was nothing left for us to say to one another except for when it was time for me to kill her stupid, naive ass.

I was maybe four or five minutes from the mall when I noticed that I needed some gas. I wasn't all the way on E, but shit, I wasn't too far from it either. I decided to stop at the first gas station that I saw. Pulling up to the pump, I parked behind this all-black Tahoe. Cutting the car off,

I reached for my wallet in the glove compartment. I was about to get out when I looked up and thought my eyes were playing tricks on me. I closed my eyes and opened them again, but when I did, I was still sitting there staring at the one and only Mia. Now either God was sending me a message or He really didn't like her. Whichever the case was, I was actually one happy-ass dude right now. So instead of getting out to pump gas, I sat there in the car and waited.

Now I didn't know what I did good, but when I saw the nigga who Keyon was supposed to be getting married to and having kids with walking out of the store, I got excited. He went to the same truck Mia was standing at as they began talking. I couldn't help the smile that was on my face. Pulling my phone out, I snapped a picture of them. This was going to get me my girl and my family back. I waited until they were in the car and pulled off to follow them.

I guess I'm not going to the mall, I thought as I followed them to what I was guessing was the hotel they would be staying at. Since I didn't want to risk them noticing me, I grabbed my hat and jacket and watched as they walked into the hotel. I hurried and got out as I put the jacket and hat on. They were too busy talking about what I soon realized was Bundy that they never saw me there. I followed them until they got onto the elevator, where they rode it to the third floor. I then hauled ass to the third floor. Before exiting the stairway, I stopped to calm myself down and to catch my breath. Only then did I walk out. I was damn near late, but I caught Mia just in time to see which door she entered. I then cautiously speed walked to the door, memorized the room number, and got my ass out of there before they saw me. I didn't want to risk the chance of that, because I knew firsthand that she would run and I'd probably never see her ass again.

Pulling my phone out, I called Jamel up. He wasn't going to believe this shit, not one bit. After everything we'd been going through to try to find her ass, she just up and shows up. I couldn't help but think that today had turned out to be one of the luckiest days of my life. All I knew was that her life was winding down and all she had were hours left.

CHAPTER TWENTY-THREE

Mia

I'd been in a funk since we found Bundy's beaten and battered body in his house. The only person I could think of who would've done something so horrible to him was Cash. I wasn't concerned about the shit, but now I was, which was why being back in Chicago wasn't such a good idea for me.

After sitting in the same spot that I had been in since I walked through the door, I decided that it was best I leave. I didn't care what Kane had to say. I wasn't trying to lose my life and leave my child behind. I was now on the phone, calling up my cousin Brittney. She was the only person I could think of who could actually help me. Then once I was out of here, I was going back to Tennessee to get my son and leave there as well. The best thing for me to do was to get far away from everybody who had some kind of dealing with Cash, Keyon included. I didn't have anything against her, but I needed to stay alive, and as long as she had Cash's daughter and I was around them, I would always be in danger. So the best thing for me to do was get myself out of each and every situation altogether.

"Hello," she said, answering the phone.

"Hey, Brit, where are you?" I asked her.

"I'm home. What's up with you?"

"I need you to come and get me," I said, walking over to the window. Pulling back the curtains carefully, I looked out of them.

"Come and get you? Where you at?" she asked.

"I'm in Chicago," I said as my heart began beating. I was more scared now than I ever was in my whole entire life.

"Chicago? Why didn't you tell me that you were here?"

"I just got here, and now I need to leave. Please come and get me," I said, practically begging her.

"All right. Where are you at?" she asked. I told her where I was as I got up and began to pack the few bags that I did have.

"Okay, I'll be waiting. Call me when you get here, and I'll come right out," I told her.

"Okay."

"Don't go parking now. Just pull up in front of the hotel because I'll be right out," I specifically told her. I didn't need a reason for her to park. That shit there was bound to get us caught up and shit.

"Girl, all right, damn," she said, laughing. "You sound like you're running for your damn life or something."

"That's because I am," I said, hanging up the phone. Just as I finished packing my bags, someone started knocking on the door. Placing the bags on the side of the bed, I went to answer the door. Looking through the peephole, I noticed that it was Ant standing there.

"What's up?" I asked him once I opened the door.

"We were about to go and get something to eat. We were wondering if you wanted anything."

"Nah, I'm good. I don't really have much of an appetite," I told him honestly. "I don't think I will have one for the next couple of days, in fact."

"All right. Get some rest," he suggested. "Kane's going to go over there and break the news to his auntie. We'll most likely be leaving tomorrow and heading back to Tennessee until it's time for the funeral."

"Okay, cool," I said just as my phone started to ring. I looked down and noticed that it was Brittney calling. The bitch must have flown down here or something. Ignoring her call, I looked back up at Ant. "That's all you need?"

"Yes. I'll holler at you later."

"All right," I said, closing the door. I immediately went around to the bed and got my bags and then headed for the door. Opening the door slightly, I peeked out of it. Once I was sure that Kane and Ant were nowhere around, I made a run for the elevators. I must have pushed the button at least eight times, and the elevator had yet to show up. Getting impatient, I turned in time to see Kane walking out of his room. I ducked into the stairway and made a run down the stairs. I didn't look back as I almost tripped and fell, but I kept on going. I was pretty sure the few people sitting in the lobby thought I was a crazy woman, but I didn't care one way or another. I kept on going as I reached the door and ran out the exit. Just like I asked her to, Brittney was waiting for me right by the door. I didn't waste one second as I opened the door and hopped in.

"Drive," I yelled. I ducked down in the seat right as I spotted Kane and Ant walking through the lobby. It was a good thing that her tints were a bit dark and that practically no one could see inside of her car.

"All right, bitch, damn," she replied, speeding out of the hotel's parking lot. It wasn't until she was on the highway that I got up. "You all right?"

"I'm good. I'll be even better when I get the hell out of Chicago," I said more to myself than to her.

"Well, where are you going?"

"When I leave here, I'm going to pick up my son, and I'm getting the hell out of Dodge. I can't take this shit no more," I said on the verge of tears. I never knew that doing this would come back to bite me in the ass, and boy, did it bite me hard. "I already booked a flight. Just drop me off at the airport. I'll take it from there."

"All right, but first I gotta make a stop at my house."

"Bitch, really?" I asked, pissed. I didn't need her to be doing shit like that when I was literally on the run.

"Girl, yes, chill. We won't be nothing but a few minutes," she replied. I rolled my eyes as I sat there trying to calm myself down. Since I was straight for now, I decided to rest my eyes a little.

After a little while, something told me to get up. I could sense I was in trouble, but I didn't know for sure. When I opened my eyes, I noticed her going in a direction that was nowhere near her house. In fact, the bitch wasn't even on the road anymore. All I saw were dirt and trees.

"Where the fuck are we going?" I asked nervously. I then looked over to her and noticed that she was pointing a gun my way. "Fuck me, Lord."

"That's the right person to call on," a voice that almost made me shit my pants said. I turned around and looked right into Cash's eyes.

"So this is how you're doing it?" I asked her, but my eyes were still on him.

"I'm sorry, Mia," she said softly.

"Bitch, I don't want to hear all that. If you were so sorry, you wouldn't be doing this shit," I told her.

"Pull over right here," Cash told her. My heart began beating loudly as I felt the car come to a complete stop. "Turn around and get out of the car."

"Cash, don't do this," I said, beginning to beg.

"Mia, right now the only thing I want you to do is get the fuck out of the car. There's nothing in the world you can say to make me want to change my mind."

"Well, what about our son?" I asked, trying to play the only card that was left.

"He'll be fine right where he's at. I'm sure Keyon is taking good care of him," he replied.

"How do you know where my baby is?" I asked, spooked.

"I'm Cash, darling. I know just about everything," he said, flashing me this evil grin. "I also know that you had Bundy, his punk-ass cousin, and some other dumb nigga rob me for my money. Then ya had the nerve to act like you ain't know about the shit. Yeah, that's right. That nigga Bundy gave you up. The way he saw it, you wasn't loyal to him, so why should he be loyal to you? Now get the fuck out of the car."

"Ca—" I began to say, but his fist connected with my mouth and silenced me.

"Drag this bitch out of the fucking car," he yelled. The next thing I knew, the car door swung open, and I was being pulled out. "Oh, get that other bitch too."

"What?" I heard Brittney yell as someone else pulled her out. "I did what you asked me to. Why are you doing this?"

"Bitch, do you really think that I would just kill her in front of you and let you go?" he asked her. She looked at me before she put her head down.

"Cash, you don't have to kill her," I said, but what I said went through one ear and out the other as he raised his gun and shot her right in the head, killing her instantly.

"Oh, my God," I yelled, trying to run, but I was stopped when one of the dude's fists connected with the side of my face. I was pretty sure that my jaw was broken when I heard that loud crack followed by my jaw dropping.

"I wanted you to suffer, but I figured that it would be best for me just to end ya life. Say hey to that nigga Bundy for me," he said right before he pulled the trigger.

CHAPTER TWENTY-FOUR

Keys

It'd been almost a month since we buried Mia, and it still felt like yesterday. I still remembered how I felt when I got the call from Kane when they went to visit Chicago. Apparently, Mia's body along with her cousin's were found in a deserted area somewhere in Chicago. Someone killed them execution style and left their bodies there, where a hunter found them a few days later. I don't even want to tell y'all how everything else went, so I'll skip a few details. Due to everything that was going on, we decided that it would be best if we postponed the wedding until a better time.

Since Mia didn't have any family, I decided that it would be best if I gave her a small but proper burial. Her family was a total bust, and she really didn't have any friends, so it was mainly me and mine. Poor CJ sat on my lap the whole time and didn't know that his mother would be gone forever. I was sure we'd have this conversation when he got a little older. I was now his legal guardian. Just like you all, I was surprised when a lawyer brought the papers to me. He also informed me that I was the beneficiary of a $200,000 insurance policy.

Of course, I had to go through a little more than the usual, but with Kane's connections, I got everything done. Now all I had to do was wait until I dropped these babies so that I could go back to work. Being at home all day was not the type of woman I was, and I didn't plan to be that way either.

Back to the Present

I heard two more shots. I waited to feel the burning sensation I'd always heard about when people got shot, but I felt none. What I did feel was water running down my legs. As I opened my eyes, they immediately landed on Cash's lifeless body a few feet away from me.

"Are you all right?" Kane asked, running over to me. Right then and there, I felt a sharp pain in the middle of my back.

"Ahhhh," I yelled, falling to my knees.

"What's wrong, baby?" he asked, trying to pick me up.

"My water broke. I think I'm about to go into labor. Go downstairs and wake my mother up so she can keep an eye on the kids."

"What are you going to do about this?" he asked, pointing to Cash's body.

"It's okay. I won't tell a soul," my mother said from behind us.

"How did—" I was about to ask her, but she placed her finger over her mouth.

"I'm surprised the kids didn't wake up after those shots. Now go on and see about my grandbabies."

"I'll call Ant and have him come over and take care of this," he told her as he picked me up and carried me down the stairs.

"Ma, call Tay and tell her to meet us at the hospital," I yelled to her.

"I will," she replied right before we entered the garage. Opening the car door, Kane placed me in the passenger seat before he ran over to the driver's side. It was a good thing that I kept a bag in my car for times like this.

"Oh, my God, Kane," I yelled once I saw that my nightgown had blood on it.

"Damn," he replied, backing out of the garage. He didn't waste one second as he pulled off and headed straight for the hospital. I was so glad that the hospital was only fifteen minutes away, because I didn't think I would be able to last any longer.

"Let me use your phone," I told him. He looked at me before he gave me the phone. Grabbing it, I dialed Tay's number.

"Hello," she said, sounding like she was about to have a panic attack.

"Did my mom call you?" I asked her.

"Yes, she did. I'm leaving the house now. Have y'all seen Ant?" she asked.

"He's doing something for Kane. He's going to meet us at the hospital," I said just as we pulled up to the hospital. "We just pulled up. I'll see you in a minute."

"Okay, cool," she said, hanging up.

Kane pulled up in front of the emergency room, where he damn near ran into the front of the building. Getting out, he hurriedly ran over to my side and grabbed me into his arms.

"Someone help me," he yelled as he made his way into the hospital. "My girl is pregnant and she's bleeding."

Not a minute after that, the hallway swarmed with nurses and doctors. They took me up to labor and delivery, where they hooked me up to a million and one different monitors.

"How many months is she?" one doctor asked.

"Five months," I answered as the rockiest contraction waved through my body.

"Get me an ultrasound," he ordered. "I need to see what is going on with these babies."

"Yes, Doctor," the nurse replied. She then left the room, but returned later with the machine, which the doctor took over. Once he saw everything that he needed to, he ordered them to take me to the operating room. Apparently one of the babies wasn't getting enough oxygen, and its heart rate was greatly decreasing. So in order for him to save both of my babies, I would have to have a C-section in the next twenty or so minutes.

"What's going on?" Tay asked, entering the room a few minutes later. Kane pulled her to the side and explained everything to her. I could see the worried look in her eyes, but she decided to play it tough. I was guessing she didn't want me to get upset. What she didn't know was that I was already dying inside, but I didn't want to make the situation any worse than it already was.

Less than an hour later, we welcomed Keeven Michal and Keyvon Mykell into the world. Keeven was two pounds, twelve ounces, while Keyvon was a solid three pounds. Due to them being early, they were immediately rushed to the NICU, where they both were placed on a ventilator since their lungs weren't properly developed. It was only when I was stitched up and in the recovery room that I let out the tears that I was holding in.

"Don't cry, mama. The doctor said that they were going to be fine," Tay said, rubbing my arm. What she didn't know was that I was crying for both my boys and the stuff that happened at the house a little while ago.

"I'm good, girl," I said, lying. I then sat there and told her everything that happened. She was glad that Cash was gone and that he was no longer a problem for Kane or me. I wanted to tell her what he said about me sleeping with the enemy, but I decided to let that go. Kane might have been his enemy, but he was no enemy of mine.

"Damn, girl," was all she said as she sat there shaking her head.

"I know, right?" I said just as the door opened. In walked Kane and Ant with flowers and balloons. I smiled, knowing that he would do anything to see me smile. He was happy that he got not only one but two boys who he could spoil rotten.

"I got a surprise for you," he said, giving me a kiss on my lips.

"What?" I asked. He walked over to the door and opened it. In walked a white dude in a black robe.

"I know you want to wait until the wedding, but I can't," he said, showing me the ring. "Will you marry me?"

"Yes," I said as a fresh set of tears rolled down my face.

"All right, come on, Pastor. Let's get this party started," Ant said, smiling.

That night, Kane and I became husband and wife. It wasn't the wedding that we had planned, but it didn't matter. The only thing that mattered was that I was happy. I now had the husband and family that I dreamed of having, and there was no one to mess that up.

The End